The WishKeeper

APPROVED

Cover art by Adam Ford

Graphics design by Elizabeth Sweeney

Published by OddInt Media

ISBN 978-0-9915961-9-5

Originally published in 2013 by Lost King Entertainment

For Dad and Carrie. The best storytellers I know.

THE WISHKEEPER

PROLOGUE

Even WishKeepers make clerical errors. An overlooked mistake, even of the simplest kind, can grow into a major problem, and when it was discovered that two children hadn't yet been assigned WishKeepers, heads rolled. Figuratively speaking, of course.

Grayson Brady and Miranda Anderson were born in the same room of the same hospital, one day apart. Miranda was the one who arrived early. Miranda was always the one to arrive early, being the much more eager and adventurous of the two. They grew up in quaint, neighboring ranch homes on a small cul-de-sac at the northern tip of a town named Abdera. A throwback little town, Abdera had a main street paved with bricks that unevenly rushed past an old Five & Dime store that had been renovated into an antique shop. The town was a tourist attraction simply for its purposefully kept historical feel–a town that never aged, only its inhabitants did. For a kid, it was a perfect place to grow up, and by the time Miranda turned nine years old she had scouted every inch of the woods at the end of her little cul-de-sac. Miranda was always searching for something. There was always a door that needed opening, an empty hallway that called her name, or an expansive forest that begged for her exploration.

     Grayson was an introvert that would rather consider his own thoughts and musings than consider someone else's. Not that he ignored his parents' love or guidance: he simply listened and took it all in. His father would secretly wish that

Grayson would talk back or pout or throw some form of a tantrum just to see a spark of life within his son. As his parents would ready themselves for bed, Grayson would overhear them chatting, worried about their son and wishing he would show the same adventurous spirit as other kids his age. While he didn't feel there was anything wrong with him, Grayson knew his life was merely on hold and it was going to be worth the wait.

When two WishKeepers were finally assigned to the children, the two fairies discovered quite quickly that they had a mountain of work ahead of them. As Beren and Elanor transferred to The Other Side for their first wish wrangling session, they didn't need to search very hard to find their WishMakers. They flew along the edge of the cul-de-sac and found Miranda and Grayson sitting alone on their respective front porches thinking, dreaming, and wishing. Nine years' worth of their wishes crowded the end of the quiet neighborhood. The bug-eyed, brightly lit wishes smiled and giggled when they finally saw their WishKeepers speeding toward them. All of their Athletic Wishes, Ladder Wishes, Purity Wishes and Money Wishes owned this little corner of The Other Side, and all Beren and Elanor could do was smile.

In the first nine years of their lives, Miranda and Grayson never had a wish granted. Their wishing lives, however, were about to begin.

1
GOGGLES, GOGGLED

Ten Years Ago

"Wings tucked, Private!" Shea's mother ordered with a charged smile.

The frozen sap of the evergreen clung to Shea's bare feet as if the icy tree were trying to keep her in one place. It was Wishing Eve in the Makers' world–The Other Side, as the WishKeepers called it—a night when all WishKeepers would leave their secret world of Paragonia and cross through the Gates to tend to their WishMakers in celebration of opportunity: the opportunity to collect millions of wishes and sustain the harmony between their world and the Makers'. It was the most important night of the year, but for Shea it was a night that would define her.

It was the night a True Love Wish was destroyed. It was the night her wings were ripped from her delicate shoulders. It was the night her mother died. And the sap of the evergreen tugged at her toes, as if begging her not to move. She should have listened.

Shea played along with her mother's orders as Elanor stood in front of her little fairy daughter, fists at her hips.

"Check! Yes, ma'am," Shea replied, standing upright and tucking her wings straight behind her.

"Goggles goggled?" her mother asked, stern.

Shea adjusted oversized aviator goggles around her eyes, "Check!"

"Wishes made?"

"Wishes granted!" she said as she stiffened a salute at her forehead.

Matching smiles rimmed their lips as the setting sun of The Other Side silhouetted Elanor's graceful wings.

"I have to go to work," Elanor said through a deep breath. It was Shea's first time on The Other Side, and she could sense that her mom regretted not being able to stay with her all night.

Shea loved the feeling of the slow, gentle swipe of her mother's fingers as they gently tickled her forehead, moving the thick red mane out of her eyes. Despite never wanting to admit it, there was an immeasurable eagerness within Shea's little body to become her mother. Every ounce was desperately impatient to be just like her. Shea watched her mom buzz her wings and prep for a quick launch.

"Hey... Mom?" Shea stopped her. She felt compelled to say something, but the words dangled from her tongue.

Elanor waited for one last peep from her eager daughter.

"I... I mean. Never mind." Shea said with a bashful smile.

"I won't be long," Elanor returned, noticing the eagerness of adolescence pouring from her daughter's eyes. "You are going to be a wonderful WishKeeper someday. But it's not today, honey. Please... promise me you'll stay here."

Little Shea nodded as wishes darted through the park behind Elanor. The impulse to fly after each and every one of them was overwhelming as Shea watched her mother zoom out of the tree and into the sea of colorful wishes. Purple, blue, pink and green, the wishes danced and darted through the park. Their playfulness was intoxicating. The evergreen did its best to keep her little feet stuck to its branch, but as much as she wanted to be a good fairy and follow her mother's orders, Shea couldn't deny her innate impulse to explore.

Present Day

It was ten years ago, but the edges of her nightmares had only sharpened. There are signposts to every memory: checkpoints that Shea forced herself to remember so that the in-betweens of that particular night were never forgotten. The little goggles game. The bleeding red of her father's tunic as he said goodbye to his wife just before she destroyed the True Love Wish. How the wind that swirled around her was black and wet, and the face that stretched out of it— their WishingKing's skull-grey face. How easily her beloved wings were torn from her back as the bright red explosion of the wish consumed her.

Bouncing between these signposts allowed her to fill in the gaps of her memory and strengthen her anger, resentment and frustration as she lay in bed, staring at the ceiling and fighting sleep. And though her thoughtful run from checkpoint to checkpoint always started with the relentless tug from the sap of the evergreen, the fire that fueled it all was not an image but an incessant reminder.

Had Shea known it was to be the last time she would have a conversation with her mom, she might have said it. She might have pushed through the little barrier in her heart that kept her safe—safe from expressing anything remotely vulnerable. She might have fought the urge to hold back the three words that, for years to come, she would grow accustomed to hating. Instead, every night she would wonder if saying those three words would have made a difference.

THE WISHKEEPER

It was impossible for Shea to release such imagery from her mind. It was impossible for her to forgive her parents for destroying a True Love Wish. And it was impossible to forget that she never told her mom that she loved her.

2
FORGET ME KNOTS

You are going to be a wonderful WishKeeper someday. But it's not today, honey. Please...

Shea's frustrated response would always echo as she woke. *If not today, then when?* It had been ten years, and 'someday' had yet to come. The pain from her cramped, stiff wings in the morning would brush the dusty echo away, and reality would return. Her broken wings would always stiffen up at night, and she got used to waking with an aching back.

On this particular morning there was a different kind of pain in her back. She needed to pull double duty – work at the Wish Nursery in the morning and manage a Gate as a GateKeeper in the evening. She had recently been promoted to GateKeeper and was relieved to no longer need to serve The Nursery on a full-time basis. It was, however, the final day of practice runs before the Keeper Performance Trials for all new recruits, and her father needed a helping hand in The Nursery. It would be another day within another year that she would have to watch other fairies attempt to become WishKeepers.

Since 'the accident', as her father called it, she and her dad had needed a new cottage to live in. Their previous home was the General's quarters, a relative mansion compared to the rest of the fairy cottages in the forest. Sprawling out over the top of a high arcing oak tree, the General's quarters were impossible to reach for any fairy that couldn't fly. Being the father of the only fairy that couldn't, Beren made the decision that a cottage at the base of the oak would be the safest place for his handicapped daughter. Handicapped daughter. Shea refused to admit such a thing, but the hidden glances and furrowed brows of her fellow fairies made it difficult to forget her mangled wings.

Shea tried to make the most of her new grounded home, and for months had begged her father to build the turret she now called her bedroom. Her large picture window was at the top of the turret and looked out into the open green valley. It was a wonderful view in most respects, but Shea purposely built a long overhang at the top of the window to shield her view of the fairies flying through the trees above her.

Walking to her window, Shea stopped, stretched and yawned. She had loud red hair streaked with bright blonde highlights, and her knee-high striped socks and green plaid skirt were stained with dirt and dried mud. She removed her tank top, pulling it up and over her head, and cringed as it slightly tugged on one of her broken wings. All that was left of her wings were dark, skeletal remains: mere remnants of the once silky extremities she had loved as a child.

She stood at the window, topless and secretly exposed to the world, and took a deep breath. Her toned arms fell to her side; they were painted with two large tattoos that dashed down the sides of her biceps. The tattoos were of stripped, broken wings, something she was proud to show off, especially since her dad hated them.

She strapped a worn, soft-leather, high-collared, sleeveless vest around her—brass buckles were covered by a thick silver zipper which she pulled up to her chin. Standing up straight, lean and athletic, she was quite a bit taller now, ten years older and on the verge of adulthood, some might say. She looked out at the peaceful valley through her wide picture window. Her nose ring glimmered and reflected the morning sunlight as models of flying machines lightly swayed in the morning breeze. Like most days, this was one she just wanted to be over with, but a sinking feeling bottomed out her stomach as she wondered if tomorrow would be any different.

A knock at the door startled her from her little meditation. She groaned, knowing who it was.

"Shea? You up?" her dad called out from the other side of the door.

"Yes, my doting father. Can't wait to embrace this lovely day." There was no better way to have her morning ruined than to receive a check-in call from her father... and it happened every morning. She never fell asleep long enough for her to actually sleep in. Could he, just once, not worry about her and start his day without slapping that dumb door?

"Well, before you go, stop down in the kitchen."

She listened to his footsteps creak the floorboards of the nearby staircase. Stop by the kitchen? Since when did her dad want to have breakfast with her? Snatching her wand from under a pile of dirty socks, she stopped at a mirror to make sure she looked just as awful as she felt. She pulled her thick hair back into a puffy, frizzed ponytail and took another deep breath. Unable to look too long into the mirror, she made sure not to make eye contact with herself. Despite all of her attempts to color her hair, cover her body with ink or jewelry, she was the spitting image of her mom and moments at the mirror never lasted very long. Aviator goggles dangled from the corner of the mirror. She grabbed them absent-mindedly, and placed them around her neck.

She smelled something surprisingly good wafting from the kitchen as she approached, and when finally creeping in, she couldn't help but snicker at the sight of her father wearing an apron and cooking breakfast over the stove.

"What in the world are you doing, Dad?" Shea said.

"Just because I'm a General, Shea, doesn't mean I can't cook a damn fine breakfast for my daughter."

Her snickering stopped. An audible sigh rippled up from her chest as she realized her dad was most likely up to something. "What do you want?"

"What do I want? I haven't seen or spoken with my daughter in almost a week. We both have a busy day ahead of us, so I thought…"

Shea knew that her dad saw her expression change, otherwise he would have continued mumbling about needing to spend time with the daughter he barely knew.

"Now, Shea, just listen for a second," he tried.

Rushing through the kitchen, Shea knocked two glasses of cherry juice from the table—albeit an accident, though it had a nice effect—and stormed to the back door.

"Shea, wait! Please," Beren called out.

She whipped around, enraged.

"I told you I was done with this! I told you I didn't want to and here you are!" Shea yelled, anger boiling.

"You owe it to her to celebrate," Beren pleaded. "To remember her."

"I remember! And I don't owe her anything!" She wanted to scream it, but the unwanted and sudden emotion gripped her throat. "And if there is anyone who owes something, it's her." She turned and stormed out of the cottage, broken wings and all.

As she pushed through the green, soft grass of the valley, she didn't care if her father was upset. She didn't care if he didn't have anyone to celebrate with. As far as Shea was concerned, there wasn't anything to celebrate. Her mother was dead, and that was that. Bounding through the rising morning sunshine, she was more upset that she couldn't shake the sadness of having forgotten her mother's birthday.

3
THE OTHER SIDE OF BITTERSWEET

Every day Shea would traverse the valley countryside on her walking commute to work. It was a long trek, but it was the only part of the day she enjoyed. No one asked her questions about her wings and she didn't have to answer to anything other than her own thoughts, and she of course always agreed with herself. She would purposely take the same path every morning, enjoying the comfort of knowing what to expect from around each corner and over every little hill. She stuck close to the edge of the forest, where the valley cradled the trees, and fingers of River Paragonia rippled clear water over smooth round rocks. She rarely looked up at the sky anymore, embracing what the ground had to offer and taking solace in how little it changed. It was nice to see things that didn't judge her or force her to change or remember a birthday she hated to remember.

The Bittersweet Bridge would mark the end of her commute, and its small wooden nameplate reminded her of the history lessons she had learned as a small fairy. She liked the word "bittersweet" but hated how it represented a moment in Paragonian history that she believed to be treacherous and deceitful, though she was the only fairy to have such an opinion. *The Other Side of Bittersweet.* The event, or really the sugarcoated lie, was titled as such. Her ancestors destroyed one hundred wishes in order to live in their beloved, secret world.

For thousands of years, her ancestors lived alongside the humans, or WishMakers as they called them, but when the Makers started to spread out and unknowingly infiltrate the woods and lands of the Earth, a new home had to be created: a home completely separate, completely secret. Shea never understood why they couldn't simply find a way to live with the WishMakers. Her father incessantly reminded her that Makers have a hard time accepting something so different, so strange. When Shea would look at her broken wings in the mirror, she wondered if her own kind was any more accepting. There was also the problem of a WishMaker discovering a Keeper's role in granting wishes. Should a Maker discover such a thing, evidently all wish granting would cease. This is, at least, what her elders told her. At this point, Shea didn't care. Her own kind destroyed wishes in order to create something for themselves, using wishes for selfish intentions. It was dark magic, even though the history books refused to admit it.

But when she would look around on her long walks to The Nursery and remember how much she loved her home, she understood the meaning of "bittersweet." It was bittersweet in that she loved Paragonia, all the while knowing it was created by questionable means.

To make it worse, Paragonia was slowly disappearing—literally. Since Shea's parents had destroyed the True Love Wish ten years ago and removed their WishingKing, little by little the forests and trees had vanished, leaving nothing more than a gleaming white edge to their land. It was just another reason to harbor the ever-increasing resentment towards her deceased mother. What was impossible to forget was the price the WishKeepers paid for their new home: a human needed to be their WishingKing. A WishingKing was a human whom, every 100 years, the WishKeepers selected to sit upon the Paragonian throne. The problem was not that a human owned such a realm, but that such a rule was necessary in the completion of the dark magic used in destroying the wishes and creating their new land. Dark magic comes with a price, and the price was to always keep a physical connection between the human world and their own, and thus a human needed to be crowned king. When their last WishingKing was removed, The WishKeepers' world slowly began its descent into nothingness.

Even just his name flashed anger and hatred through Shea's little body. The Keepers selected a man named Erebus to be their WishingKing because of the supposedly powerful wishes he had made in his lifetime. It didn't take him long to get greedy and want the wishes for himself. And when a True Love wish was made, oh how he wanted it. Shea would never forget his face and she would never forget that he was the real reason she's handicapped.

Erebus was cast away to the Maker's world after her parents destroyed the last True Love Wish, and she'd heard the rumors of how he had taken over The Other Side. She shuddered at the thought of what that world must look like—consumed by his fog, dark, hopeless. Quickly she would remember her broken wings made it virtually impossible for her to venture to The Other Side, despite her desperately wanting to. By the time this thought had clamped around her brain, she would find the other end of the Bittersweet Bridge and the front gate of the Wish Nursery directly in front of her. She never tired of the same thoughts, the same musings that ricocheted through her mind during her commute. As desperate and gloomy as they were, she grew used to them, as if they were supportive, best friends. She didn't have any real friends, so she was thankful for how easy the thoughts returned every day. By the time she made it to The Nursery, she needed to say goodbye to her friends and begin the monotony and annoyance of sweeping and cleaning the wish pens, and adding sprinkle feed to the meal spouts.

THE WISHKEEPER

The Wish Nursery was a massive compound of thatched roof barns, wooden stables, and small ponds that rimmed the base of the far eastern edge of the Paragonian Mountains. It housed every wish brought from The Other Side. A decade ago, The Nursery was overflowing with wishes. Now it was nearly empty, and sad and lonely. The only thing Shea enjoyed about working in The Nursery was that it was easy to get lost and hide from the surrounding world... most days, anyway. On this day, The Nursery would be bombarded by a slew of Keeper recruits trying to impress their commanding officers by acting as though they knew what to do inside The Nursery. None of them really knew what to do with the wishes they'd wrangled, and Shea tried to stay out of sight any time the recruits came around. It wasn't just because of how dumb their questions were, but more the wide-eyed, second looks that were filled with disgust as they noticed Shea's charred wings. The inevitable bullying and name-calling was one thing: words were easy to ignore. The spoken word didn't push against the chest as much as the silent one. *Freak, loser, disgusting imp.* Names were just names and Shea had gotten used to them. Dumb questions could be dodged, too. *Can you feel them at all? How do you get around if you can't fly?* She would always smirk a little when that last one was asked. *I have my ways.* The smirks, though, only brought more abuse and sideways glances. A hardened exterior may deflect an onslaught, but even the toughest armor can be chipped away over time, and the never-ending wordless stares were the most difficult to avert.

She felt bad for the hopeful recruits, for their relentless hope and optimism. They were idiots for believing that a wish could be granted. Every day she was reminded of how dismal their fulfillment situation was – not one wish had been granted in almost a year and she saw firsthand what happened to wishes when they went unfulfilled.

As she placed her wand into the Time and Attendance slot outside the main gate, Leroy, the ancient guard that had been stationed at the stable gate for the past century or so, would always greet her the same way: a wink without looking at her, a click of his teeth, the tip of a non-existent cap and a line of, "Evenstar to the rescue." Shea hated that fairy.

Shea finally felt like she was awake enough to function outside of her thoughts and when she spoke to Leroy for the first time in ten years, she thought he was going to faint.

"I'm not here to rescue anything and can you please just call me Shea!" she yelled, not giving Leroy a chance to start his greeting.

The anger from her recent argument with her father and the sudden remembering of her mother's birthday was still thick in her throat. She immediately felt a little guilty for snapping at him, but when he stared at her, Shea quickly realized that there was a very good chance he had never before noticed that her wings were broken. His look darted back and forth between her eyes and wings, and he was suddenly completely incapable of even a stuttered word. Shea felt a rush of disappointment. This might have been the only fairy in all of Paragonia who didn't know her wings were the way they were simply because he had never actually looked at her. She felt like cursing out loud, but simply left the stunned fairy at the gate and went inside.

"Evenstar! You're back. Good to have ya," a curly haired, dopey-looking Nursery Hand called out. He had a bright blue, puppy dog-like wish tugging on a spell that connected to the end of his wand. The wish's tongue was wagging with excited breaths. Its bulging eyes were tightly shut as it concentrated on the game of tug-of-war. An Athletic Wish was one of the more annoying wishes to manage, though Shea always had a silent love for the

Athletes. She liked how much they enjoyed showing off, but more so how difficult a time the Hands had while trying to keep them in their pens. Shea never had a problem with them.

"I'm not back, Rufus. And stop pulling so hard on him. He just wants to play," Shea replied as she walked through the main gate. Rufus relaxed his grip a bit and the Athlete stopped tugging.

"Sure looks like you're back," Rufus said.

"I'm not!"

"Shea. Shea Evenstar, miss. Miss Shea." Tully always greeted everyone three times before starting his obsessively compulsive conversations. Shea called him Three Times Tully as a friendly joke, but since he never understood why she called him that, the joke just simply became a name.

"I know my orders today, Three Times. No need for roll call, thanks." Tully was The Nursery supervisor and Shea never blamed him for being constantly nervous. Security Posts were to be manned and operated throughout The Nursery, and Roll Call was necessary to ensure that each Nursery Hand understood his or her responsibilities every day. Shea felt that roll call was virtually pointless, seeing as though so few wishes were in need of tending in the first place. Still, it wasn't easy managing the wishes, much less the Keepers that came and went on a daily basis, so Shea was at least relatively willing to be patient with Tully. On a day when moronic recruits were going to be shuffling in and out, Tully's anxiety was expected to be at an all-time high.

"Yes, you know your post orders, I appreciate that, Miss Shea, but your post orders have…"

"Damn. They're early." Shea spotted a group of roughly ten young fairies flying toward The Nursery. They each had bright, excited wishes attached to wrangling spells, as if they'd caught a balloon with a rope. It was always clear which recruit had wrangled a Money Wish. They were rarely

16

THE WISHKEEPER

able to stay in rank. A few recruits were tossed, pulled and whipped in every direction as they tried handling their Monies. Impossibly rude and having no regard for the wishing process, Money Wishes had a green glow and a pointed, cone shape. Ugly as trolls, Shea thought. Even though the wishes didn't speak—they squeaked more than anything—the Monies had a way with their squeaking that was incessantly annoying.

"But, uh, Miss Shea, your post orders," Tully tried to continue.

"Only ten this year. The Keeper force is really kickin' butt, eh, Tully? Rufus!" Shea called out. "You've got some Athletes coming your way. A couple Ladders too. I'll handle the Purities."

"You always handle the Purities," Rufus grumbled and tied up the Athlete he'd been struggling with.

"Relax. I'll take the Monies too."

Shea removed a wand from her side, released a deep, annoyed breath and called out, "Purities and Monies over here! Ladders and Athletes, to your left!"

The recruits split up and flew toward various areas of The Nursery. Two groups careened toward Shea, but only Tully was nervous. Shea rolled her eyes as she watched them fly in. Two fairies had Purities wrapped in wrangling spells. They landed perfectly in front of Shea, barely out of breath.

"Went for the easy ones, eh?" Shea said to the two female recruits. They looked at each other, blushing, knowing that they did, in fact, take the easy route.

"Don't worry. I would have done the same thing," Shea said, still keeping her eyes on the incoming recruits struggling to bring their Monies.

Purities are pink, peaceful, consistently happy little wishes that always float directly toward their Keeper. They rarely put up a fuss and would rather help a WishKeeper than hinder any part of the wishing process. They represent a Maker's wish for health, spiritual and family prosperity, and so on. Rather boring, Shea thought, but they are quite easy to manage.

Shea lazily waved her wand from left to right, sending yellow sparks in an arc above her. The Monies dashed to the sparks, forcefully pulling their recruits. Not one recruit landed on his feet. It was just another attempt to try and show off. Recruits assumed that wrangling a Money Wish would give them high marks, but the wild and obnoxious wishes usually ended up embarrassing them.

One recruit crashed to the ground and rolled to Shea's feet. He still had the wish wrangled with a spell, which was somewhat impressive, but Shea didn't bother addressing him as he quickly stood up and gathered himself.

"Purities inside, through the main hall, to the right and into the Purity Garden."

The two female recruits walked their happy little Purities into the main hall of The Nursery while the rest of the recruits had their arms yanked and tugged while awaiting orders.

"OK, the rest of you..." CRACK!

The sound of a whip pulled her attention to a tall, muscular young recruit about twice her size. He did it again—CRACK! The recruit whipped his spell like a rope and cracked a wrangling spell, over and over, around the small Money. The wish winced as he did it again.

His nose was sharply pointed and his bright green hair was spiked to a tip at the top of his head. He looked like the typical WishKeeper that was trying too hard, but despite the obvious efforts to look the part, Shea could tell this recruit was probably one of the few that would actually complete the training and move on. He was cocky, strong, and tall—all of the things that just made Shea hate him even more. She wanted to crack a whip at him, slash a bloody cut under his eye, and ask him how it felt.

The blood drained from her knuckles as she tightened her grip around her wand. It sparked just enough for the recruit to notice. Even though the monotonous Nursery work annoyed every little bit of Shea, she did still love the wishes. Mishandling them was unacceptable. Seeing a WishKeeper treating them with disrespect—punishable.

"What's up with your wand? Malfunctioning?" the recruit said, shaking his head, purposely taunting. "You should get that checked out." He knew she didn't have any authority over him, and loved every bit of it.

"Follow me, please," she said through a clenched jaw, trying to ignore the self-righteous recruit. Shea's reaction the last time a recruit mishandled his wish had led to her dismissal to well-washing duty for a week. On top of not wanting to scrape bird crap off of unused wishing wells, she just wanted her Nursery duties to be over. The sooner the better.

She waved them down a wide, weed-covered path. It wound around the edge of the main hall toward a large pasture lined with ivy-covered fences: the Money pens. She took a couple steps, but paused and heaved a frustrated sigh as she noticed a skinny little recruit trying to keep up.

"You," she addressed him, annoyed. "What kind of wish is that?"

"Uh," he blushed, and looked up at his wish. A bright purple wish was circling his head like a hawk. "A Money?"

"What color are Monies?" she asked, even more annoyed.

His little brain was working overtime. "Green." He quickly noticed his was purple. "Oh…"

"Again, what kind of wish is that?" she asked, rolling her eyes.

His face was blank.

"Ladder Wishes represent?" she asked, impatient, waiting for a reply. Nothing. "Since when am I your Wish Instructor? Come on! Maker career advancement. Home improvement. Education! What's wrong with you idiots?" More blank stares, though the muscular, pointed-hair recruit was laughing. She sighed again and continued down the dirt path.

"I should have wrangled a Death Wish. The crippled Nursery Hand wouldn't be so disrespectful," the muscular recruit mumbled with a smirk as he jabbed the fairy next to him.

Cripple. It made her boney wings tingle every time she heard the word. When she was younger, it would make her run away to a secluded corner of the world and cry the anger away, but she had since learned to harness her anger.

Her blood boiled as she quickly bounded toward him, wand sparking. Tully yelped and jumped in front of her.

"You may just get your wish, punk!" Shea yelled. Her forehead barely reached the middle of his chest as she stared up at him.

"Miss Shea!" Tully cried. "You're scaring the recruits, miss. And, please, your post orders!"

"Scaring? Yeah." The cocky recruit didn't budge, laughing over Shea's outburst.

"I know my post orders, Tully! Just let me do my job!"

"Your post orders have changed!" a voice called out from behind Shea. Beren was behind her and nothing about his glare was happy.

"General Beren. Sir. General, sir," Tully said, nervous.

Shea rolled her eyes, and sent a lazy salute to her dad.

"We need all of the GateKeepers reporting to their respective Gates, Shea. There's one recruit left to cross over, but we've lost sight of him. You're done here."

"Thank you," Shea said, already stomping toward The Nursery exit.

"Hey," her dad called out. He approached her with a low, serious voice. "These recruits just risked their lives for a training session. You have no idea how difficult it is to wrangle a wish."

"Yeah, they have it so tough. I really feel bad for them," Shea said. Her snarky remark was not what her ill-tempered father wanted to hear.

"Drop the attitude!" he yelled. "It's this kind of attitude—"

"Those wishes aren't even real! They're training-wishes!" Shea yelled back.

Beren paused, fuming. He released a tension-filled deep breath. "If I ever hear you talk back to a recruit like that again, you're done and will never leave the house. You understand me?"

"Whatever," Shea said as she spun and continued her brisk, frustrated walk out of The Nursery. No Keeper ever used her Gate and she was more than happy to leave and spend the rest of her day relaxing. She secretly hoped that the recruit lost on The Other Side wouldn't come back. It would be one less WishKeeper wannabe to worry about.

4
THE RECRUIT

Thane rushed through a frozen forest, jingling icicles as he flew. Fleeing something, he kept looking back with the hope of evading whatever was chasing him. With a pink Purity Wish in his arms, the athletic Keeper-in-Training with his sharp shoulders and tall frame looked a bit awkward holding such a feminine wish, but he didn't care. He needed to cross over and quick.

Despite Thane's nervous tendencies, throughout his childhood he was heralded as an up-and-coming Keeper to watch. He never forgot how proud his parents were when General Beren visited their home in a recruitment effort. The General told his parents that Thane was the youngest fairy ever to be recruited for the Keeper force and that they should expect great things from their son. It was every son's wish come true to genuinely please his parents, parents who were both top WishKeepers in their own right. It was the second most memorable day of his life. Second only to the day Beren pulled him aside during a vigorous training run to bear the news that his parents were missing in action on The Other Side. He knew what that meant. They weren't missing. They were dead. He never appreciated the false hope that came with such a claim of "missing in action," but before that day there was never a moment of hesitation or doubt within Thane. As the years passed, the highly touted recruit quickly sank in the recruitment rankings. Little by little, despite his naturally gifted abilities, he lost confidence. Now, suddenly, here he was gripping a Purity Wish tight in his frozen arms, and lost. But this was just a training session, and training wishes are always placed in pre-planned areas of The Other Side so that instructors can monitor the safe return of any recruit. There was always a safety net. He was always safe.

Not this time.

He hurled himself onto a nearby branch as neon spells zipped over his shoulder. "Oh, just stop following me!" he complained out loud. His assailants flew past him, about a dozen or more flashes of shadow.

Crouching against the tree, Thane got a look at what was tailing him. Lost Fairies. He'd only ever heard stories about them: stories that would keep him up at night when he was young. Well, he wouldn't admit it to anyone, but the stories still kept him up at night. He'd heard that thoughtless minions of Erebus had helped take over the Other Side. With charred, black, bony wings, they couldn't fly. They ate small fairies in their sleep. That last part was unconfirmed, but as Thane stared out from his little perch, trying to hold back the shakes, he was beginning to believe every bit of the stories.

Dust trailed behind them as they flung themselves through the air. They wore black robes with hoods that covered their pitch-black faces. Their wings were gnarled and broken. They didn't fly as flying goes, but instead used their wands like grappling hooks, spiraling thick spells from tree to tree, swinging and propelling themselves through the air like dusty, shadowed rogues. More than just Erebus had taken over The Other Side.

The job was simple, really. You're assigned a WishMaker. Every wish he or she makes needs to be tracked, monitored and wrangled, if strong enough. Thane was taught in his wrangling classes that most wishes were wasteful little wisps from lazy Makers, but every now and then a fully formed wish would be worthy of bringing back. Thane remembered how much anxiety pulsed through him when he first heard that a Keeper's job was to manage all of its Maker's wishes. Although he was thankful that only some were strong enough to hold any meaning, it still didn't make a Keeper's job any easier. There were stories of such eager and wishful Makers that their designated Keepers would go mad trying to wrangle all of their wishes, but none of what he had learned mattered at the moment. Since Erebus had taken over The Other Side, hardly any wish was wrangled and brought back to The Nursery. A Keeper was lucky to retrieve any at all, and since Thane had just wrangled his very first wish, even if it was just a training wish, nothing was going to stop him from completing his mission, except for maybe the army of zombie fairies currently surrounding him.

A hundred yards in front of him was the giant oak. A soft white light vibrated and pulsed from high up in its trunk. This was the Gate that his general had marked for the recruits' return. Finally, he'd found it. He would get ridiculed for days once he got back to headquarters. *If I get back,* Thane thought. The last Keeper to finish the Trials was always hammered with cocky insults. He wasn't sure if he was more worried about returning to the ridicule of his fellow recruits or the Lost Fairies swarming him. Nonetheless, he had to get to the Gate and needed to gather a little courage before doing so.

He had a tendency to talk to himself, especially when complaining. Looking at the brightly lit oak tree in front of him, "Let's just shine a bright light and tell everyone exactly where I'm headed. Come on!"

*   *   *   *

In the main surveillance office of the Fairy Intelligence Agency, a massive circular room rimmed with maps and radars, sat a WishSentinel. A WishSentinel surveys various regions of The Other Side and tracks the positions of WishKeepers as they tend to their Makers. On this day, the Sentinel was relegated to tracking the recruits. Thane was still struggling to get back and the Sentinel couldn't help but get a little worked up watching Thane. The Sentinel had spent all morning monitoring the trainees' whereabouts and even though he had finally found Thane, his patience was quickly receding.

On the screen in front of him, he watched Thane crouch along a tree branch, holding his little pink wish.

"Don't just sit there! Get up! The Gate's right there. Go!" the Sentinel called out.

"You know he can't hear you, right?" said a voice from across the room.

The Sentinel spilled his tea a bit while standing and saluting.

"Yes, right, sir. Of course, sir", he reacted.

The years had not been kind to Beren, and Shea's growing rebellion wasn't helping his aging process. He looked even more exhausted on this particular day, his dead wife's birthday and all. His hair was streaked with grey and his eyes revealed too many sleepless nights. "How's the trainee doing?"

"He needs assistance, sir. He'll be surrounded any..." the nervous Sentinel started.

"At ease. Sit," Beren said as he picked at his teeth with a stick. He bent over and eyed the surveillance screen that showed Thane still crouching.

"It's Thane's fourth Keeping trial. He blows this one, he's done. No aid," Beren said, emotionless.

"Yes, sir. He actually has a wish this time, sir. A Purity."

Beren rolled his eyes at the news. A Purity: not much of a challenge. He removed the stick from his teeth and looked a little closer at the monitor. Indeed, there was the little pink wish.

"Better get goin', kid."

* * * *

Mustering as much courage as he could, Thane slapped the bark of the tree, trying to pump himself up.

"Here we go, Thane. Last chance to—whoa!" He jumped back just as a green spell blasted the side of the tree, missing his face by inches. He sharpened his eyes to a squint and dashed off the branch, soaring toward the oak. Green spells lit up the darkness of the frozen forest as he dodged, twirled and lunged for the glowing Gate. Crashing to a thud at the base of the tree, the wish bounced out of his arms. A Lost Fairy's spell exploded, just missing the floating wish. Thane was lucky this was a Purity: it floated right back to him. He cast a wrangling spell around it and pulled it in.

"No, no, no, get back here!"

He gripped it tight and pulled it close as he looked out at the snow-soaked forest.

Hundreds of Lost Fairies dangled from branches, loosely holding grappling spells and hanging from every tree like bats poised to pounce. They were waiting patiently, daring him to make a move.

"Oh, boy."

Thane slowly aimed his wand as if to fire, but instead quickly turned toward the tree behind him and blasted a spell. It connected to the vibrating Gate. Blinding white light beamed and filled the forest. Thane smiled at his hungry attackers as they covered their faces and fell from the trees like dazed gnats. He laughed and, shoulder first, hurried through what he thought was an open Gate but, "Ow!" He slammed his face against the tree. It didn't open.

"Oh, come on!" he begged. He slammed his shoulder into the tree again as if trying to open a locked door. The light of the Gate slowly faded and the Lost Fairies recovered, blasting back into the trees.

"Open! Open, please!" he cried and slammed his shoulder into it repeatedly. Nothing but solid tree bark.

A deep black shadow slowly crept over him, blotting out the light of the Gate entirely. Thane turned and looked. Directly in front of him, stemming from the snowy ground and growing ever larger, was a black-hooded, enormous shadow. Erebus morphed into his hooded shape, his bright red eyes peeking out of a hooded cloak. At one time Erebus had been human but, since his fall into greed, his evilness had changed him into nothing more than shadow. Thane knew all about Erebus and the WishingKing's fall from grace. He was barely seven years old when Erebus was cast away and the True Love Wish was destroyed. But even though he knew about Erebus and had heard the stories of his demented control over The Other Side, he had never seen him before. Very quickly he was reminded why he never wanted to. He could only stare, fighting back unexpected tears, as the shadow of their one-time king towered over him, grinning.

*   *   *   *

The WishSentinel covered his face with his hands, now genuinely worried about the recruit. He couldn't watch.

"Why isn't the Gate opening?" he cried.

"Whose Gate is that?" asked Beren, frustrated and almost as worried as the Sentinel.

"I don't know!" yelled the Sentinel, completely losing his cool.

"What do you mean you don't know? It's your job to know! Whose Gate is it?"

The Sentinel realized his foolishness and quickly flipped through a clipboard, "Oh, wait! It's... it's here somewhere, I mean, of course I know whose Gate..." The Sentinel kept rifling through the clipboard as Beren leaned toward the surveillance monitor, getting a better look. Looking hard at the screen, Beren realized on his own who the GateKeeper was. His fists clenched with frustration.

"Here!" yelled the Sentinel. "The GateKeeper is... oh, dear."

"Assemble a Keeper force! Now! Get him out of there," Beren demanded as he flew out a nearby window.

The Sentinel, still panicked, threw away the clipboard and rushed toward a nearby communication monitor. "Yes, sir!"

5
THE WINGLESS WONDER

High up in an ancient oak tree, a slight breeze rustled the leaves of the Paragonian forest. The sun was shining and the sky was a perfect clear blue. The simple sounds of birds chirping to their friends were interrupted by a beeping alarm somewhere below. A call that no one was answering.

BEEP BEEP BEEP!

A few leaves, knocked from the grip of their oak companion, lazily floated down as a hand tugged a nearby branch with a grunt. A faded, muddied black boot gained its balance on another branch and pushed off. Climbing and climbing, someone was ignoring the incessant alarm.

Finally finding the topmost branch, the fairy climbed up. Pulling aviator goggles over her eyes, Shea took a deep breath. Her shredded wings were silhouetted in the setting sun falling behind the mountains in front of her. At the tallest point of the ancient tree, Shea balanced on a thin branch and leaned. The valley spread out beneath her. It was a deadly drop, to say the least.

"Let's do this," she said as she readied herself. She snatched her wand, held out her arms straight to each side and with a deep breath....

BEEP BEEP BEEP!

The alarm below was getting louder and, annoyed, Shea muttered some form of a frustrated curse word. Impatient, she pulled the goggles off, clamped her wand between her teeth and climbed down. Finally plopping down near the middle of the tree, she straightened her skirt and rolled her eyes. In front of her was a vibrating, pulsing white light. The other end of a Gate.

BEEP BEEP BEEP!

"Yeah, yeah! Relax."

*   *   *   *

Thane leaned against the trunk, never taking his eyes off the taunting Erebus towering over him. "Uh, knock, knock? Please?" he said, begging the oak.

Thane's eyes were fixed on Erebus. Staring into his eyes, he could feel the cold loneliness that perpetual darkness brings, and a rush of hopelessness swept through him.

Erebus smiled, slowly raised his black, shadowed arms and curled a foggy finger. His Lost Fairies charged. They blasted themselves onto the branch, diving at Thane. Punching and kicking his way through the onslaught, Thane was handling the pawns well, still gripping the wish with his other hand. But this hand-to-hand combat wasn't going to last: it was one hand against many.

Erebus crept closer, like a devouring fog. He was inches away before Thane exploded a powerful spell and sent his attackers careening off the branch.

"Get off me!" Thane screamed in frustration.

Erebus recoiled at the light, but with the blast of the spell Thane lost control of the wish. It was loose and though he dived for it, Erebus was quicker. He whipped a wave of black fog at Thane, using the darkness like a weapon, and blasted him back against the tree. A Lost Fairy snagged and recovered the floating wish. He placed it in Erebus' dusty black palm and, like a thunderbolt, the wish cracked and exploded. Its energy pulsed through Erebus. Breathing in, he consumed the energy of the wish.

Grey and lifeless, the wish slid out of Erebus' hand and fell, disintegrating in the wind. Peering back at a dizzy

Thane, the shadow king slowly reached for him again. The Lost Fairies swung to the branch and approached, menacing, surrounding him.

"Don't you wish to stay, little Keeper? You would do well here," said Erebus.

"I'd rather die," returned Thane, out of breath.

Erebus smiled, "Really? Then your wish is my—well, you know what I mean."

All of Erebus' black fog raged toward Thane. It poured over him like a tidal wave, but the sudden exploding light of the Gate blocked the rush of darkness. It opened and pulled Thane through.

*　　*　　*　　*

Crashing to the other side of the Gate, Thane was thrown to the ground, knocking Shea over. They collided, rolled and slid through the grass, tangled.

"Easy on the reentry, geez!" cried Shea.

"Easy on the—are you kidding me?" Thane picked himself up. He charged toward Shea, wand pointed. "I was just staring into the eyes of my death!"

"Oh, stop being so dramatic!" countered Shea.

"You lazy, no-good—" This time, Thane sprinted at her.

"Go ahead, say it!" Shea replied, begging for a fight.

"Wingless gimp!" Thane yelled.

Enraged, Shea jumped on his back and swung her fists. Her knuckles tumbled down upon Thane's forehead. He tried grabbing Shea's wild fists, surprised at how much those little fists actually hurt. He spun himself, begging gravity for a little help, but she was stuck to him, relentless.

"Get off me!" Thane screamed.

"That's enough!" a voice yelled as a green spell knocked the wild duo to the ground. Grabbing Thane and pulling him away, Beren swept in and broke up the fight. "You're twice her size, Thane. Knock it off!"

"Sir, because of her we lost another wish! My wish! Why is she guarding a Gate? She can't even –"

"At ease, private!" Beren cut him off.

Thane backed up, following orders, but, heaving breaths of frustration. Beren pointed at Shea, pissed. A wooden stump lay behind her. "Sit down," Beren ordered.

Thane gruffly took a seat on the stump, not understanding it was meant for Shea. Shea, still out of breath, just stared at her father.

"Thane," Beren said, not wanting to have to correct him.

"Oh, her. Yes, sir," he said standing, realizing the seat wasn't for him.

"It's not my fault Big Nose lost another wish," Shea said.

"I said, 'Sit down!'" and this time Beren wasn't holding back. Shea finally obeyed the order. "Please tell me, how often do we bring wishes back?" Shea rolled her eyes in response, prompting Beren to ask again.

"How often?"

Thane chimed in, "It's been a while since we've—"

"I'm talking to my daughter!" Beren barked. Thane clamped his mouth shut: saluted.

"Not very," Shea finally answered.

"An understatement," Beren continued. "A wish is lost today because of your carelessness."

"I opened the Gate, didn't I?" Shea returned.

"You're done. You're off GateKeeping duty."

"What?" Shea yelled.

"You're too much of a liability, and with the lack of wishes coming in, I can't risk the—"

"A liability? I could be twice the Keeper this one is if you'd just let me try and—"

"Then prove it!" Beren's yell startled Shea. He had been mad before, but this response held more than just the madness of the current situation. He calmed a little and looked at Thane. "You. This is your fourth trial with nothing to show for it."

"I was ambushed, sir. And if the Gate would have… and Erebus!"

"No excuses. You hesitated! You let the lost ones surround you and didn't maintain control of the wish."

"You let Lost Fairies surround you?" Shea mocked. "They can't even fly."

"Yeah, keep talkin', wingless!" Thane yelled.

"Enough! Home! Now!" Beren barked.

With that, Shea pouted, jumped off the stump and bounded toward the woods.

Beren sighed as he watched his daughter leave, then turned toward Thane.

"You want to be a Keeper?" he asked.

"Of course, sir. I had it this time, I just…"

"Stop talking. You've got one last chance. You know my daughter?" Beren asked, already knowing the answer. Thane bit his lip, trying not to say the wrong thing. "You've got your first Keeper assignment."

"Keeper assignment?" Um…"

"If you can keep her, you can keep any wish," Beren floated away. He was done with this conversation.

"But what do I do with her?" Thane asked, hoping it was a joke.

"Keep her safe and out of trouble. You do that, you'll get your Keeper wings," yelled Beren, already halfway to the agency headquarters.

"Safe and—? Yes. Yes, of course, sir," Thane muttered.

6
THE BABYSITTER

Flying along the bottom of the forest, Thane searched for Shea. "If this is what it's come to, chaperoning a whiny, stuck-up brat who thinks she's better than me, then maybe I don't even want to be a Keeper," Thane thought out loud. "Seriously, this is ridiculous." He stopped flying and looked around. The forest was empty but for a chipmunk munching on an acorn nearby. It stopped chewing and stared at him.

"What are you lookin' at?" Thane asked the chipmunk, daring. It continued to stare at him as if it knew something Thane didn't. "At least tell me where the red head is, please," Thane continued. At that, a branch fell and bonked Thane on the head. Leaves tumbled down, then another branch. Thane looked at the chipmunk again.

"You're a big help."

The plump chipmunk eagerly went back to munching on its acorn. With a frustrated sigh, Thane looked up and saw the sunlight glimmer off of a moving object in the trees. Red hair shined and another twig fell. He kicked off the ground and reluctantly flew up into the tree.

Gritting her teeth and grasping branch after branch, Shea climbed, determined not to look down. "A liability. I'm the liability? Maybe wishes haven't been coming in because he sucks at his job. Like I'm the reason wishes aren't fulfilled," Shea complained to herself as she climbed. Quickly stopping, she noticed a caterpillar on the branch that she was about to grab, "Move, please! I'm climbing here." The caterpillar barely budged. "I'll smoosh you, I swear," she warned, but the caterpillar obviously didn't understand the threat. A frustrated grunt from Shea and she stretched for another branch.

"You're lucky I don't feel like having bug guts on my hands today."

Just as Shea was about to grip a different branch, Thane appeared, floating, out of breath. "Whoa!" Startled, Shea missed the branch and almost fell, holding on to the other with one hand.

"What was that back there? Not only did you almost get me killed, but—" Thane grabbed Shea by the waist and helped her right herself.

Once settled, she pushed his hands away, "Are you following me or something? Leave me alone."

"My name's Thane. Nice to meet you, too," Thane said.

"I know what your name is, stupid," Shea replied, eyeing another branch to continue her climb.

"I'm pretty sure it isn't 'stupid' but whatever. And, yes, I'm following you," Thane said. Shea was already mid-climb.

"Take this." She handed him her aviator goggles.

"Sure. I mean, would you stop for a second and listen please? The general ordered me to—" At that, Shea slipped and almost fell. Thane screamed, a bit like a girl.

"What is your problem? Scared me half to death!" Shea said.

"Sorry, I just—what exactly are you doing?"

"I'm climbing a tree. What does it look like I'm doing? And what order did the great general give you?" Shea asked, patronizing, and reaching for another branch.

"From the looks of it, detention," Thane replied, more to himself than to Shea. The climbing fairy finally reached the top of the tree. She took a deep breath and surveyed her surroundings.

"Goggles, please. What do you mean, detention? You leading a Lost Fairy support group or something? You already know them so well." As Thane gave her a dirty look, he handed over the goggles.

"He ordered me to keep you," he replied.

"To what?" Shea asked, genuinely not understanding. She looked down, put the goggles over her eyes and took another deep breath, ignoring Thane's explanation.

"Yeah, but listen, I've got one last chance at getting my Keeper wings, so would you just work with me here?"

Shea looked at him. He was actually kind of cute for a hopeless recruit. She stretched her arms and looked out at the valley below her. Without caring about his request and after a brief teeth-filled smile, she jumped—a free-fall dive.

Suddenly panicked, Thane froze, not knowing what to do. Finally, he dove after her.

Shea barely dodged branches as she nosedived, weaving through the air and tearing through dangling leaves. She loved the rush of the wind against her cheeks, the whipping sound the leaves made as they whizzed by. She'd almost forgotten about her annoying companion until he finally caught up.

"Hey, don't you think this is a bit dangerous since you can't—"

Shea pointed her wand directly at his face. He flinched as she blasted a spell just past his cheek. The spell caught a branch and attached. Like from a grappling hook, Shea swung away from Thane. It was definitely not her first attempt at this as she flung herself from branch to branch just as the Lost Fairies did, but she showed even more skill and expertise, turning it into an art form. Thane zipped through the trees, trying to keep up. The chase was on and Shea loved every second.

"Would you just let me explain?" Thane cried out, but before he could continue a giant maple leaf crashed into him, covering his face. He couldn't see as he struggled to rip the brown leaf off. Finally tearing it away, he searched for Shea and saw her grappling far ahead. Like a determined arrow leaving its bow, Thane zipped after her.

"C'mon, Big Nose! You're supposed to be keeping me, right? Better keep up!" Shea taunted.

A wrangling spell suddenly crashed around her, gripping her tight at the waist. On the other end of the spell was Thane and, like a cowboy throwing a lasso around a calf, he tugged. Shea was stuck and falling fast.

Thane pulled and reeled her in, but they continued to plummet to the ground at a rapid pace. He pulled and pulled, tugged and tugged, gritting his teeth as they fell. Finally bringing her in close, he hugged her, squeezing, buzzing his wings to try to slow their descent.

Grunting as hard as he could, Thane's powerful hug was suffocating Shea.

"Would—you—let—go?"

Thane opened his eyes. He stopped the fall about a foot above the ground. With their faces inches apart, Thane quickly let go. She gasped for air and fell to the forest floor. "What are you doing? You could have killed me!"

"Killed you? I just saved your life!" he replied through heaving breaths.

"I was doing just fine!"

Thane was still out of breath and walking off the sudden heavy workout. "Seeing as though you almost ended mine earlier, now you owe me double."

"What do you want?" pleaded Shea.

"I told you. The general ordered me to keep you. Do you do this a lot? Because I almost had a heart attack."

"You're actually serious!" Shea said. "Like a babysitter?"

"He wasn't incredibly specific. Just told me to keep you out of trouble."

"Unbelievable! I'm done with him!" And with that, Shea bounded away, done with Thane, too.

"Wait. Are you going to the fulfillment ceremony tonight?"

"Just stay away from me."

"I can't. Orders. And it's the first ceremony in almost a year. I'd really like to go."

"Then go! I'm not stopping you." Shea continued to hurry through the forest.

"Fine!" Thane yelled, unable to hold back his frustration. Shea returned it with her own, "Fine!"

"Hey!" Thane yelled, "I have my orders, and I can't let you—" With that, Shea stopped, put her hands to her hips and stared, daring him to continue.

"Would you just come with me, please? Make this whole thing a lot easier. And if the wish is fulfilled, there will be a really fun party after." Thane smiled, as if the party would completely change Shea's mind.

"Bye, Big Nose." Shea hurried off through the forest leaving a frustrated Thane behind. His disappointment ran deeper than just failing at his job: he felt that maybe he actually wanted her to attend the party with him, orders or no orders.

7
UNFULFILLED

The night sky was lit by a bright full moon when Shea was sitting along the edge of a small oval lake just outside the Wish Nursery. The moon's silver glow illuminated The Nursery's main barn built into the base of the mountain. The Nursery resembled a stable, but was cleaner, more comfortable and without the smell. Wishes had no need, as some might say, to relieve themselves as some stable-bound animals tend to do. They were quite comfortable there, and despite the open-air construct of the grounds, the wishes were bound to this place. There was no worry of a wish escaping. The Keepers welcomed the occasional roaming wish, as exploration aided the wish in its growth process. The wishes knew their place and were happy to be there. Because of this purposely relaxed set of rules and no real need to police The Nursery, Shea always felt the role of a Nursery Hand was virtually pointless, unless some worthless recruit needed help. Throw some wishing dust feed into the meal pens three times a day, keep the place tidy and pretty much just sit and stare.

Assigning a Keeper to The Nursery was either a reward for a young Keeper wannabe, or a demotion. Having just been fired from her GateKeeper position, Shea was surprised her father didn't even demote her back down to Nursery Hand. Despite its peaceful surroundings and serene landscape, this wasn't a place where Shea wanted to reflect or relax. She had to do something. Sitting with only her thoughts to keep her company would drive her insane. A burning desire to escape, explore and, in general, leave Paragonia and everyone in it, inflamed inside her.

Above the stables and in plain view was Exclamation Pointe. A large, flat rock cliff that protruded out from the top of the valley mountain like a shelf, Exclamation Pointe was the final resting place of all soon-to-be fulfilled wishes. Fairies of all kinds were preparing for a ceremony, flying about and eagerly awaiting their first granted wish in almost a year. The magical source of the early creators' spell—the dark magic used to escape The Other Side—resided atop Exclamation Pointe. Upon completion of The Bittersweet Spell and the creation of the new world, a marble statue of a WishKeeper was placed in front of a white waterfall that splashed into a small, stone-ridged pool. The Keeper statue remained nameless on purpose as it wasn't meant to represent one Keeper, but all Keepers. As a small fairy, Shea dreamed of having that statue named after her, after all of her heroic, brave accomplishments in WishKeeping. She hadn't looked at the statue since her mother died and she had no intention to do so any time soon. Every wish since The Bittersweet was brought to the statue for its exclamation—its fulfillment or non-fulfillment. While beautiful, the exclamation statue had become a source of impending anxiety in recent years since its judgment of presented wishes had been harsh, to put it lightly. No wishes had been granted in nearly eight Wishing Seasons and its glistening pool was slowly receding, evaporating and disappearing. For Shea, it was just another catalyst for her anger. Acting as if she didn't care was her only defense against such anger.

She sat along the grassy shoreline of the lake, staring at the effervescent reflection of the full moon as playful wishes buzzed along the glass-top water. The shimmering lights of the wishes reflected like water-bound shooting stars.

Angrily wiping a tear from her cheek, she couldn't let go of the notion that suddenly she wasn't even good enough for The Nursery, a place she never wanted to be in the first place.

She looked to her left at a Purity Wish that was hesitant to join her. It bounced a couple times, getting a bit closer. It wanted to sit with her, but could sense Shea didn't want visitors. This Purity had a slight yellow tinge to it. Any wish with a hint of yellow marked that it was near the end of its life cycle and either ready to be granted, or about to disappear and go unfulfilled. These days, most wishes in The Nursery had a yellow tinge—a sad reminder of an impending and unavoidable doom. It was something all too familiar to Shea, and she'd grown numb to the many yellow-stained wishes.

The Purity Wish's long eyelashes fluttered above its big bulging eyes and it looked at Shea as if to ask if she was OK. Even from a Purity, Shea didn't want any sympathy. Noticing Shea's aviator goggles nearby, the Purity nudged them toward her inch by inch until finally they were close enough for Shea to reach. It snuggled up to Shea's hip and she couldn't help but pet the little pink ball of fluff, despite her foul mood.

Shea looked at the wish, expressionless, but another tear formed in her eyes. When Shea picked up the goggles the Purity's smile expanded, thinking it was helping. Shea, for a moment, looked at the goggles and, frustrated, tossed them away. The Purity, thinking it was a game of fetch, happily bounced after them.

Behind Shea, Thane cautiously approached. She gave him a dirty look, quickly stood, and walked toward The Nursery. He picked up the goggles as he followed her, snatching them out from under the Purity's mouth.

"What?" Shea asked as she opened a stable Gate.

"I'm just doing my job."

"Try keeping some other hopeless case."

"You're the only one I know," Thane returned playfully.

Shea ignored the banter as she entered the stable. Even if she wasn't technically a Hand anymore, she couldn't just sit and stare. Especially since her new babysitter was hovering over her. The compound was lined with pens, most of them empty. A few dimly lit wishes slept nearby as Thane hurried in after her. A couple of the wishes woke and perked up, like puppies.

"And I don't have anyone to watch the ceremony with," Thane continued.

"Yeah, well, neither do I and I like it that way. And could you clam up, please? You'll spook the wishes."

"Right, sorry. I made you this." Thane held up a poorly formed cupcake with an unlit candle on top. It looked like a half-melted mushroom.

Entering a pen labeled *Money Wishes – West*, the largest by far, Shea followed a dirt path through the middle. A few dozen Monies zoomed about, excited to have visitors. They darted around Shea, bopping her on the head, snickering and hollering. Pranksters, to say the least.

"Confident little things, aren't they?" Thane said.

"Money Wishes. Zero manners," Shea replied as she pulled her wand from her sheath.

"It's customary to make something for a friend before a fulfillment ceremony. So... here." Thane handed her the cupcake.

"We're not friends. And it looks like it's dying," Shea said, barely looking at the gift. She stopped at a stone table in the center of the pen and placed her wand into a hole in the center of it. As she tapped the end of the wand, yellow sparks showered up like a wishing dust sprinkler. The wishes loved it, whooping and hollering as they swooped through.

"I'll just leave it here for you then," Thane said as he placed the cupcake on the stone table. He removed his wand and lit the candle. "Here's to wishes coming true."

"It's been forever since we granted a wish. They don't come true," said Shea with more frustration than remorse, and swatted at incoming Monies.

"Some do." He looked at her and tried to get a smile out of her. No good. High above them, they watched fairies fly toward Exclamation Pointe.

*   *   *   *

A crowd of Keepers in the thousands hovered in anticipation as Beren approached the wishing pool with a bright blue wish in his arms, an Athlete. The most basic of wishes, Athletes represent personal gain or advancement. Most wishes are of an Athletic type; material items such as bikes, cars, or some other meaningless WishMaker object. There was nothing overtly special about this particular wish. Its wishing time had simply come and its Maker believed in it enough to allow for the Keepers to grant it. But to the fairies, this wish represented the possibility of breathing life back into their world. As the stone statue of the WishKeeper held out her hands as if in a perpetual state of waiting for something, the crowd of onlookers held its collective breath.

The pool was rimmed with ornate stone and the statue stood within a grotto built into the side of the mountain—its once gushing waterfall dropping barely a stream from the shoulders of the rock embankment. The lifeblood of wish fulfillment, Exclamation Pointe looked out over the entirety of the Paragonian valley. On the other end of the valley, resting in darkness, was a massive human-sized castle; the castle of the WishingKing. Dormant and silently lurking, the castle loomed as a symbol of Paragonia's prominent past, and yet stood as an incessant reminder of how even the truest of hearts can be darkened. Now, in the place where a million wishes had been granted, where on a regular basis wish-granted light used to burst within the hands of the Keeper statue, the fairies floated with baited breath, crowding Exclamation Pointe and hanging their hopes on one little Athletic Wish.

Beren hovered above the pool. A faint breeze whistled through the nearby evergreens as the crowd hushed. He raised the Athlete above his head, offering it to the waiting statue. "You are the giver of hope, the bringer of dreams, the one who gives flight to the grounded chance. May you forever be granted," he said, as he released the wish.

The Keepers eagerly watched as the Athlete cautiously floated toward the statue.

Beren backed away as the light of the pool shined in his eyes. The wish lightly bounced and finally rested within the palms of the Keeper statue. A rumble echoed around The Pointe as the Athlete lit up, shining brighter and brighter. The rumble grew louder and the light stronger until—poof.

The wish disappeared and the light quickly faded.

Failure and rejection dripped from Beren's eyes and the crowd of onlookers was stunned. The wish had not been granted. So much hope and anticipation stripped away once again. A few hiccups of tears chirped throughout the stunned crowd. Beren continued to stare, thinking maybe this was a mistake. Maybe it wasn't over yet. Maybe there was still hope. Maybe... just maybe.

*　　*　　*　　*

Thane stared at nothing in particular, dumbfounded. He floated past Shea, who tried to hide her disappointment, but it didn't matter. It was the wave of frustration that rushed through her that truly upset her. Why is anyone surprised? Why such hope when they knew what was most likely going to happen anyway? Some of the Monies nearby suddenly popped and disappeared: a little disaster that they were all too used to seeing, which only reinforced Shea's bubbling frustration—any time a wish isn't granted, other wishes are doomed to disappear. They might as well all just go away. Why wait?

"I guess you were right," said Thane as he floated away.

The small cupcake's candle still burned. The flickering light of the flame bounced, as if unaware of the sad news. With tears welling up in her soft, frustrated eyes, Shea grabbed the gift. Wanting to throw it into the pond, she found she couldn't. She stared at it, hoping that sheer will could vanquish it, since she couldn't even muster a quick breath. The false hope of the flame continued to bounce. Was there anything she could do? Not for her home or fellow fairies, but for herself?

Finally, she blew the candle out.

8
ANOTHER CHANCE

The moon was at its highest point in the night sky, casting a cold grey shimmer on the glistening pool of Exclamation Pointe. Beren stood alone along the stone edge, staring at the water, but his thoughts were elsewhere.

"What do I do, Ellie?" Beren said out loud. "You'd know what to do. You always did." He sighed audibly and brushed his fingers through his graying hair.

Quietly approaching and noticing her dad talking to himself, Shea took a cautious step around the dirt-paved exit path. It was the first time she'd been up to The Pointe in years, but she knew her father would be there. He may have been the last person she wanted to talk to, but she needed to do something. She was hoping that the recent unfulfilled wish might soften her dad a bit and allow for an actual conversation about her possibly joining the force.

"Hey. Dad?" said Shea quietly. He didn't respond and continued to stare at the statue. "I'm—I'm sorry about today. I'd like to try again if you'd let me. I can be a Keeper, Dad, I just—" Shea continued, but Beren suddenly woke up.

"Did you know there used to be a waterfall here? It poured into the pool. There was a constant beacon of light shining from this Pointe. Your mom called it, 'the heart of Paragonia.' I always liked that."

Shea took a seat along the edge of the pool, scared to look at her distraught father. She glided her hand along the water as he continued. "With every wish we lose, the shallower this pool becomes."

"I know. That's why I—" her eagerness was cut off again.

"It's my responsibility to keep this pool filled. To keep our fairies safe. The only thing keeping us from being overrun by Erebus is… what?" Beren asked, but it was obviously a rhetorical question and Shea didn't bother answering. "Granting wishes. You realize that's what we do, right? The more we grant, the stronger our borders become."

"I know, Dad, and I'm…"

"Every wish is of extreme importance! Every wish! And when a Keeper allows one to be destroyed, it equals the death of a dozen others," Beren continued, frustration brimming.

"I already know this. Why are you—?"

"Because you'll get your second chance when you realize your responsibility to this realm!" Beren yelled, this time looking directly at his daughter. Shea knew there wasn't, or shouldn't be, a response to this. She held her tongue.

"We'll discuss your detention tomorrow. You can walk home from here," Beren said as he flew off over the edge of The Pointe, leaving his daughter alone.

The thought of starting over, working her way up through the ranks from the very bottom, kissing the butts of every commanding officer, much less her father: it was excruciating and nauseating, and there was no way she could do it again. All just to maybe guard a Gate for the rest of her life? Something needed to happen, but the familiar feeling of helplessness was overwhelming as she sat and dangled her legs over the edge of The Pointe. How ironic, she thought. The Pointe. What was the point of all of this, really?

Watching a shooting star streak across the sky over the dark and empty castle in the distance, she found it impossible to accept that anything was pointless. All she ever asked or wished for was a chance. But she might just need to create that chance on her own.

9
BROKEN

A thick, heavy snowfall descended over the cul-de-sac. Street lamps lit up Abdera's snow-covered streets and, though Christmas lights on the small cottages of The Other Side did their best to brighten the neighborhood, it appeared sad and run down. A once-happy little town, though never bustling, Abdera's comfort had leaked away over the past ten years. The familiarity and ease that once emanated from its corners were gone, and the quiet that was left was loud and unnerving.

A small single-story cottage with a wrap-around front porch was the only house without Christmas lights. The sidewalk and steps were untended and drifts of frozen snow were cut through with lazy footprints. The quiet of the cul-de-sac juxtaposed with the argument going on inside the house.

While they didn't know their True Love Wish had been destroyed ten years prior, the couple did know their marriage was crumbling. It was all wrong. All of it. They were supposed to be happy. They were supposed to be in love. One little unfulfilled wish can't possibly affect an entire lifetime, right?

A small candle flickered on a dusty table as Miranda rushed by, a suitcase in her hand and tears streaming down her face. Grayson followed her like a pleading puppy as she picked up odds and ends, shoving them into a half open purse. Miranda had long, stringy black hair, and her eyes were wide, oval shaped, and glistening from hours of crying.

They were rimmed with exhausted redness, and begging for whatever extended argument they'd witnessed to just simply end.

Grayson didn't have a hard edge on him. He was simple, tall, and yet just a shell of a once-energetic young man who thought he'd found the love of his life. There was a light in his eyes that beamed with an inability to accept that he may have been wrong. As he pleaded with his wife, trying to keep her from storming out, he felt that it wasn't just a girl he was begging to keep, but a way of life that for so long had felt perfect. She, along with the life he thought he knew, was slipping through his fingers.

"Please don't do this, Miranda," pleaded Grayson. He looked older than his years as he grabbed Miranda's coat.

"That's the point, Grayson! I can't do this. Not anymore," replied Miranda as she tugged the coat away. She threw it over her arms and shoulders and hurried to the door. Grayson pulled again, stopping her.

"We loved each other once, right? We can again. Just have to work at..."

"I can't work at it anymore, Grayson!" she said. "We never see each other! When we do talk, it's nothing but arguing, and you spend every moment in the basement painting whatever it is you're painting and meanwhile I'm working two jobs just to—"

"I've got some bites on my work and if all else fails, I'll get a job."

"Selling artwork to pay dentist bills isn't a bite! And all else has failed," returned Miranda as she turned toward the door.

"Please, Miranda! We'll spend more time together. We should have your parents over for Christmas dinner like we used to. Let's just fix this."

"You hate my parents," Miranda replied. "And spending time together—it isn't that easy."

"Hate is a pretty strong word," said Grayson. Miranda rolled her eyes and turned back to the door. He stopped her again, "Please! It'll get better."

"How?" asked Miranda. "We're broken. When does it get better?"

"We're not broken. Maybe a little bent, but just— please don't run away," begged Grayson.

Years of comfort. Years of ease and stability. A simple touch. A look that could strengthen a day's chances of success. Like their little town, Grayson and Miranda were slipping away. Even though on the surface it may have seemed obvious why, deep down the confusion was enough to break them. Miranda saw all of this in one flicker of candlelight that bounced from Grayson's eyes to her own. Something deep down was wrong, missing. The stare was prolonged by Grayson's firm grip on her hand.

She let go.

"Merry Christmas, Grayson," she said, but as a goodbye. A finality.

Swiftly, she flung the door open and hurried down the snow-covered porch steps, rushing to the driveway. Grayson could only watch, desperate, but out of options. He stepped out into the icy winter air and slowly sat on the hard-packed snow of the porch and stared as Miranda climbed into her car. It was cold, but he didn't care.

A swirl of red light slowly formed above his head as he sat. It flickered like an old light switch that was flipped on again after years of non-use. Fluttering to life, a red ball of light appeared above him. The red light twinkled and reflected upon the muddied snow and yellow street lamps. Grayson didn't notice the light, but its burning blistered within him.

Breaking down into tears, Miranda pushed herself into her car, trying to catch her breath. The crying overcame her as she stared at Grayson through the frosty windshield.

How could this be happening? I'm leaving the love of my life: my best friend, she thought.

As she sat in her frozen front seat, fighting and choking back the tears, a red light flickered above her, too, swirling into shape and finally twinkling to life. Breaking each other's gaze, there was nothing left to do but leave.

Between them, hovering in the air in the middle of the frozen front yard, the two red, flickering bulbs connected and morphed into one powerful red light. The wind picked up and swirled through the cul-de-sac. A True Love Wish was growing between them and it whipped the snow into a whirlwind. It popped into form and spun in a circle between the two heartbroken lovers. Faster and faster, it whirred and spun, creating a loud hum that echoed throughout the neighborhood until it exploded into a giant red beacon. It fired up into the winter sky.

The beacon blasted its blaze for a short time and finally disappeared, leaving a wild stallion of a True Love Wish spinning between Grayson and Miranda. The still winter night rushed back in as Miranda started up the car. The roar of the engine sputtered grey, foggy condensation into the street. The wheels crunched through hard-packed snow as she backed out of the driveway and drove away. Grayson couldn't bear to watch her leave. He picked himself up off the frozen front steps and limped back into the house.

The wish stopped spinning and zoomed toward Grayson, only to be cut off by the front door slamming in its face. Turning on a dime, it zipped down the wet street, chasing after Miranda's car. The wish was bright red, and oblong in shape. Its aerodynamic form enabled it to flash through the air faster than any other wish. It gained on Miranda, getting close to her rear bumper, but slushy grey snow splashed up and crashed it to the pavement.

Dizzy, the wish popped up out of the mud, shook the slush off and searched for Miranda's car. No sign of it.

The wish looked in the direction from which it thought it had come, but Grayson's house was out of sight. The empty, wet street glistened under a Christmas star decoration dangling from a street lamp. The star blinked a slow, pulsing red and green. Icicles hung from its lowest point. A winter wind buzzed the little wish's fuzzy, oblong shape, and as much as it searched desperately to find a glimpse of its Makers, the True Love Wish was lost. Confused and not knowing where to go, the sad little wish floated away into the cold winter night.

Away in the corners of the neighborhood, the darkness rippled.

10
BEACON

BEEP... BEEP... BEEP

Something woke Beren from a soft snore. Groggily reaching for a star-shaped device on his bedside table, he grabbed his wand and fired a soft spell at it. He sat up, rubbed his eyes and ducked as the device exploded a holographic image out of its top. The image showed a WishSentinel failing at keeping his cool and a wild Fairy Intelligence Agency situation room behind him with staff members running about, papers floating to the ground and panicked yells from Keepers barking orders.

"Easy!" yelled Beren, still trying to wake up.

"Yes, sir, sorry, sir!"

"What's going on over there? You know how early it is?"

"Yes, right, very early. Sir, there was a signal and all the lights on the panels are blinking and it might be because of the signal but it can't be, sir, because that would just be crazy, but then we noticed—" The Sentinel wasn't exactly being professional at this point.

"Officer. Officer! Speak like a normal fairy being. Please!" Beren begged. "Tell me what's going on... slowly."

Down the hall from Beren's bedroom, Shea could hear her father's voice. She was lying in bed, still awake. She perked up her head and listened to the garbled voice, but couldn't quite make out what Beren was saying. Jumping from the bed, she grabbed a rope and swung down to the bedroom door. She landed as quietly as she could and cracked the door open just an inch. Putting her ear to the opening, she listened.

Beren was standing now and definitely awake as he barked responses to the panicked Sentinel. "Erebus is always busy at night. You know there's nothing—"

"Yes, but, sir, the signal!" replied the Sentinel now inches from the camera. His face almost pressed up against it.

Beren was refusing to listen to the Sentinel. "How many times have I trained you in how to manage the WishPanels? It's old equipment. You have to jiggle the—"

"It was a beacon, Sir!" the Sentinel barked.

"A beacon?" replied Beren, uncertain.

Opening the door a bit more, Shea whispered to herself, repeating her father's question. "Beacon?" With delicate toes and risking the inevitable creaking of the floorboards, Shea crept to her dad's door and leaned her head against it.

"Show me the WishPanels," ordered Beren. The Sentinel hesitated. "Now!"

Shea pushed her father's bedroom door open just a bit. She couldn't help it—curiosity getting the best of her. Through the crack, she watched the hologram image swerve and show the main surveillance room of the F.I.A. A massive system of panels lined hundreds of feet of wall space, showing maps of various towns and cities. Blue, green, purple dots, pink ones too—they covered each panel except for one.

The particular panel of interest to Beren showed a black fog slowly moving across a radar screen. The fog edged closer and closer to...

"The cul-de-sac. Show me another panel. The city," ordered Beren. Worry was building inside him as the camera moved to an adjacent panel. Though denser with various buildings, regions and populace, it was almost entirely clear of the black fog. "It has to be a glitch. None of the other panels... why would Erebus go back to..." said Beren, thinking out loud.

"But, sir, it's impossible and, well, it just can't be." The Sentinel moved the camera closer to the fog-heavy panel. It was obvious to what the Sentinel was referring. Two red dots blinked—one pacing within a small cottage, another moving quickly down a small neighborhood street.

Shea, spying through her father's door, stared wide-eyed at the image. Luckily for her, Beren was too engrossed in the panel to notice her.

"The WishMakers. It's Grayson and Miranda, sir," said the Sentinel, stuttering in his own disbelief as a pop-up bubble of words appeared on the screen above each red dot. *Grayson Brady: Home, Alone, Despair. Miranda Brady: Car, Alone, Confusion/Despair.* Shea couldn't read the notes on the screen, but Beren could.

Beren sat, pale-faced, unable to comprehend, but he knew his Sentinel wasn't lying and that his WishPanels were never wrong.

"How many fairies know?" Beren asked as calmly as possible.

"Uh..."

The Sentinel turned the image toward an office full of WishSentinels, office fairies, Keepers and then some. They huddled in a corner, staying as far away from the panel as possible as if the two red dots might bite. Beren groaned.

"The Keepers on The Other Side. Get them back here. Immediately," ordered Beren. He threw on a robe and hurried out the window. The star-shaped device shut off as

THE WISHKEEPER

Shea slowly opened the bedroom door. She watched her father fly away. Breathless.

11
THE CAPTAIN

Ten Years Ago

"Mom!" yelled Shea as she stood at the edge of the swirling storm. Her daughter's plea haunted Elanor's eardrums as she looked at Beren and felt Grayson and Miranda's quivering, doomed True Love Wish in her arms. *I can't look at her,* she thought. She forced herself to keep her eyes and thoughts on her husband as Shea screamed again. Beren is the only one who would ever understand. Her WishMaker's true love, their future, their most important wish, rested weightless in her arms and she was going to destroy it.

"I love you," Elanor whispered, and though Beren couldn't hear the words over the surrounding storm, she knew he would feel them. Most often, a goodbye needs nothing more than a wordless look. Her wand charged up. The spell wrapped itself around her wrist and sparked, inches from the True Love Wish.

Erebus roared toward her, and tossed Beren to the ground. She watched her husband struggle to stand, and with the fog rushing toward her, Elanor's eyes never strayed from him. Her wand charged and charged. Its power was so strong she could barely hold on. She wished it hadn't come to this. She wished she didn't know....

When she watched Beren dive on top of Shea, it woke her from her stare. "Shea," she said quietly through a sudden bursting of tears. Erebus' blackness consumed Elanor as she looked down at the True Love Wish before closing her eyes. The wind whirled and raged around her.

"I'm sorry," she choked.

She let the spell go and it ripped into the wish. The blast was enormous, and once the blinding light reached her eyes, Elanor only remembered the pain.

*   *   *   *

The darkness of the sky lifted and gave way to a silver screen of dotted stars. Elanor was lying on her back. The snow all around her was melted and barely a rustle of Erebus' storm remained. Beren and Shea were gone. The wish was gone. Her life as she knew it only moments prior was gone as well.

Brown, wet grass surrounded her in a perfect circle, and her wings—nothing but charred, mangled skeletal remains. The night was calm and windless. The stars blinked, but Elanor didn't. She was barely breathing when a shadow stretched over her.

Limping, Erebus stopped and stood over her. He was completely shadowed, almost shapeless, but retained the form of a demented man wearing a pointed, hooded cloak. He looked down at the barely conscious WishKeeper, lowered a shadowed hand just a bit, wrapped black fog around her, and lifted her up. Elanor was limp in his shadowed palm as he turned and stepped into the darkness of a tree's stretching shadow. Morphing into the blackness, he disappeared.

Taking shape again, Erebus reappeared at the base of an ancient oak on the other end of the cul-de-sac. He looked up. A Gate was flickering like a scrambled, broken image above him. He placed Elanor on a branch, setting her down. She stirred and moaned through the pain of her broken body.

"My Elanor. Wake up, my Elanor," Erebus whispered.

She rolled onto her side and blinked through a crippling headache. Quickly sitting up, she crawled away from the staring Erebus as he loomed over her.

"Shea. Where is she?" she pleaded, but stopped suddenly when she backed into the trunk of the tree. She felt for her wings. Looking over her shoulder, she saw the bones. Panic slowly set in.

"They're gone. All gone now," said Erebus.

"You did this. How could you?" asked Elanor through the pain, exhausted and desperate.

"My research got the best of me, Elanor. Literally, the best of me." He smiled an evil grin as he pulled in a deep breath. As he let go of the breath, thick black fog rumbled down his shoulders and chest like the smoke from a volcano. "But that was quite the heroic act, destroying a True Love Wish. A necessary sacrifice, I suppose. You have helped me see the light, however," he continued, grinning.

Elanor forced herself to stand. Every muscle ached and the throbbing in her shoulders pulsed with every beat of her heart. She looked up at the blinking Gate above her and, out of habit, tried to fly. She cringed, and what was left of her wings barely moved. Falling to her knees, she cried out. A wave of nausea pulsed through her.

"Don't bother. Your friends have done something even I did not expect," Erebus said. "They closed the Gates. All of them. Unprecedented, really. I will have to have a little talk with your husband."

"Beren. He—" tried Elanor, but the pain was too much.

"It's just you and me now. *My* Elanor." A black fog rolled out of Erebus. Darkness reached up and out of him, swirling toward her. She tried to back away, but it consumed her.

59

THE WISHKEEPER

*　　*　　*　　*

Present Day

Within the Fairy Intelligence Agency, The WishSentinel watched through a hologram, fresh off the news of a newly made True Love Wish. His General's orders to retrieve all Keepers from The Other Side still rattled his brain as he grabbed a microphone device and flipped a switch. Two WishMakers had made a second True Love Wish. How could this be? He had heard the stories of their first True Love Wish and how it was destroyed: sacrificed, if you will. But to make a second one—impossible. But was it? He was dizzy as he grabbed the microphone.

"All active duty Keepers, this is not a drill. All Gates will close in T-minus five minutes. This is a breakout call. Return to headquarters immediately."

He slapped the switch off and stared at various monitors. On the screens, he watched WishKeepers react to a device on their belts and bolt away. "Come on. Get out of there," he said with what little composure he had left. He stared at another monitor. A WishKeeper was perched on top of a street lamp. He hadn't noticed the breakout call yet and continued surveying his location. The Sentinel watched, impatient and desperate, as the street lamp Keeper didn't budge.

Atop the street lamp, the WishKeeper watched a teammate tracking a lazy Ladder floating above a nearby home. To his far left, another Keeper was doing the same with an Athlete.

On his belt, the WishKeeper's radar device blinked and beeped until finally he noticed it. He looked at it, confused at first, but followed orders. He waved down his teammates and sparked his wand, sending a sharp red flare quickly into the sky. The lightly falling snow muffled the sound of a beater car rumbling along the unplowed street below as the two other Keepers noticed the flare. They darted out of their positions and followed his lead.

The trio of Keepers flew in formation through frozen branches and came to a clearing. An old maple glowed with a shimmering Gate in the middle of the tree. Just as they darted into the clearing a swarm of Lost Fairies launched and propelled themselves, firing spells at the retreating Keepers, cutting them off. The blasts lit up the little pocket of the forest.

Faster and more agile, the Keepers dodged and weaved through the onslaught, but they were outnumbered. Forced to break rank, they fired defensive spells back at their attackers, desperate to make it to the maple, until one of the Keepers was tackled and pulled to the icy ground.

About to finish off the tackled Keeper, the Lost Fairy with his wand raised high was blasted back as the two other Keepers grabbed their fellow soldier and rushed back into the sky. Hurtling through grappling Lost Fairies and wildly aimed spells, they were seconds away from the Gate until...

A menacing Lost Fairy dropped down from a higher branch and landed directly in front of the Gate. Taller and more athletic than the others, he held his wand loose in one hand and leaned a thick, heavy crossbow against his shoulder. A black, form-fitting cloak draped the rest of him, and his hood skewed any light from his face. Black, charred bones protruded from his back. The wing remnants were gnarled and twisted as if hundreds of battles had battered them into regression. This was no ordinary Lost Fairy and the Keepers knew it. This was The Captain.

The WishKeepers drew their wands and charged. The Captain didn't flinch, as if eagerly awaiting the fight.

The Keepers blasted spells in unison. Three spells careened toward The Captain. He ducked to his left and dodged one, blasted the next spell with a counter, then caught the third blast with his bare hand. Smoke sizzled from his burning palm. The Captain slowly turned his head and looked at his competition. Now it was his turn.

He dropped the lame spell, blasted his own wrangling spell around the neck of one incoming Keeper, and pulled and propelled himself, using the Keeper like a hook to swing up and above his attackers. He swung the neck-wrangled Keeper and slammed him into a tree. Letting go of the spell and starting to fall, he fired another wrangling spell at the second Keeper and with the same technique hurled himself back toward the Gate, shooting the Keeper with his crossbow as he soared.

Careening toward the tree, he stuck his crossbow deep into the bark, perching himself along the trunk and wrangled the third incoming Keeper, also around the neck. This time, he held the final Keeper up, choking him to death. Every move was effortless, as if The Captain was simply observing everything he was doing. He was coldly watching them, free of judgment.

A black wind whipped through the trees and swept the strangled Keeper out of The Captain's grip. A familiar foggy hand wrapped around the Keeper's waist.

"It would be in our best wishes to let this one live. Your Gate awaits," he said to the caught Keeper. "Go tell your hero General his time has come and I hold true to my promises," said Erebus, calm but threatening.

The Keeper was suddenly free and didn't hesitate. He swept toward the Gate and disappeared through it. The Captain watched him leave, staring at the diminishing light as the Gate shut.

"You wish to leave, do you? To fly through with him?" taunted Erebus in a cool tone. He swiftly grabbed The

Captain and squeezed a tendril of fog around his neck, raising him up. "You waste my time chasing useless Keepers and birthday wishes while the first beacon in years shines on The Other Side!" he said as he slammed The Captain to the ground. He leaned his black face inches from The Captain's and slowly whirled fog around the fallen Lost Fairy.

"You want to leave? Then do as I say!" Erebus yelled, and the fog suddenly straightened The Captain to attention, under a spell, unnatural.

"Find the Makers, bring me True Love and you can go. We can all go," Erebus finished. He swirled into the blackness of the night and left The Captain alone, still stuck in the spell.

Fighting the curse, The Captain slowly turned his head toward where the Gate shined within the maple. He stared at it for a breathless moment, then quickly propelled a grappling spell into a nearby tree and launched himself away.

12
FAIRIES DON'T MAKE WISHES

It used to take Shea all morning to climb the wall of the castle in order to sneak into its library. Because of the overgrowth of vines sprawling over its mossy stone, her climb was a bit easier these days. Through daily repetition she had memorized every crack, step, reach, and balancing act needed to get to the third story, where she squeezed through the oversized mouse hole under the stained glass window. She liked to think that a mouse got so hungry for knowledge one day that it couldn't help itself and gnawed right through the stone. Now that she had become so good at grappling, her ascent up the northwest wall wasn't as tiresome, and it gave her extra time to devour the thousands of books within.

Shea wasn't what most consider an avid reader. She wasn't interested in others' stories, only her own. It was a sickness that drove her to the library on a daily basis. A sickness that she grew to love: one that stirred her stomach, tingled her spine and pumped her angry blood. While most of her peers were too frightened to cross over to The Other Side, Shea was determined to do so. Every unread book represented a possibility, a hope, that despite her disability, there was a loophole or a precedent set by a past WishKeeper that she could emulate. A precedent that she could use to prove that just because she couldn't fly doesn't mean she couldn't Keep wishes. While nothing had yet been found on the subject, there was a vast resource of available skills, spells and tips that she had secretly practiced for the past ten years.

The library was enormous—so big, it took the dust and spiders much longer to cover it compared to the other rooms of the castle. Over the years, Shea had divided the massive library hall into stacks of books: "Boring," "Possibly Not So Boring" and "Awesome." The "Boring" stack was much larger than the "Awesome" stack, but adding to the "Awesome" stack was what kept Shea returning to the library every day. However, books with titles such as *The Flying Machine, The Physics of WishMaker Flight* and *Spells For The Lazy Keeper* had captivated her.

On this exciting day, Shea wasn't climbing her "Awesome" stack; instead, she was slipping and sliding up and down the "Boring" stack, mumbling to herself.

"Where is it? I know it's here somewhere!" Tossing aside books such as *Why Do We Just Call Them 'Trees'? A Nature Guide to Paragonia*, and *Release The Giant Within; Self-Help for Wizards*, she let out an impatient grunt and craned her neck to look up at the towering shelf in front of her. This being merely one of a hundred towering shelves, she was looking for a needle in a haystack.

Blasting a grapple spell three shelves up, she heaved herself to the shelf and landed on the edge. Inching along, she wiped dust from each book's binding, searching. "Come on. Where are you?"

"Shea! What are you doing in here?" yelled Thane from out of nowhere.

Startled, Shea slipped and fell. Thane rushed beneath her, arms out. She quickly blasted a grapple spell and connected to a random book.

"Don't you know we're in a library? You can't just sneak up on someone and scream!" Shea yelled at Thane as she dangled.

"The king's library is off limits."

"The so-called king is long gone. Don't think he'll mind—whoa!" Shea accidentally pulled the book from its shelf and crashed to the heap of "Boring" books below. The dislodged book toppled over her.

"Shea!"

"I found it!" chirped Shea from under the book. The little fairy pushed over the giant book and flipped through its pages. "Evenstar... Evenstar. Where is... got it!"

"Found what?" asked Thane as he looked over her shoulder. At the top of the page he read, *WishKeepers and WishMakers – Lineage.*

"Something happened last night. Something huge," said Shea as she continued searching the pages. "There! I knew it!"

"I just know we can't be in Erebus' library. It's strictly off—" Thane stopped short as Shea's wand was suddenly digging into his neck.

"I don't care if this was once his library: it's not anymore!" yelled Shea as she flashed angry eyes at him. Realizing the placement of her wand, she pulled it away and relaxed a little. "Sorry."

"You're crazy, you know that?" Thane rubbed his neck.

"I said I was sorry, OK?"

"Then tell me what happened and why you're in... here."

"Do you believe in fate?" Shea quickly asked. Thane could barely say "um" before Shea continued, "Like, no matter the choices you make or what happens in your life, you're supposed to be something? Or someone?"

"Yeah, I—maybe," tried Thane, but Shea cut him off again as she read from the book.

"WishMakers Miranda Anderson and Grayson Brady, assigned at human age nine by the order of the WishKeepers to first class fulfillment officers Elanor Willowind and Beren Evenstar, respectively." Shea looked at Thane.

Thane wondered out loud, "They were nine when they were finally assigned Keepers?"

"Just—would you listen? My parents met when Miranda and Grayson were kids. Because they spent every wishing moment together, so did my parents! My parents eventually married and had me!" She flipped to the next page. It was a huge family tree with notes of which WishMaker belonged to which WishKeeper within the family history of Shea's parents. A note next to *Elanor Willowind* read, *First WishMaker Assignment: Grayson Brady, Maker Year 1991.* The same type of note was next to Beren's name, noting Miranda as Beren's first assignment. Only four years prior had Erebus been crowned WishingKing.

"My parents were assigned their first WishMakers in the Maker year of 1991. They were fresh out of training when they were assigned Miranda and Grayson," explained Shea, still just as excited, but her enthusiasm waned as she considered how eager her parents must have been. They were no older than Shea at the time, full of hope and enthusiasm to take on their first assignment. They were fresh and optimistic with a bright, unknown future stretching out in front of them. Their daughter wasn't even a flutter in their hearts.

"Huh. Neat. I wonder if my gram's family is in here," said Thane, leaning toward the book.

"Can we stay on point, please?" Shea said as she stopped Thane from turning the page.

"Well then, what is the point?"

"Just read that." Shea impatiently pointed to a note at the very bottom of the page.

Thane sighed, annoyed, and read the text, "By fulfillment law, at parental death, the family WishMakers are passed to final heir—Shea Evenstar. And... that's all it says."

"What do you mean that's all it says?" Shea pointed at herself, "Final heir!"

"It's an old book in an old library that we're not supposed to be in," Thane said, trying to close the book and obviously not understanding what Shea was not-so-cleverly trying to explain. Shea grabbed the page from him.

"Grayson and Miranda made another True Love Wish last night."

"The deep end, and you just jumped off it," said Thane, confirming she was officially nuts.

"I'm serious!"

Thane was barely listening at this point. "If every day of my Keeping you is like this, I'm gonna be dead before I even become a Keeper."

"I heard my dad talking with the F.I.A.!"

"Look, I think it's great you're looking up your family history and I know how hard it is to lose a parent, but WishMakers don't make two True Love Wishes. It's impossible. And it would mean that –" Shea cut him off again.

"That it's my wish! By wishing right, I'm the one who has to grant it."

Thane stared at her. Even if what they were reading was correct, and even if she may be right, it was too much for him to fathom. With a quick rip, Shea tore the page out of the lineage book.

"Shea!" scolded Thane.

"Fate. Remember?"

The eager, broken-winged fairy rushed out with the paper flapping at her side.

Shea walked with a purpose across the grassy glade. Behind her was the dilapidated stone castle, and Thane trying to keep up. In front of them was the headquarters of the Fairy

Intelligence Agency. A thatched-roof structure huddled within the branches of a massive oak tree. With four tiers above the base and turrets towering over five corners, it was quite huge, even by fairy standards.

As Thane caught up to the purposeful Shea, he tried to slow her down. "Even though the rules are clearly stated and you are evidently the rightful heir to the wish, General Beren is too, so let's just think about this for a second."

Still marching, Shea interrupted, "Two WishMakers, two WishKeepers. Since my mom is... my dad needs me, OK? And I can't think anymore! It's all I've been doing my whole life."

"Yes, but sometimes stopping to think helps you make the best decision because you can't just walk into the F.I.A. and tell the General that it's your wish," said Thane, thinking he was making sense.

"Watch me." Shea quickened her pace. Thane stopped and dug in his heels.

"Shea. You can't fly!"

Spinning on her heels and staring at Thane, rage swelled within her. She charged at him, red-faced.

"Don't you tell me what I can or can't do. This is my wish! Who's gonna grant mine, huh?"

He was stunned that such a small fairy could be so intimidating. "But... fairies don't make wishes."

"Well, I do! And none has come true," her reply seethed through her teeth. She quickly turned and continued her speedwalk to the F.I.A.

Thane followed, making sure to keep his mouth shut.

13
A GENERAL'S PLEA

Nine Years Ago

Ever since Beren lost Elanor, he had never been quite the same. Word had gotten out among his Keepers that the General would occasionally go missing for hours at a time without any report to the F.I.A. He knew there were rumors about him: rumors that claimed he'd lost his spark. Not the spark of energy he once had as a young fairy, but the spark that keeps a fairy sane, intact. For Beren, it was just easier to let his troops and civilian fairies talk all they wanted. There was a spark that was missing, but it had nothing to do with his sanity.

Every night in bed he would stare at the empty space next to him with his hand outstretched, caressing the sheets back and forth, back and forth. It was all he could do to make himself fall asleep. Somehow the soothing nature of the slow waving of his arm eventually made him tired enough to overcome the insomnia, though it didn't always work. The only good thing about insomnia was that he wouldn't have to manage his nightmares, even though his worst one was relived day after day—forgetting her.

On the one-year anniversary of Elanor's death, The Other Side was covered by a grey, clouded summer sky. Determined, Beren stepped through a fir tree's Gate and looked out over the small town of Abdera.

He set a cautious foot onto the skinny fir's branch and pulled back a few needles. Peering out into the park, he covered his head with a brown hood and flew off toward a rusty well a few hundred feet in front of him. A wooden bucket dangled from a mangled leather rope, onto which he jumped and slid down. Carefully peering over the bucket's edge, he looked down into the blackness of the well below. Voices could be heard, though nothing discernible, just muffled orders barked by a low, angry voice. About to climb down, he quickly ducked when a figure in all black launched itself up and out of the well. The figure used a grappling spell to pull himself out and landed, sure-footed, on the green grass a few feet away.

Beren stared at The Captain, partially in awe and, in an odd way, longing. Flying out of the bucket, Beren slowly and quietly landed behind him. Beren removed his wand and though it was ready for a fight, Beren wasn't. The Captain whirled around and, lightning-quick, armed his crossbow. It was pointed at his face before Beren could raise his wand.

The Captain motioned for him to drop it, but the General refused. Beren tried to look into the darkness of the hooded cloak, but a thick shadow cast away any light from The Captain's face. He was a dominating figure, The Captain. A couple inches taller than Beren with arms, as if unnaturally stretched, that seemed even longer than they should be. Walking toward Beren, pointing an arrow at his forehead, The Captain was forcing Beren back. Step after step, they stared at each other until, finally, The Captain, with a quick thrust, pushed his crossbow inches from Beren's sweating brow.

Beren crashed to the ground and looked up at The Captain. The General's eyes were begging for something. *Please*, they said. *Please*. The Captain stood over the fallen Beren, pointing his crossbow at his heart.

"Elanor," Beren said. "She needs to come back. Please." Tears welled up in the General's eyes. He didn't raise his wand. He didn't dare The Captain to make a move.

He just stared at him—a husband wanting his wife to come home.

The Captain flinched. Beren noticed that there was a pause as if The Captain was contemplating more than just his plea. There was something deeper. Something he didn't understand. Finally, The Captain slowly lowered his bow, stared at the tearful Beren and walked away.

By Beren's sudden heaving breath and rush of tears, it was as if he'd rather The Captain had shot him dead than simply leave him be. He watched the lean and tall Captain walk around the well and launch into a nearby maple. Gone.

14
THE HOPE

Present Day

Because of Erebus' ten-year hold on The Other Side and the ever-growing danger of attempting a wish wrangling session, fewer Keepers were willing to risk everything for their Makers' wishes. Shea thought it was cowardly and shallow for a WishKeeper to refuse to cross over, but as the years passed and more and more Keepers were killed or went missing, she knew why they were refusing to cross over. Even though she knew why, it still didn't make it right. Here she was, desperate to be a Keeper, and so many of them were dropping from the ranks, refusing to perform their duties. *Quitters*, she thought. She watched her dad try to re-gather his forces, only to eventually accept that he was lucky to have any Keepers at all. It was just another reason that Shea was so eager to convince her father that she should be given a shot.

The remaining force was a mixture of brave heroes with an undying devotion to WishKeeping and, to put it lightly, egotistical crazies. Shea knew her dad couldn't wrangle this True Love Wish on his own. If he were lost, the core of WishKeeping, and Paragonia in general, would crack and fall to ruin, but Shea refused to tell her dad such a thing. It made her uncomfortable admitting that her dad was right, but they didn't have a WishingKing on the throne and their borders were vanishing more and more every day. While the True Love Wish brought a chance to rebuild and rebalance their realm, there was also the very real and very dangerous possibility of its falling into the wrong, shadowy hands. It was too much for Shea to think about, because if she focused on all of the bad things that could happen, she'd never get the chance to prove herself. Fear wasn't an option.

Every Keeper knew this wish was their ticket to regaining their strength, but only Beren's elite crew of WishKeepers was willing to make the sacrifice. The Forlorn Hope was the self-named troop of WishKeepers that were willing to continue their sacrifice in order to wrangle as many of their Makers' wishes as possible. Shea would roll her eyes when Beren called them The Hope. He didn't like the negative connotation of the word "forlorn." Nonetheless, The Forlorn Hope continued their missions on a daily basis and even though her dad ignored the forlorn aspect of its name, it kept proving its negative meaning since each day a few of its members would cross over to The Other Side and never return.

Squeezing their way into a crowded War Room, Shea and Thane pushed through the panel-lined main room of the F.I.A. headquarters. It was packed shoulder to shoulder with members of The Hope yelling and shouting, one opinion after another. Shea could hear two particular members attempting to aid their General in calming the crowd. They always kissed their General's butt and even though Shea despised brown-nosers, she couldn't help but want to join their ranks.

"It's not just any wish!" yelled Foster.

Foster was famous for being one of the tallest WishKeepers in recorded Paragonian history – even taller than the mythical Norderon of Greenway. While Shea was slightly below average height, standing at a petite six inches, Foster more than doubled that at thirteen. Many arguments stemmed from his assurance that he was thirteen and a quarter inches instead of the thirteen that was labeled on his recruitment sheet. His argument was the clichéd, "thirteen and a quarter inches 'in boots,'" but everyone knows Keepers, Shea excepted, don't wear boots. Though Foster's voice had a nasal tone, it was impossible not to notice it simply due to the fact that his mouth was at least a couple inches above everyone else's.

"We don't have nearly enough wishes coming in and we all know what a TLW could mean for us!" yelled Goren.

Goren, another WishKeeper, wore all green from head to even his toenails. Most Keepers were annoyed by Money Wishes, but Goren prided himself on granting his Maker's countless financially based wishes. He was massive, too, though still two inches shorter than Foster. They called him The Bull since barely an ounce of fat could be found on his body. His green cloak couldn't hide his bulging biceps, which were almost as big as his calves. The loud, rambling shouting of the crowd meshed into one continued complaint and, truthfully, Shea didn't feel Foster and Goren were helping matters.

Goren and Foster were always together, though they would never admit they were friends. A third Keeper completed their trio of mates: Avery. Avery was a terrifying beauty. Some fairies bind a heart with comfort, joy, and peace, but Avery's long, thick black hair and her deep ageless eyes were almost as dark as her black cloak, and left her fellow Keepers wondering whose side she was really on. Much like the rarity of a fairy that donned red hair representing a True Love Wish, Avery's thick black, shoulder-length mane matched that of a Death Wish.

This was the sixth type of wish that no one, including Shea, ever talked about. Just the mere thought of it would send shivers down even Shea's spine. She had never encountered one and didn't even know where they hid them. In all of her time at The Nursery she'd never come across one. She never liked to admit any kind of fear, but since most fairies were frightened of a Death Wish, she at least had company if the topic ever came up.

Shea knew Avery wasn't evil in a general sense, but only because she and her father were the only fairies that knew much about her. Prior to the destruction of the True Love Wish, Avery was a much different fairy. When Shea would ask her dad about what happened to her, Beren would just leave it alone and say that what she had been through was something that didn't need to be repeated. She knew only that her dad was content with having her on board as a Keeper. Avery never complained, and, actually, as opposed to Goren, who never shut up, rarely spoke a word. The unsaid word is sometimes scarier than a reply and Shea hated that idea. Avery never explained herself nor said much of anything, and it drove Shea crazy. Avery was the epitome of the unknown, and she liked it that way—just another reason most fairies were scared of her.

Shea was determined to get to the front of the crowd, unfazed by the hollering, but Thane was just trying to keep up. After his fourth "excuse me" he lost sight of Shea, who was forcing her way to Beren. The General stood on a pedestal doing a poor job at calming his force of Keepers.

"I am well aware of our current situation," said Beren at a volume barely loud enough to reach the front row.

"You can't handpick the Keepers! It has to be put to a vote!" yelled one purple-haired male Keeper with a sharp, pointed jaw, knowing that Foster and Goren were two of the Keepers Beren had already selected for the mission.

Thane finally pushed his way to the front and grabbed Shea by the arm just before she could make her way to her dad. She flung her arm away from his grip just as the yelling continued.

"The selections have been made," said Beren trying to keep his cool, but his impatience was bubbling to a boil.

"Favoritism!" the yells continued.

"Oh, shut it, pixie! Jealousy is a waste of time," Foster yelled back. The word "pixie," especially within The Hope, was a lashing insult for any WishKeeper. None of them considered themselves cute, or bubbly, or even friendly for that matter. To be called a 'pixie' was a genuine threat to any Keeper's bloated ego, and the word ricocheted across the crowd of frenzied soldiers. Pushing and shoving, Shea could barely keep her balance, and the roars from various insulted Keepers were deafening.

"There is no favoritism here and there never has been!" yelled Beren. "It's the most important wish..." His voice dwindled to a grumble as he watched his corps of troops rioting directly in front of him.

Shea watched her father amidst the push and pull of the crowd. His eyes were set deep within his skull, rimmed with sleepless nights and devoted worry. Yet they were clouded with thoughts that juxtaposed with the surrounding chaos. A sudden calm rolled over his glassy eyes as he quickly looked up at the crowd.

"The wish must be destroyed!" yelled Beren. His voice echoed throughout the War Room. One by one, the members of The Hope heard their General's sudden order and stopped, unable to believe what they just heard.

Shea wanted to gasp, to cry out, but it wasn't just Thane pulling her back, it was the grip of uncontrollable anger and resentment that wouldn't allow her to string together the words. A hush fell over the frenzied crowd. Goren and Foster turned to their General, already knowing this bit of information. Avery rolled her eyes, happy the crowd finally shut up.

"Are you all prepared to do such a thing? If Erebus gets his hands on this wish, it's over. For all of us. The Keepers I selected have been briefed and, though heavy hearted, understand their mission."

Shea pushed her way to the front of the crowd and rushed to her dad. "You can't destroy it! Not again! It's Grayson and Miranda's second True Love Wish!"

"Shea!" he said, in a raspy whisper. Shea could tell he wasn't prepared for his daughter to hear this news yet. "You need to leave. Now! This is strictly F.I.A. business," said Beren, trying to move on.

"No, it's my business! I have the right to decide what to do with this wish!" Shea's voice squeaked in desperation. This was it: her chance to prove to her father that she could be the Keeper he'd always expected.

Beren's quick look almost gave him away and Shea noticed. She knew her dad was aware of the lineage rules and this was exactly the time and place to discuss it. He couldn't avoid it. Murmurs and light chuckles cascaded through the crowd. *The General's daughter suddenly feels like she's important.*

Goren couldn't help himself. "That's brilliant. Yeah, OK, General, I'll step down and let the wingless wonder do my job instead." Foster tried to hold back a laugh, but without success. Avery gave him an annoyed look. This just enraged Beren even more.

"You hold your tongue, private!" he bellowed. Goren's confidence melted from his face, if only for a moment. Beren was already dealing with his daughter's small rebellion. He didn't have the energy or will power to also deal with his troops' smart comments.

Shea unfolded the page from the lineage book and handed it to her dad. He refused to take it.

"It's our wish. I'm a rightful heir," said Shea.

"Don't do this," replied Beren through gritted teeth.

Shea raised her voice, making sure the quiet crowd could hear. "By fulfillment law, at parental death the WishMakers are passed to final heir. Read it!"

"Stop!" Beren pleaded.

"You told me to prove myself, so here I am!"

"You're not a WishKeeper, Shea, and you never will be!"

It was a dagger to his daughter's bleeding heart and it was exactly what he shouldn't have said. Avery was no longer watching Shea—she knew her General's words were hurtful—but instead locked on to Beren. Even she was surprised by the sudden outburst. Her by-the-book General was blatantly ignoring Paragonian law, much less basic lineage.

Shea was speechless. In front of all of the fairies she looked up to: all of the fairies she wished to emulate, even the ones who made fun of her on a daily basis. Now even her own father didn't believe in her. She stared at her dad. Not with anger. Not with surprise, but in confusion. There was one thing of which she was ever sure. Hesitation had been a part of her daily life since she could remember, but she had never hesitated in thinking that her dad believed she could one day be the Keeper he always wanted her to be.

Bursting towards the exit, Shea pushed the silenced crowd out of the way and hurried out, barely holding back tears. She hated knowing that Thane was following, but a slight glimmer of gratitude struck her unexpectedly. At least someone was on her side.

Addressing the crowd, Beren didn't have to raise his voice this time. "It's done. My selections, gear up. We cross over at sunset." While the rest of the Keepers started to file out, Avery stood motionless, deep in thought, and staring at her General.

Thane hurried out of the F.I.A., pushing past the exiting Keepers, and tried to keep an eye on the retreating Shea. She was in a full sprint across the valley and though Thane knew he could easily catch up, he let her be. He knew his orders, but he also thought Shea would hate him even more if he followed.

He took a deep breath, considering his options, and turned to head home. Avery was standing, stoic, in front of him when he turned around and had his mind not been worried about his friend, he might have let out a little yelp. She glared at him, famously not saying a word, letting Thane say something first.

"Um, so, hello, Avery," he said, after a few long moments of staring. It was all he could come up with other than, "you're really weird and scaring the crap out of me." She continued to stare and finally took a deep breath, accepting that she would need to carry this conversation.

"Your handicapped friend... how is she with a wand?" she asked in a low, monotone voice.

Thane was surprised to feel a wave of anger flow through him. *How dare she call her handicapped?* Oddly enough, this calmed Thane and erased any strangeness he felt about the sudden conversation.

"You'd be surprised," he returned, confident.

Avery dug her hand into a pocket of her cloak and suddenly Thane's confidence began to retreat. Who knows what oddities Avery kept within that thing. Instead of a wand, she removed a blank, rolled piece of parchment, unfurled it in front of him and stared. She wasn't staring at him, but rather at nothing in particular. Suddenly calligraphic words appeared on the parchment, sprawling out into sentences that ended with, *See Winston, The GateKeeper.* Avery rolled the parchment up and handed it to him.

Absentmindedly, Thane took the parchment, unable to avoid Avery's dark eyes. He opened it and was about to read, but she spoke again; this time in a much more calming voice than he'd expected.

"Retrieving True Love goes beyond our rules of WishKeeping."

He read the parchment and looked back at Avery. "Winston? You want us to cross over."

"I want you to do what you know is right," she said, and without another word flew off, leaving Thane with a dozen unfinished thoughts.

15
THOSE THREE WORDS

A shaft of golden light beamed its way through Shea's opened picture window. Rifling through her things, she stuffed items into a small pack. "He calls himself a Keeper? And a General? A leader doesn't destroy the one thing that—oh, forget it!" she yelled as she whipped a water bottle across her room. She looked up at the dangling models of flying machines hovering over her head. They swayed back and forth in the breeze. The strings that kept them attached to the ceiling were all she could truly see. Stuck to one spot. Destined to stay where they were. To stay what they were. Fake.

She jumped, ripped one from the ceiling and threw it as hard as she could. Before it could explode against the wall, she ripped another one down, then another.

Thane flew to her window, flinching as Shea destroyed her room. He didn't think she noticed as he landed on the window seat, but she collapsed into her cushioned chair, covering her sobbing eyes. "Go away, Thane!"

"I'm sorry. I just—" he said. Shea didn't know if she wanted him to leave because she truly did hate him or if she was embarrassed that he was seeing her this way. He just sat there, staring. *At least say something!*

Shea tried to compose herself, and took deep breaths as she stood and went back to her small pack, tossing a few more items in.

"I... I have something for you," Thane said, trying to stay businesslike. If he showed any amount of sympathy for her, she'd punch him.

"I don't want it," Shea said with a snort.

He nodded, and motioned to leave.

"Wait," Shea quickly added. "Toss me those." She was referring to her aviator goggles. They were easily within her reach, but he complied anyway.

After she grabbed them from his hand, Thane reached into his pocket, pulled out the rolled piece of parchment and placed it on her chair.

"By definition, a WishKeeper tends to, protects and aids a wish in its fulfillment process."

Wrapping her goggles around her neck, Shea ignored the parchment, or at least tried to.

"I was given a mission and every Keeper sees his mission through to the end," Thane continued.

Acting like it was a nuisance, she snatched up the parchment and read it out loud. "Rules of engagement while on The Other Side." It was a list of official rules and regulations regarding a WishKeeper's actions and orders while pursuing wishes. She looked at him, confused.

"I'm supposed to Keep you, but that doesn't mean I can't help you. Meet me at Winston's Gate in twenty minutes," he said as he tried to turn back to the window before she could reply.

"I don't need your help."

Thane stopped, looked at her and swiped the parchment out of her hand. "Yeah, ya do," he said with a smirk.

Shea watched him fly out the window. She tied her pack shut. She didn't want to smile. She hated even the thought of a smile, but there it was and it wouldn't leave her alone.

Thane landed, stopped and looked back up at her window. The parchment was in his hand and he couldn't believe he was about to do what he was about to do. Winston's Gate. He hadn't thought of actually helping Shea. All this time he was simply following orders: keep her out of trouble. His General specifically ordered him to keep his daughter safe, but now he was about to do the exact opposite—bring her directly into the line of fire. *Retrieving true love goes beyond our rules of WishKeeping. Avery was right and so were the members of The Hope. This isn't just another wish and it isn't a means to an end. Destroying it will only put a patch over a leaky hole.*

He knew where Winston's Gate was and he knew he was about to take the biggest gamble of his most likely short-lived WishKeeper career. His General was wrong, and he was going to defy his orders and help his friend grant a True Love Wish.

As Thane launched himself into the air and zipped toward the opposite end of the valley, Avery sat, perched in a nearby oak. She watched him fly away, pulled her deep black hair into a tight pony tail, and sped off.

Just as Shea was about to grab a rope ladder dangling out her window, there was a knock at her bedroom door. She paused, knowing who it was, and felt her anger return.

"Shea...?" she heard her father's voice from the other side of the door. "Listen," he continued, "about earlier: There's just too much to explain and you wouldn't understand. Not right away, anyway."

Gritting her teeth, she knew he would treat her like a child. Like a little pixie that would never understand. Oh, she understood alright, but she didn't have time to listen to apologies, nor did she want one.

"Your Mom," her father continued. "She was better at this. Always knew what…" he mumbled. "You're all I've…"

Shea waited for it. Even though she didn't want to hear her father say it, she couldn't get herself to leave. Maybe she did want to hear it. Maybe she wanted to hear her father say those three damned words even more than she wanted an apology. The quiet of the room was deafening as she held tight to the rope ladder.

"We'll talk when I get back. OK?" he said.

Tears poured from her puffy blue eyes. He couldn't say it. Like father, like daughter, and the realization only made her angrier. She stared at the rope, dripping uncontrollable tears, and finally climbed out the window.

"I'm sorry." Her father's apology hung in the air, waiting for a reply, but Shea was already gone.

16
AVERY'S SECRET

Ten Years Ago

At WishKeeping recruitment time little was known of Avery Waterstone other than the fact that her bright pink eyes and thick pink locks brought a smile to everyone's face. She was a smile personified, and though the term 'living life wearing rose-colored glasses' may be construed in a negative light, Avery delighted in seeing the beauty in everything and everyone around her. There wasn't a drop of hurtful or spiteful blood within her, and she did all that she could to bring happiness to anyone she encountered. She had been Erebus' WishKeeper before he became WishingKing, and her joyful and agreeable attitude was the main reason Erebus loved her so much, and why he promoted her to Regent quickly after his crowning. After switching from WishKeeper to Regent, she practiced joyfully her responsibilities of general supervision over the conduct and welfare of all Keepers. Though it was more of an assistant role and she held no real power within Paragonia, she didn't mind. Spending each day with her WishingKing and managing the well-being of the Keepers suited her Purity-like self perfectly.

It was three months before Miranda and Grayson's first True Love Wish when Avery's life changed. It didn't bend or tilt slightly, rather it ruptured like a dormant geyser finally releasing a thousand years of tension. The rain that day spattered against the castle's windows and her king wasn't feeling well. It was odd for a WishingKing to be sick at all since every WishingKing had a specific life span of exactly one hundred years of perfect health, even up until the end. Avery brushed it off and surmised that the changing of the season and wet, chilly weather must be bringing out the sniffles.

She buzzed a cup of hot, steaming tea to him as he sat bundled up in bed and placed it on his end table.

"Thank you, my Avery dear. This blasted cold just won't seem to go away, I'm afraid," Erebus said, wiping his nose with a hanky.

Avery smiled, removed her wand and spun in a loving circle around the cup of tea. "May the sun shine all day long, everything go right, and nothing go wrong," she said in a sing-song rhythm and clinked the cup of tea with her wand. Nothing grand or magical happened, but her smile was infectious and Erebus couldn't help but giggle.

There was a knock at the door and Erebus motioned for Avery to answer. She happily bounced her way over, but the door pushed open before she could open it herself. Sopping wet and in an obvious nasty mood, Elanor swept in carrying a bright Purity. Before either of them could greet her, Elanor's complaints rolled off her tongue. Avery was suddenly frozen still.

"Your Majesty, I always appreciate our meetings, but flying across the entire valley in pouring rain just to present you with one little Purity seems to be an incredible waste of time. If I may speak freely, of course," Elanor said, wringing the rain from her long, red hair. She looked exhausted, was completely soaked, and if she hadn't been talking to her king, she probably would have yelled what she just said instead of pushing it through her wet lips.

Avery floated, caught among a hundred feelings. Her usual, natural smile faded to an open-mouthed stare. It wasn't magic of any kind that held her there, at least not of the fairy kind. It was a magic of a much more ancient and natural conjuring. It spilled from her heart and rushed through every vein with an energy unmatched. She had never met Elanor, though she had heard her name discussed within the everyday management for her king, and until now Elanor was just another WishKeeper doing a fine job. Avery floated, one hand intertwining the other as if she tried catching her breath but missed. She couldn't stop staring at her. Had she ever seen anyone so beautiful?

"Ah, my Elanor," Erebus said, ignoring Elanor's bad mood. "Thank you. I truly appreciate your hard work and dedication, and I apologize for taking you away from your Keeping duties to tend to a sick old man. Have you met my Regent, Avery Waterstone?"

Avery twitched at her name and bowed her head quickly. Elanor looked and shot a forced smile. "Hey," she barely tossed the greeting to Avery. While she didn't mean to come across as cruel, Elanor was a naturally impatient fairy and didn't understand why her Purity wasn't snug in The Nursery by now. "Your Majesty, if you don't mind?" It was a request to get on with it.

Erebus sat up and repositioned himself. "Of course. Avery, will you retrieve the Purity, please?"

"Retrieve…?" Elanor didn't understand.

As bashful as bashful could be, Avery blushed her way over to Elanor and hesitantly reached out her hands, expecting Elanor to give her the Purity. The little wish, with its wide happy smile, had no idea there was an argument brewing. It grinned a calming smile at Avery as she approached, and it was the first time Avery felt a rush of jealousy. She'd rather someone else was smiling at her, not the wish.

"Your Majesty, really, I don't have time for some form of class or lesson so that your new Regent may learn more about wishes or whatever it is you—" Elanor was suddenly cut off. It was the first time Avery or Elanor had ever heard their king raise his voice.

"Hand over the wish, Elanor, and you may go! If you have such critical goings-on more important than helping your king, then just get it over with!"

The chamber echoed with his sudden outburst and snapped Avery from her enraptured stare. They both looked at Erebus, confused, surprised to say the least.

"I'm sorry, Your Majesty, I just—" Elanor tried.

"Please," Erebus said, a bit calmer. "I respect your wishes to get back to work; please respect mine to do the same."

Elanor blinked through the confusion and followed orders. She bowed, and slowly gave up the wish. Avery accepted the little Purity with loving arms, and when Elanor connected eyes with her, her cheeks flushed again.

"Now then, I expect you have work to do. Thank you, Elanor, and I apologize for my outburst," Erebus said, gathering his breath.

Avery backed away, cradling the Purity, and even though Elanor had plenty to add and questions to ask, she felt it prudent to leave them be and floated through the chamber doors. Love-struck, Avery looked at the open chamber doors, secretly wishing Elanor would come back. She didn't understand these new feelings—this sudden rush of excitement. It felt as right as anything she'd felt before, though something on the surface told her to ignore it. Few things in life are truly impossible, but Avery had just discovered one of them—ignoring a sudden crush.

"Avery," Erebus said, again snapping her from her paralyzing thoughts. "Bring me the wish, please."

She did as she was told and floated to her king. As she flew closer to him, her newfound crush for Elanor slowly dissipated, and the strangeness of the situation came to the forefront. Never had she handed a wish to her king before, and truly, there was never a reason to. A WishingKing never handled the wishes physically. There was the monthly inspection of The Nursery, of course, but more for the inspection of treatment and cleanliness of the stables than the actual wrangling of the wishes. That was a Keeper's job.

Pausing at his bedside, she hesitated as the old king reached out his palm. His eyes were bloodshot, wide and what Avery could only define as desperate. She couldn't help but pull back as he reached his palm a bit further.

"Please, my Avery. You wish for your king to be well again, don't you?" The king's tone was filled with guilt, but not of the personal kind. He meant for her to feel it.

She nodded her head and an uncontrollable feeling came over her—the opposite of what she had just felt while looking at Elanor. She wanted it to stop; almost silently begging for it to end, but it was too strong. Unconsciously, she placed the little wish into the king's clammy palm and quickly floated backwards. There was something wrong about his hand. The cracking of blissful naïveté can be a painful process and Avery had never felt it before, but it was fear. For the first time in her life, fear overcame her.

Erebus sat up in bed, leaning forward over his cupped hands. They covered the Purity, and while it looked like Erebus was being delicate, Avery knew this was wrong. This shouldn't be happening. The room filled with a darkness that had nothing to do with how bright or dark it could be, but more of an emotion. The room vibrated with a hollow, deadening pulse.

Avery couldn't fly backward any further as she bumped into the stained glass window, rain crashing into it. The sound of the raindrops filled the room with a deafening hum. Avery watched her king consume the wish. A black flash of shadow stretched from his hands, and with a quick crack of thunder, the darkness pulsed through him like a filthy wave.

A deep breath from Erebus released the tension in the room, but not the moment from Avery's wide eyes. *What had just happened? What did my king just do?* He breathed deeply again, and moved his thick wool blanket away. He climbed out of bed, still cupping the wish in his hand, and stood. Erebus looked at little Avery shaking, pushing herself against the foreign comfort of the cold stained glass, and opened his hands. The once happy little Purity was nothing but a grey, lifeless ball of dust. He tilted his palm and the ashes of the wish fell unceremoniously to the floor, becoming nothing more than something else for Avery to sweep up later.

"Your WishingKing feels much better now," Erebus said, staring bright-eyed at the scared little Keeper. "You must promise me something, Avery. No one can ever know about this. It will be our little secret. Something only you get to share with your WishingKing."

He leaned in close. Avery's breath was quick and labored, and all she wanted to do was rush to Elanor and tell her how sorry she was. She shouldn't have taken the wish from her. To tell her... just to tell her. She had never cried before, but Avery felt what must have been a tear trickle down her face. Little did she know, she would grow accustomed to tears, as a torturer does to pain.

"Speaking of secrets, I have discovered one. Have you and the Keepers been keeping something from your WishingKing?"

Avery shook her head, genuinely not understanding what her king was referencing. *What secret? I would never keep anything from my king.*

"The sixth," Erebus said, demented and eager.

Her desperate little head was suddenly filled with scrambled thoughts. *Not the sixth. He couldn't mean...* She shook her head again, more to erase the possibility that this is what he meant than to actually answer him.

"I chose you as my Regent, Avery, because I love your dedication to the truth. Lies do not fit you, my Avery," he continued, staring at her with wide anxious eyes. "You will tell me where they keep the Death Wishes."

Creeping out from under his cloak, a black fog enveloped Avery, wrapping her up in its thick, wet smoke. Panic swept through her. *Why would my king do this? Why would my beloved WishMaker make me tell him such a thing?*

Her eyes crackled with a black shadow and her head perked up, looking intently at her king. "Behind The Pointe, there is a cave," she said, as if in a dream. "All wishes of Death forever will be saved." The fog rushed away from her, retreating back under his cloak. Erebus stood upright, smiling as Avery's black eyes continued to stare.

"And you will retrieve for me such a wish," Erebus said.

*   *   *   *

In the following months all of the Keepers noticed a difference in their happy little Regent. A darkness fell over Avery, and her famous smile became more and more rare. She was a prisoner to her own devotion to ignorance, and every time Erebus requested another Death Wish, she felt the one-time joy and love in her heart disappear a little more. Eventually, she became almost robotic and while the other Keepers assumed it was simply a matter of a heavy workload and busy schedule, Elanor was the first to notice a real change. The dark circles under Avery's eyes were one thing, but there was something within them that worried Elanor. She and Beren took her in, inviting her to supper, tea and the occasional party. For Avery, the only time a true remembering of emotion or love crept back in was when she spent time with Elanor and her family, and yet Elanor continued to witness the slow decay of the happy little soul firsthand, and true worry began to sink in.

It was the night of Wishing Eve when Avery came to Elanor, unexpectedly. When she would look at Elanor, she felt the agony of love. The agony that she knew would always be with her, and somehow the cold curse that Erebus had set upon her became a comfort. At least she wouldn't have to feel, to long, to love. The curse of the unrequited. It was too much to bear, and she cared too deeply about Elanor to burden her with futility. She loved her too much and couldn't allow Elanor to feel any amount of guilt. It was time to come clean.

She and Beren were readying their packs for the busy night and Shea was pleading with her parents to let her cross over with them, pouting and throwing a fit each time they said no.

Despite how quiet and introverted Avery was, Beren and Elanor felt that she was a part of their family, even only after a short three months' time. The pink-haired Regent stood in their living room, looking so thin and frail that a slight breeze might knock her over. After appeasing their tantrum-throwing child, allowing Shea to cross over if she agreed to go to her room and stop complaining, they sat Avery on the couch and listened to her confession.

Avery told them Erebus' plan and how he had been using Death Wishes to grow in strength and power. What truly frightened them was her admission that she was the one retrieving them for him. Too exhausted to cry, Avery sat and stared, thankful to finally be rid of at least one secret. She didn't tell them the whole story, however. She didn't tell them that Erebus was planning to capture a True Love Wish and combine it with a Death Wish.

Why didn't Avery tell them that night? Did she assume they were smart enough to protect a True Love Wish if one was made? She assumed correctly, of course, but as she sat in their living room awaiting disaster, a hint of a relieved smile spread across her cheeks. She couldn't do it anymore and one burden was finally released. The second burden would simply have to be hidden.

Elanor and Beren argued over their next move while Avery watched, barely listening. Grayson and Miranda were "ripe," as they called it. Ripe for what everyone was hoping for, a True Love Wish. It's impossible to predict when such a wish will be made, but like trying to predict the weather, it was at least possible to track. Because it was Wishing Eve and wishes are always a bit stronger on such a night, Beren and Elanor agreed that it was very possible their WishMakers could make a True Love Wish that night.

They planned every precaution possible. After Avery explained to them that Erebus didn't have a new Death Wish—he hadn't given her the order yet—they agreed that positioning guards at the entrance of the Death Wish cave was necessary, and that Erebus needed to be removed.

"He's gone," Avery said, in a monotone voice. She was listening to their plan, though barely awake.

"Gone? What do you mean?" Elanor asked.

"I went to his chambers tonight, checked The Pointe, The Nursery, everywhere. He's gone," she said, sure of herself.

"I'll order the guards, but we have to go, Ellie. It's getting late and my troops are waiting," Beren said, grabbing his bags. "We don't have time to search for him. Avery, I want you to stay here tonight. Shea is coming with us, so you'll have a little peace and quiet. Just relax and we'll take care of this." A worried look washed over Elanor's face, but there was nothing more to say, and they had a busy night ahead of them. Grayson and Miranda were about to make a True Love Wish. Snatching their things, they left Avery in the darkness of the General's Quarters.

THE WISHKEEPER

Outside the F.I.A., after Beren prepped his WishKeepers for the crossover and detailed everything, including Erebus' plans, he pulled a WishSentinel aside. Charlie was a new Sentinel, recently added to the ranks. He was an eager, young soldier and because he hadn't had much training with the WishPanels yet, Beren gave him peculiar orders that had nothing to do with headquarters. Though Charlie didn't understand why he needed to stand an armed post outside of his General's own home, he followed orders and gave a quick salute. He was off with a flash, excited to be a part of his first official Wishing Eve as a soldier.

Beren confirmed Elanor's worry, sharing a glance. They had to take every precaution, regardless of how much they trusted their friend, Avery.

When Elanor huddled within the surrounding storm the night she destroyed the True Love Wish, Avery saw it all. She didn't stay where she was told that night. Instead, she hid within a tall fir tree at the end of the cul-de-sac and watched, stone-faced, as the monster Erebus grabbed Beren. She watched as Shea screamed for her mother not to destroy the wish. She watched Elanor's wand charge up and destroy it. She watched as Shea's wings were ripped from her back.

Avery didn't hear Elanor tell Beren that she loved him, but she knew. She knew that Elanor didn't love her the way she wished she would, and she knew, the moment that wish of true love was destroyed, her own love was as well.

Avery stared with lifeless eyes as the heat of the explosion warmed her cheeks. She crouched, unmoving within the fir. Her Erebus was gone. Her Elanor was gone. And so was her ability to cry.

17
THE STREET LAMP

Four Years Ago

Rarely does the end of a thing happen in an instant. More often than not, glimpses of such an end flash, sparkle and twinkle in a multitude of ways. They are hardly enough to cause alarm, or change, or even any kind of action. For Grayson and Miranda, it was a slow evolution of a feeling that rolled into rising anxiety, but their lifelong friendship glossed and rounded the sharp edges of what was actually happening. Their true love was dying. The fact that it took almost six years for either of them to finally take notice was mostly due to their inner need to ignore such a horrible thing. Little did they know it had been six years since their True Love Wish was destroyed.

Grayson had never admitted to himself that he was truly in love with someone until the day he finally proposed to Miranda. Even after years of their friendship and eventual courtship, it was as if he was never able to break the barrier of allowing himself to go there. It was always too much. It was always too dangerous, as if he would somehow lose himself in the admitting. As if the protection he was hiding behind was enough to keep him intact, in form, and safe. But when he held that ring in his hand the night he proposed—the ring that Miranda had technically bought him many years before as part of a funny little birthday present—it struck him. He didn't know, at first, what it was that bowled him over. It, being the truest, most delicate and yet life-altering feeling a man can have, rippled through every inch of him like a crack of quiet thunder after a soundless bolt of lightning. It burst through whatever impenetrable barrier he had created, and allowed him to cross. And when he realized that the "it" wasn't something inside of him at all, but was instead the girl across from him, he knew. He knew she was the bringer of all that quiet thunder.

And yet, no matter how many drinks he shared with her, meals they laughed through, or quiet moments they shared on their park bench, the explosive feeling that for so long had been commonplace was slipping away and a new feeling was emerging. Hope. As if he was hoping to gain back something he had lost. But why should he hope for the retrieval of something when that something was already right there next to him? And isn't hope a good thing? Not when a man's hope edges too close to fear, a fear founded on the worry of losing her. And yet he had unknowingly trained his brain to go back to the hope even without knowing he had returned to it. When he would say even the simplest of hellos or wish his wife goodnight, his heart would sink, knowing that unexpected feeling of hope was there, somewhere in between the letters of every spoken word.

Sitting there, on their park bench, Miranda looked at Grayson as he sketched in his notebook. She watched his hand scribble a chalk drawing of a maple whose leaves had all but fallen. It was late autumn. The park was covered in flashes of gold and brown from the layers of leaves that blanketed the dying grass. A hint of winter was in the November air, but the humid, moist smell of the fallen leaves helped hold on to the last few days of a comfortable fall. Miranda was staring at Grayson's wedding ring as it reflected the overcast sunlight.

"I love him. Right?" she thought to herself. It was suddenly strange to see the ring. She hadn't examined it with much thought since her wedding day: a day that felt like a lifetime ago. Looking at her own ring, she lightly caressed it, hoping that it would bring back the heart-filled happiness it once represented. Nothing moved within her as she stared at it. Just silence from a soul that once shouted with love. "Where did it go?" she thought.

"It's getting a little cold. You can head back if you want," Grayson said, still scribbling in his notebook.

His comment broke her from her thoughtful gaze. She didn't want to stop staring at her ring, as if there was a chance of ending the silence within her if she continued to stare. She looked at Grayson—something inside wanted to smile, but her mouth didn't seem to follow orders.

"It's probably the last day we'll be able to come out here for a while. Before the cold comes, I mean. I know how much you like it. I don't mind staying," she said as she sat back against the bench and pulled her legs tight to her chest, trying to gather a little warmth.

Grayson looked at her squeezing her legs. "Miranda, you're freezing. I drag you out here every week. You don't have to stay." He went back to his notepad and continued sketching.

The sun was ending its path across the sky and behind them a street lamp blinked to life. Miranda looked up at it. There on the bench where they first kissed, the street lamp used to signal that their time was up. They used to react like clockwork to the lamp without saying a word, taking each other's hand and walking back to the house. This time Grayson was telling her to head back without him. Was that the memory they were forgetting? Was their time up?

Nodding her head, she slowly stood and tucked her cold hands in her coat pockets. "Yeah, I guess it is getting a little chilly. Anything you want for dinner?"

"You don't have to make anything. I might take a walk in a bit, so I'll just stop down at the store and grab something. But thanks," he said, finishing with a slight smile.

She nodded again and was about to lean in to kiss him on the cheek, but her feet wouldn't move her forward. Swaying for a bit, she stepped back, "OK. I'll see you at home."

"OK," he replied, and continued to sketch.

Miranda walked away, crunching the leaves beneath her. Grayson pulled his eyes away from the notebook and slowly turned to watch his wife make her way to the sidewalk. He knew that there should have been a feeling—of any kind—rekindled within him as he watched her walk alone under their street lamp, but there was nothing. She shouldn't be walking alone, he knew this, but why didn't he get up? Why didn't he follow?

Within the maple a few meters in front of Grayson, Beren huddled behind a branch, watching. Though his eyes weren't filled with tears, there was anguish in them. Pain. Frustration. His emotions were too connected to understanding what was going on between Miranda and Grayson and, more importantly, why. It was six years since he had lost Elanor and it was six years since their wish was destroyed.

Unable to watch, he leaned his wand against the bark of the tree. A Gate quickly flashed open. The cold wind was beginning to take over the park, and he couldn't witness the slow expiration of his WishMaker's true love.

The flash of the Gate vanished as Beren stepped through. Grayson looked up into the tree. Did he notice something? It was probably just a trick of the eyes. Diving back into his sketch, he continued without a second thought.

18
A FLASH IN THE DARK

Present Day

Trudging through the thick valley grass and repositioning her well packed bag over her shoulder, Shea made her way to the edge of the Paragonian forest. She saw Thane pacing underneath a withering old oak with roots that reached out a few twisted feet toward the brink of the valley. This side of the valley was in danger of vanishing all together. The borders used to span several miles to the north, but now only a mere quarter mile away their bittersweet realm was disappearing. The ancient oak was simply waiting to fade away.

Her nervous friend had not yet noticed her approach. "*Friend?*" Shea thought. "*Why is he doing this? Is he really just following orders? He's kind of funny when he gets nervous.*" Shea quickly halted, took a deep breath and tried to regain her composure. "This is for real, Shea. Get yourself together," she said out loud to herself, as if a pep talk was needed to get her into the right frame of mind.

Thane noticed Shea standing there and most likely that little bit where she was talking to herself. This prompted Shea to straighten her skirt, stand up straight and march toward him.

"Great. So we'll get you debriefed," Thane started, but Shea had an agenda and she wasn't going to let him run this show.

"Let's get a few things straight. Just because I'm letting you help, doesn't mean I need it. Once we get to the Other Side, it's up to you if you want to stick around. And if you say one thing about my wings, I'll make your giant nose even more crooked than it already is. Got it?" she said in one quick breath.

Touching his nose, Thane asked, "It's crooked?"

"Are you going to debrief me, or what?" Shea demanded, still in business mode.

"If you're gonna have an attitude, I'll let you figure out how to cross over without me." Thane was willing to banter, but he wasn't willing to give up control just yet.

Shea readjusted her pack. "Fine. Sorry. Go ahead."

"Apology accepted. Barely. Now listen closely." Thane looked at the parchment Avery gave to him. He already knew the rules by heart, but it helped to reference notes, if only to avoid a glare from Shea. "Keepers cannot allow Makers to see them, they cannot come in physical contact with Makers and must not, by any means, interact with or speak to any Makers."

"OK, I get it. Makers are off limits," Shea returned, wanting him to go on.

"A wish will always remain close to its Maker and once the wish is secure, Keepers must immediately find a Gate and return home," Thane continued to read. "The wish is immediately brought to Exclamation Pointe for inspection then placed within The Nursery for monitoring."

"OK. What else?"

"What else? Other than Lost Fairies and Erebus killing Keepers and eating wishes? That's about it," Thane said, and even though he was saying it sarcastically, he was serious.

"I'm not worried about Lost Fairies."

"You should be," warned Thane.

Trying to ignore his comment, Shea looked up into the tree. It was massive, well over one hundred years old, and dwarfed Thane and Shea as they stood among its gnarled roots. Another deep breath rolled out of Shea as she stared up into the leafless tree.

"So, you're sure about this?" asked Thane, giving her one last chance to bail.

The red-haired fairy just smirked, raised her wand and fired a hot grappling spell up into the tree. Thane shook his head with a smirk of his own and launched himself after her.

They both landed on a thick branch. Its bark had been gnawed and pecked by some kind of a hard-nosed bird, most likely a woodpecker. A hollowed-out, empty nest rested at the crook of the branch and trunk. Casually sitting against it with his legs crossed, arms folded and eyes pleasantly shut was the oldest fairy Shea had ever seen.

For as long as the Keepers have been guarding wishes, GateKeepers have been guarding the Gates that connected Paragonia to The Other Side. Before Erebus reigned as WishingKing, every tree in Paragonia connected with another in The Makers' world. Be it a fir, maple, oak, evergreen, palm, apple or cranberry, the Keepers were free to cross over through any tree they liked. Because of the sheer number of possible Gates, the rank of GateKeeper was basically like that of a parking meter maid. It was the simplest form of military rank among the Keepers, but as the years passed, more and more Gates were shut. By the time Erebus betrayed his Keepers and the True Love Wish was destroyed, fewer than one thousand Gates were still active. Considering the scope of The Other Side and the need of the WishMakers, the dwindling number of Gates made WishGathering that much more difficult.

Most GateKeepers were forced to find other work and thus left the Keeper force altogether. A new force of

GateKeepers was needed to guard the Gates due to the ever-growing danger and threat that spread throughout The Other Side. They were shutting out the very world they depended on, but what choice did they have? Erebus was growing in power and if he was able to break back into Paragonia and destroy the wishes that were awaiting fulfillment, it would be a very quick end to the Keepers and any chance of a WishMaker's wish ever coming true. Their bigger worry was the power of Exclamation Pointe. It was the lifeblood of their realm and, like any power, it could be harnessed for all the wrong reasons.

Winston, the old fairy, was a grandfathered GateKeeper. His father and his father's father before him were GateKeepers and, at one time, Winston was the most skilled of them all. Beren kept him on more as a relic, but his Gate was never used. A GateKeeper's true skill was in his ability to gather news and make reports and Winston knew it all. That is, if he ever woke up.

Thane and Shea stared at Winston as he slept. His beard covered him like a blanket, a ratted up old driver's cap sat sideways over his left eye, and his chest rose and fell as soft as a breeze.

"Winston, I presume?" Shea asked.

"Winston's the oldest GateKeeper in Paragonia. I used to come up here when I was little and he'd tell me stories of The Other Side. Now he just kinda sleeps all day."

"So… what do we do?" asked Shea, not under-standing why Thane brought her to see the oldest of old GateKeepers.

"We wait," Thane said, as if Shea should have known this already.

"Wait for what?"

"Well, there's a reason no one uses his Gate anymore."

Winston let out a great, soggy, snorting snore like a buzz saw and very suddenly the side of the oak tree opened. A Gate quickly appeared and then just as quickly disappeared as Winston ended his fat snore.

"See?" said Thane.

"See what? The old fairy snored."

"He has a tendency to snore the Gate open. It doesn't stay open for very long, though, but every now and then..."

"Are you serious? This is your plan? To wait for him to randomly open the Gate?"

Setting his hands at his waist, he replied, "With no help from you, I'm not a Keeper yet. Non-Keepers aren't able to open Gates. So what do you propose we do?"

Shea's annoyed sigh was almost as loud as Winston's snore. He snored again, and the Gate opened and closed with a flash.

"If we treat it like a game, like a timing thing, we just might be able to—" Thane started, but Shea wasn't in a waiting kind of mood.

"This is ridiculous." She ripped a dead leaf from a nearby branch and tiptoed to the sleeping Winston.

"Don't wake him up! I'm already in deep enough trouble helping you cross over. Last thing I need is a Gate-Keeper reporting back to headquarters."

"Just shush," she whispered as she crept over. She reached the tip of the leaf toward Winston's nose. It was tricky aiming the pointed end of such a large leaf without simply mashing it against the sleeping fairy's face, but she managed to tickle his nose.

SNORE! Winston let out a long-winded, raspy, snot-filled snore. The Gate flashed open and Shea quickly dropped the leaf, grabbed Thane's arm and pulled.

"Go!" she yelled as they rushed toward the Gate.

They met nothing but thick, brown bark and smacked their faces against the tree. Dazed, they stumbled back. Thane fell and sat, holding a blood-dripping nose.

"Ow."

Maybe the timing game wasn't going to work after all.

* * * *

At the other end of the forest, Beren paced in front of his chosen members of The Hope. Among the dozen troops, Goren's robes were pristine as he proudly awaited orders. Foster's bright blue tunic matched the color of his intense, confident eyes. The setting sun streamed its light through a massive white birch tree. Shafts of the golden light cast long, skinny black shadows across the branches. It was a day Beren would rather forget, but he knew more were ahead of him that he feared would only be worse.

The WishKeepers were standing at attention, each holding mini WishRadar devices that tracked the Makers on the Other Side. Avery stood, arms crossed at her chest, her black, hooded cloak pulled over her head. Though her face was all but masked by the heavy hood, her thick, deep eyes were fixed on Beren. Her demeanor was one of nonchalant indifference, but her eyes studied her General as he paced. The mobile radars blinked in unison as Beren stopped pacing and addressed his troops.

"Erebus guards the Gates, but it's a good possibility he has all of his forces out searching for the TLW. Regardless, upon entry, be wand ready. Your WishRadars will lead you to the Makers."

He took a second to look each of his Keepers in the eye. The mission had already been addressed, explained and scrutinized enough: there was no need to review. They knew what was at stake, and what had to be done. Even more, they knew what they were up against. Beren and Avery exchanged a long, hard stare. The General respected the WishKeeper's intensity, which was one of the reasons he had selected her for this mission, but this was a different stare: one of unexpected irreverence that was quite uncommon, even from stone cold Avery.

"Let's go," Beren said, still studying Avery's eyes.

The General turned to a nearby GateKeeper. He was as ancient as the woods, wearing a long blue robe, with perfectly kept white hair and sharp, pointed wings. He stood perfectly still, eyes closed, eventually drawing two wands out from under his robe and motioning from left to right as if he was pulling back an invisible drape. The Gate shined a bright white light, drowning out the golden light of the sun.

One by one, the Keepers filed through. Beren nodded to the GateKeeper and took a step toward the Gate. Pausing for a moment, he looked over the peaceful Valley behind him. Early evening starlight twinkled on the horizon and the General couldn't help but wish Shea were there to see him off. His eyes surveyed the valley for any sign of his daughter, but it was a futile search. He took a deep breath, nodded again to the GateKeeper, and stepped through.

*　　*　　*　　*

The sun was behind the valley mountain range as Shea and Thane sat along Winston's branch. Not much had changed, though Thane's bleeding nose was clearing up. Blotting it lightly with a cloth, Shea sat cross-legged in front of her wounded friend.

"*His nose isn't that big,*" she thought. "*He's kinda cute, I guess. Oh, stop it, Shea, he's here just because he wants his stupid Keeper wings.*" Her inner dialogue was loud enough for Thane to notice. He smiled when she looked in his eyes, and a bit more when she quickly looked away.

Winston let out a great snore, popping the Gate open for a second. "That one might have worked," Thane said casually. Their eyes met again as Shea dabbed the cloth around his nose.

"What can you tell me about these Lost Fairies, anyway?" Shea asked as she quickly put the cloth back into her bag. There was too much of a connection between their eyes. Shea had a mission to complete.

"What happened to 'I'm not worried'?" Thane mocked.

"I'm not. It's just strange they wouldn't come back, is all."

"My Gramms says they're WishKeepers trapped on The Other Side and Erebus now controls them. But she also thinks gnomes are spying on her when she eats, so…"

"Why don't you ever talk about your parents? You always just mention your grandma." Winston let out another snot-filled roar, popping the Gate open and closed.

"They were WishKeepers. Went to The Other Side one day and, well, they're not here anymore." It was years ago and Thane had accepted the loss of his parents. It was difficult to think of what kind of zombie-like state they might be in. He secretly hoped they had been killed, but of course he never shared that with anyone. It was upsetting enough not having them around, but to think they were still alive and somehow trapped was even worse.

Finally meeting his eyes again, Shea was surprised to see that even though they were deep in thought, his eyes weren't crying or filled with rage or anger. They were just thinking. This made her mad, though she couldn't exactly explain why. Realizing that she had more in common with Thane than expected may have been part of why this angered her. She couldn't muster much of a reply other than, "Sorry." As the word came out, she knew that she meant it. She knew that Thane was tied to her in some way and as much as she didn't want to accept anyone's help, she was glad he was with her.

"I believe in what you're doing, you know. Even though it's for different reasons, that wish shouldn't be destroyed," Thane said.

"Different reasons?"

"You're not the only one who's affected by this. There's more than just a wish at stake here."

He was right, but Shea hated to admit it, even just to herself. It was still her wish, though, and her need to grant it was just as important as any other need, right?

Thane wiped his nose and sniffed. The bleeding had stopped. He stood and stared at their sleeping GateKeeper companion. Winston was just as peaceful as when they had first arrived. Little whistles chirped from his vibrating lips as Thane, with his hands at his hips, mustered a plan.

He picked up the leaf again. "You might have had the right idea before. What makes someone snore? They can't breathe, right?"

"We're not suffocating a GateKeeper, Thane," Shea replied, already put off by any scheme he might have.

"Of course not, but what if we help him breathe?"

"Then he wouldn't snore anymore and obviously the snore is what opens the Gate!"

"Yeah, but..." Thane slowly crept to the old fairy, dangling the leaf over Winston's face. Ever so gently, Thane tickled his nose. Tickle. Tickle. SNORE! It was the biggest one yet and exploded the Gate wide open. Quickly, Thane grabbed Winston's arms, pulled them up over his head and repositioned the ancient fairy on his back.

The Gate stayed open. "He just needed a more comfortable position," Thane said, smiling at Shea.

"Thane! You actually did something right!" She punched him on the shoulder. The white light of the Gate shined in their eyes, inviting them to jump through. Shea picked up her pack, flung it over her shoulder and slowly joined Thane at the precipice of the opened Gate.

Without looking at Thane, and keeping her wide eyes on the unknown depths of the vibrating light, she softly placed her hand in his. It was big, oddly soft and dwarfed her own, swallowing her little hand up, and there was a sudden feeling of proper placement, as if her hand was meant to fit in his. The tight squeeze she gave felt natural. For the first time ever, she felt she was exactly where she needed to be. It was strange how easy it was to hold his hand. The acceptance. When he squeezed back... if she thought about it for too long, she may never let go.

"Let's go," he said.

With a few quick steps, they jumped.

Neon green spells lit up the darkness of the Other Side. They had jumped into a thick pocket of the woods among scrawny, leafless branches—and smack in the middle of a battle. Lost Fairies swarmed the area, flashing explosive spells at charging WishKeepers.

Unable to gather herself, Shea couldn't latch a grappling spell as she careened toward the frozen winter ground. Disoriented, Thane knocked into random tree branches while trying to stay afloat. He caught a glimpse of Shea falling.

"Shea!" he screamed.

"Thane!" Shea screamed back just before she crashed to the ground. The impact knocked her out.

Panicked, Thane zipped through the debris of exploding spells, dodging the relentless fury of the Lost Fairies' attacks. The WishKeepers were outmatched and outnumbered, but Thane didn't care, he was only concerned with reaching Shea, seeing her lying on the ground, her pack still tied to her back, her wand balancing in her limp hand. "Oh, please. Please, no," Thane said as he dashed to her.

He lifted her into a sitting position and thankfully she let out a painful groan. "Hey! Get up! Shea, come on!"

An explosion overhead knocked two Keepers out of the sky. They fell hard to the ground, unconscious. He recognized one of them—Avery. Thane knew he couldn't hesitate. Just as he tried to pick Shea up, a spell exploded against his chest, knocking him back, out cold.

"Thane!" Shea squeaked. Amid the chaos, Shea crawled to her friend and looked out at the battle around her. Lost Fairies propelled themselves through the air. Blast after blast resounded as WishKeepers tackled Lost Fairies to the ground, spun and dodged incoming spells, and countered with blasts of their own.

Now what? But before the desperate thought could allow an answer, two Lost Fairies swooped down and landed in front of her. Wands pointed, they slowly stalked closer. Charging up, their wands sizzled with energy, aimed directly at Shea's chest. Just before the wands could fire, the Lost Fairies were knocked to the ground, pushed by something – someone. It wasn't a Keeper, but The Captain.

He towered over Shea like a threatening avalanche about to crumble. His pitch-black cloak covered him completely as he stared down at her. The wind rushed through the woods as Shea stared at him. The Captain held the gaze for longer than Shea expected and, for a second, Shea didn't know if he was going to make a move or not. As Shea reached for her wand, The Captain drew his. He aimed it at Shea with a steady hand, charging it up. Even though Shea couldn't see through the darkness of The Captain's hood, she felt that he was dealing with an unexpected hesitation, questioning whether or not the shot should be taken.

BLAST! Breaking Shea from her stare, a spell exploded against The Captain's chest and blew him back. He fell hard to the ground. Shea looked behind her and saw Avery sitting up, wand pointed, with a wisp of smoke rising from the end of it.

Before Shea could react, she noticed the look on Avery's face wasn't that of triumph, but instead confusion and horror.

Shea looked back at the fallen Captain, where Avery was still staring. The Captain's hood had fallen back off of his head. He shook off the blast, and Shea met eyes with her enemy.

Elanor. Her long red hair whipped in the winter wind. A heavy gash of a scar crossed her face, and her eyes – they were blacker than her cloak. She sat up and looked at Shea.

"Mom!" Shea screamed. Was this real? It was the last image she remembered seeing—her mother's scarred face and deep black eyes staring at her. Two spells blasted Shea and Avery back, leaving Shea unconscious and Avery writhing in pain. Two Lost Fairies rushed Shea, picked her up, and escaped.

Elanor stood, placed the black hood over her head, paused and looked at Avery dazed on the ground. There was barely a glimmer of recognition from Elanor, but despite the pain from the wand blast and before she passed out, Avery whispered, "Elanor." Like at their first meeting, Elanor, cruelly, ignored her and hurried off.

19
THE PROMISE

Four Years Ago

The last time Beren said goodbye to Elanor, wind battered his face as he dashed through a damp, dark alley on The Other Side. He was chasing something and as he emerged from the alleyway he paused in the middle of the empty small town. Abdera's main street, paved with uneven, aging bricks, glistened from a recent autumn rain. Wet, brown leaves stuck to the gutters of the quiet street, and Beren hovered without concern about being spotted. The town was well on its way to decay and by this time, six years after the destruction of Grayson and Miranda's wish, it was already a virtual ghost town.

Desperately searching for whatever he was chasing, he spun around, looking both ways until—there! Just past the Five & Dime store and headed toward the water tower park was a black flash of dust swinging into a tree. Zipping off like a bullet, Beren followed.

The water tower stood like a watchman in the center of the park as Beren flew into one of the evergreens. Catching his breath, he searched the other trees for whomever he was tailing. A cool November breeze rustled the trees as he pulled back a few needles to get a better view, but just as he was about to launch, the end of a crossbow dug into his back.

Beren didn't flinch. He knew who it was. Raising his hands up as if to surrender, Beren paused for a moment, took a deep breath and then quickly spun, grabbed the crossbow from The Captain's hands and tossed it to the ground, disarming her. The Captain quickly reached for her wand, but Beren was faster. He exploded a powerful bright spell at her feet, and knocked her out of the tree.

Elanor's hood had fallen back, revealing her scarred face and thick red hair. She was dazed, but not unconscious. Beren quickly flew down, picked her up and rushed out of the park.

Finally settling within a maple at the end of the cul-de-sac, he placed her softly on a branch and looked down. Below them, Miranda and Grayson were sharing a bench—Grayson sketching and Miranda sitting quietly. He knew they would be there at the end of their cul-de-sac. It was their street lamp, after all. Beren caressed Elanor's face as she slowly woke up.

"Ellie... Ellie...?" Beren pulled his hand back as she groaned. Quickly reaching for his sheathed wand, he wasn't sure if the blast had done the trick. Was it his wife, or was it The Captain?

Elanor opened her eyes. Like a retreating storm, they swirled with a hurricane of black fog. She was waking up, but fighting the release of whatever curse was controlling her. She looked at Beren, clenched her jaw and snatched the wand from her side. Though weakened, she sprung to her feet and fired a spell at Beren. He blocked it with a counter of his own, dashed behind her, grabbing and locking her arms.

"Look! Look at them! You know who they are. You know!" Beren wrestled to keep her still. He was referring to Miranda and Grayson, and though Elanor looked down, it didn't seem to faze her—she tried ripping away from his grip.

"You know them, Ellie!" For a moment, she stopped struggling and stared at Grayson. "Your WishMaker. He belongs to you. The real you. And he needs you, honey. Please."

THE WISHKEEPER

Elanor always knew Grayson was special. She would giggle as his parents whispered to each other at night about how their son never cried or threw a tantrum, worried that something was wrong. She would watch his mother softly enter his room two or three times a night just to check that he was still breathing. As a teenager, Grayson kept Elanor extremely busy with Athletic Wishes since he didn't fit in very well at school, but once he began spending more time with Miranda, his wishes became consistent Purities. She loved the boy that never cried, and as she stared at Grayson sketching, ignoring the love of his life, something awoke inside of her. Her eyes stopped swirling with fog and instead filled with tears.

"And you know me. It's me, Ellie. Your Beren." He whispered through tears of his own, desperate to wake her. She slowly turned around. Her quivering hands touched his cheeks and she stared into his eyes as if waking from a nightmare. Her eyes were clear of the fog, for now.

She grabbed her husband in a tight hug. "Beren… Beren, please."

"I'm here. I'm here," he said. "Come on. We have to go." He tried letting go, but Elanor wouldn't. She held on to him, knowing this could be the last time she ever woke up.

"Beren… you have to stop."

Slowly pulling away, Beren searched her eyes. "Stop?"

Beren had been coming to The Other Side, relentless in his attempt to free Elanor from her curse, for six years. Six years of desperately fighting and losing battle after battle. It was only a year prior when he accidentally and momentarily woke her from her state by exploding a bright light around her. Ever since, he had returned every day trying the same tactic. The time he would get with her would be brief, but it was all he could think about, and he wasn't going to stop until he broke the curse for good.

"I can't stop, Ellie. It's weakening! Every time you wake up, the fog retreats for a little while longer than the last. It's going away, Ellie. If we can just get you—"

Elanor quickly cut him off. "No more, Beren! It's too painful. Knowing that I'll only turn back and forget all over again."

"You'd rather forget completely? To live in this fog? This evil?" Beren was tired of this conversation. Every time Elanor woke up, she begged Beren to leave her. He was tired of trying to convince her.

Elanor rubbed her temples in pain. Even though the fog had lifted, the headaches would never go away. She sighed and sat on the branch, staring down on Miranda and Grayson. "Shea?" Elanor asked.

Sitting down next to her, he was able to relax for a bit. Albeit they usually covered some kind of trouble she was in, their conversations about their daughter were a welcome reprieve to fighting this blasted curse.

"A pain in my side as usual. She's turning more and more into her mother every day."

This made Elanor smile, but she couldn't hold it for long. "Have you—?"

"No." Beren knew what she was asking. "I don't know how to tell her."

"Don't. Her mother is dead." She continued to stare.

"No, she isn't. She's right here next to me and we can keep it that way," Beren said, trying to hold back his frustration.

"Look at them, Beren. We ruined them. I ruined them," Elanor said, referring to their WishMakers below.

"We can fix it. I don't know how, but we can." He put his arm around her, but she flinched and stopped him. Staring into his eyes, Elanor knew this had to be the last time this ever happened. It had to be the last time she ever allowed her husband to have false hope or to believe in something impossible. She stood up, just as Miranda stood. The street lamp had popped on and Grayson was telling her that he was going to go for a walk later and that she didn't need to make dinner.

"This needs to stop, Beren," Elanor demanded. "Shea needs you. I don't."

"Elanor, please."

"Go home, Beren!" Stepping back, a wave of dizziness swept over her. She buckled in pain as black dust fell from her shoulders. Grabbing her head, she cried out.

"Ellie!" Beren yelled. He grabbed his wand and lunged for her, but she stopped him with her dusty hand. She was turning.

"Go!"

"I'm not leaving you!" Beren barked even louder, but suddenly and swiftly, Elanor stood upright. Her eyes were filling with black fog. The remnants of the real Elanor were quickly fading.

"Don't ever come back," she said in a low, steady voice. "Promise me, you'll never return."

"I can't."

"Promise me!" Elanor screamed through her final set of tears and aimed her wand at his chest.

Fighting anger and tears of his own, "I—I promise."

She pulled the black hood over her head, covering her face. Fog swirled around her with a rush of wind: The Captain was back. She slowly raised her wand up and just before she could fire a grappling shot, Beren reached and grabbed her hand.

"I love you, Elanor. Always."

She looked down at Miranda and Grayson. Miranda was walking away from the park, leaving Grayson alone. The Captain snapped her hand away from Beren and fired a spell into a nearby tree. She was gone, again.

Falling to his knees, Beren couldn't hold back the desperate, angry tears. He slapped the side of the oak and tried to compose himself. Taking a few deep breaths, he looked one last time at Grayson, wiped away the tears and aimed his wand. He slowly stood, and walked through the bright light of the opened Gate.

20
THE TRUTH COMES OUT

Present Day

Thane lay motionless with his face pressed against the cold, muddied snow. The sun was rising on another frigid winter day. Thane's cheeks were beet red. He groaned as he slowly woke, cupping his forehead with his palm, hoping the headache would soon go away. Opening his eyes, his blurred vision could barely make out two bare feet patiently standing a few inches from his face. Blinking through the headache and following the feet up, his vision returned as he looked up at Beren.

"Oh boy," Thane said as he immediately tried to stand.

"'Oh boy' is not how you address your commanding officer," said Beren, hands at his hips.

Thane pushed himself off the ground and saluted his General. "Sir! I mean, sir!"

"Are you hurt?"

"Yes sir. I mean, just my head kinda..."

"Good." His remaining members of The Hope were surrounding Thane, all battered, bloodied and war torn, but still intact. There were nine still left, and though Beren knew two were taken by the Lost Fairies, a third had disappeared entirely. He knew it was Avery, but he had to deal with Thane before searching for their lost member. Goren grabbed Thane's arm as Beren ordered, "Put him in detention. I'll deal with him when I return."

"Is Shea OK, sir? We got split up."

"What do you mean, split up?" He was surprised to even see Thane on The Other Side, much less hear this. He slowly turned back around.

Thane's headache suddenly pounded a bit harder as he remembered it was supposed to be a secret mission. "Oh, boy."

"Keepers!" Beren yelled, never taking his eyes off Thane. His crew lined up at attention behind him, awaiting orders. He spoke to Thane, "I don't care why you came here or what your intentions were or what greater good you think you're fighting for. Tell us exactly what happened." He stared a hard, meaningful set of eyes at Thane, trying to hold back an overreaction.

"She—I think she was taken, sir. When I saw you, though, I thought maybe—" Thane's explanation, no matter what he said, wouldn't suffice.

"What you think doesn't matter right now! Did you see what took her?"

"I was knocked out, sir. But... Lost Fairies were..." Thane said softly, knowing he was in for it and that his chances of ever getting his Keeper wings had just flown out the window. Even worse, his friend was gone and it was all his fault.

"Escort the non-Keeper back to the Gate." Goren grabbed Thane again and yanked his arm.

"But sir, I—"

"I told you to keep an eye on her. Your mission is over."

"Sir, I was just doing my duty as a WishKeeper to assist in the fulfillment of a wish."

"You're not a Keeper, Thane, and Shea isn't just another wish." Beren walked away and motioned for his Keepers to follow.

Thane wasn't sure what erupted inside of him, and even though it was uncalled for, he felt he needed to speak up. He felt his General needed to wake up. Something just snapped.

"What do you want her to do, sir? She finds out a family WishMaker is in trouble and she does what she has to do! If there's anyone who's a true Keeper, it's Shea!"

"You don't know the situation and I don't have time for your ignorance. Get him out of here!" Goren pulled Thane away, but the eager and suddenly spirited trainee wouldn't give in.

"I do know that you're the only family she has and that maybe you should start acting like it!" Thane knew he had crossed the line. No one ever talked back to the General, much less made such a personal comment as the one he had just screamed.

The surrounding Keepers looked at each other and stepped back. Goren let go and hid behind Foster. Their eyes were wide as saucers, knowing Thane was in for it. Beren bounded toward Thane. Rage brewed from deep inside as he stared at him.

"You want to be brought up to speed, Thane? So be it."

The General took a couple slow steps back and launched up into the air, holding his wand tight. Pausing for only a moment, he charged up his wand as bright as it could shine and drove it straight into the frozen ground. Explosions rippled through the forest as all of the surrounding trees detonated with wild, golden light. Gates were opening everywhere. Each tree was suddenly a hot, golden light, vibrating with a loud hum. The wind picked up and howled as Beren stood, staring at Thane.

"Years ago, Keepers could come and go as we pleased, through any Gate at any time. The veil between Paragonia and The Other Side was thin, free and clear," he said in a low, serious tone. He whipped his wand left to right and all of the Gates slapped shut. The golden light vanished, but the wind continued to wail. "But our beloved WishingKing decided his own wishes were more important. We were forced to lock the Gates shut, leaving only a secret few open."

Sprinting toward Thane and jumping behind him, he grabbed him around the waist and squeezed. As he raised his wand up, a blinding light blasted from the end of it. A rippling wall of energy surrounded and barricaded each tree. Talking directly into Thane's ear, Beren continued through gritted teeth, "And we trapped him here in the WishMaker's world to keep Paragonia safe. To keep young Keepers-to-be safe." He let go of Thane and turned him around. "We knew Erebus was unable to touch the wishes prior to a Keeper's intervention, but we underestimated his treachery."

Thane was suddenly blown to the ground as Beren unloaded a massive spell on his Keepers. He raised all of them up, suspending them in air, caught in a painful spell.

"Sir!" Thane yelled, scared of the madness that was quickly emanating from his General.

Beren dropped his Keepers and let them loose, but cast a more powerful spell around Thane and raised him up instead. Thane struggled to break free, and when his wings burned with red light, he screamed in pain, "Please! Stop!"

"Our king captured and tormented his Keepers. Torturing them until they begged for mercy!" Beren yelled. "He destroyed their wings, their hope, their confidence!" Smoke billowed from Thane's wings as he growled through the pain. Beren was losing control: all he could think of was Elanor. Elanor kept flashing across his memory: how he'd lost her, over and over again. His rage mounted until, BLAST!

A wild, purple spell exploded against Beren's back and knocked him down. Released from his spell, Thane fell hard, crying out as he smacked against the ice. Goren and Foster unsheathed their wands, looking for the source of the explosion, but they were too slow. A flash of black hurled itself on top of Beren. Avery was suddenly strangling him.

"You've known! Haven't you? You've known this whole time!" she screamed as her hands wrapped around the General's neck.

Foster rushed and threw Avery off. Goren grabbed and restrained her as she flailed her arms, wanting nothing more than to beat Beren into a bloody pulp. Thane watched in panic, still cringing from the fall.

"Avery! Avery, stop it!" Goren yelled, trying to calm her. He was only adding to the mayhem. Foster helped a bloodied Beren to his feet, afraid his General might answer with an attack of his own. Beren pushed Foster's helping hands away.

"Let her go! It seems Private Avery has something to say, so let her say it!" Beren was out of breath and still angry, but he'd given in at this point. Let everyone know what his secret was: he didn't care anymore.

Avery pushed Goren away and tried to compose herself. Watery, angry eyes flashed at Beren. "How could you? How could you leave her here if you've known all along?"

"You're overstepping your bounds, private. You don't—"

"I loved her!"

Her scream ricocheted against the surrounding ice of the trees. "When everything was falling apart, she was kind and thoughtful, and understood what I had to put up with. Whom I had to put up with!" She screamed the last part only to keep herself from breaking. With what little strength she had left she continued, "And you left her here... with him."

Thane finally had something in common with the members of The Hope. None of them knew what was going on, and they looked at each other for any help with solving this new riddle.

Beren slowly approached Avery. After a pause, he slapped her. He was known as a powerful general among his Keepers. No one crossed the General, not because they were afraid of him, but because they respected him. He was loved because he brought order and hope to the WishKeeper corps, but something in him cracked that day and his Keepers saw it. Avery was so surprised by the slap, she barely felt the sting.

"For the past ten years I have spent every waking and sleeping moment broken. Every moment filled with a desperation to, just once, hold Ellie again. If you think I walked away from that night without hope of bringing her back, you're the same naïve fool I met years ago." Beren wasn't angry anymore. Partly because he understood Avery's anger, but mostly because she simply didn't know. She didn't know what he'd been through. How could she know?

"But you've done nothing about it?" Avery's voice cracked.

"She wasn't left here, Avery. She—"

"She's still here, isn't she?!"

"She chose to stay here!" His yell was louder, firmer, and ended it.

Walking over to Thane, the General helped the confused young fairy stand.

Thane could tell that his General was exhausted, and with this new information suddenly revealed, he couldn't help but feel terrible. The other members of The Hope didn't know what to do or how to react while seeing their commanding officer so grounded, so... real. There was an unexpected level of respect they suddenly had, though they still couldn't help but feel sorry for him.

"Are you OK, Thane?" Beren asked, softly.

"Yes, sir," was all Thane could muster.

"Avery, I am sorry I struck you. That shouldn't have happened. None of this should have happened, and yet it did. And now we have to do something about it. It's all we can do: just keep moving forward," Beren said, as he looked at his fellow WishKeepers.

Avery wept for the first time in ten years and let go of tears that had filled to an unbearable level ever since Elanor had disappeared. Goren and Foster watched their quiet friend break down and didn't know if she needed space or a shoulder. Beren softly walked over and hugged her.

"Shea is here, Avery. She's alone, frightened and confused. She needs your help. Can you help me find her?" he said, with his arms still wrapped around her.

She caught her breath and pulled away from her General. She nodded and he understood it to be more than just an agreement, but an apology. Nothing more needed to be said.

Calming with a deep breath, Beren addressed his troops, "The Keepers who are trapped here struck a deal with Erebus. A deal that I did not approve."

"A deal, sir?" Thane asked, happy to be clear of the heart-aching moment.

"Deliver the next True Love Wish to him in exchange for their freedom. But they're too blinded by their own will to survive to understand that a True Love Wish is all Erebus needs to reclaim Paragonia and all wishes everywhere." Beren looked through the dense pocket of the woods as he finished. Thane stood next to him, trying to sort out all of this new information.

"Then wouldn't helping Shea retrieve her wish be even more important—"

Beren didn't bother to let Thane finish. "It's not her wish. Shea isn't the final heir. Not yet anyway," he responded.

"If she's not," Thane wondered aloud, "and other than you, who does the wish belong to?"

"Her mother." He looked at Avery when he said this. Her eyes flickered with what little life was left in them, and she realized the magnitude of the situation. Erebus needed Elanor to retrieve the wish for him.

Beren started off toward the park at a slow and tired pace. "If you're going to help your friend, Thane, you'd better not just stand there."

Beren's Keepers followed their leader as Thane watched them march by. Since they weren't going to put him in detention, he couldn't help but smile, but the reality was that Shea was in trouble and this helpful little journey was going to be a lot different than he initially planned.

Avery approached him, wiping a final tear away, "I'm sorry. If I'd known…"

"It's OK," Thane said. "Shea would have figured out how to cross over without my help anyway. I'm glad you gave me that note."

They nodded and followed The Forlorn Hope into the thick of the woods.

21
A MOTHER'S CURSE

Elanor woke in a dark, brick-rimmed chamber. A constant drip from an unseen leak splashed into a puddle near her straw bed. A small candle's flame danced across the walls as Elanor sat up. She was still wearing her black robe, and a gash from Avery's spell had ripped a hole in its thick material. Looking around the room, she didn't know where she was for a moment, but she dragged her feet over the side of the bed, remembering. Rubbing her eyes and temples, she took a deep breath.

Ever since Beren's last visit four years ago, on random nights Elanor would wake up in a cold, harsh sweat. The curse was weakening and though the release of the fog would be brief, it was occurring more and more often. She couldn't decide if it was a good thing or a bad thing—she would just as well forget it all than recall the horrors she had performed for her shadow king.

She popped her head up, quickly remembering the events of the night before.

"Shea…"

Searching through the darkness of the cave for her wand, she finally found it, put it in her sheath, and approached her chamber door. Pausing for a moment with her hand on the handle, she wasn't sure what to do. Her daughter was in the room next door. The daughter who thought she was dead. The daughter whose life she'd ruined when she destroyed Grayson and Miranda's wish. "*What would she think of me?"* she thought. "*This... this thing I've become.*"

The look on her face changed from desperate to resolute, and, placing the hood over her head, she opened the door.

Rushing through a narrow cement hall lined with torches, Elanor passed by guards, who saluted. Though Elanor was clear of the curse for the moment, she kept the allure of The Captain and did her best to walk upright, strong and confident. The curse gave Elanor a more powerful and taller stature, but when it cleared, she simply looked like any other ex-Keeper with gnarled wings. She hoped the guards would overlook the slight physical transformation.

"Captain," said one of the guards. "The prisoner is waking up." The tone and cadence of the guard's voice was odd and jumbled, like a song was slightly skipping on its player.

Elanor halted. Shea's chamber door was just behind her. She had no intention of entering, and had the curse still been in effect, she would have ignored the comment and let the guards deal with it. Instead, she stopped and couldn't bear the idea of her daughter, scared and alone, waking up in pain in a strange, dark place.

Hiding her face from the guard, she didn't say a word and slowly walked to the door. A small barred window was at eye level and the guard started to open the door. Elanor quickly pushed it shut. She couldn't go in. She couldn't let her daughter see her like this.

Peering in through the bars, she watched Shea roll over in bed. Her daughter was still dazed from the blast, sick from whatever painful spell the Lost Fairies had exploded on her. The room was much smaller than Elanor's, and much filthier. There she was. The little fairy that was so eager, and so hopeful. Elanor's little aviator.

She couldn't hold back the tears, but luckily her hood shaded any emotion from the nearby guards. Shea rolled over again and revealed her shredded wings. She was dirty and battered, and Elanor couldn't take it. She looked away, took two steps back and told the guards through choked tears, "Leave her." She rushed down the hall and into the darkness.

The door to Shea's cell was left slightly open. Elanor had unlocked it without the guards noticing.

*   *   *   *

Even though the winter sun was shining, it did little to warm the small town as Elanor launched herself from tree to tree. She rushed as if leaving this place forever couldn't happen soon enough. If she could just disappear and never be seen again.

She cried through her reckless and wild grappling, finally landing awkwardly in a tree just on the edge of the cul-de-sac. The cul-de-sac where it all started.

Looking down from the tree, Elanor saw Miranda and Grayson's quaint little home resting within mounds of plowed snow. It looked cold and lonely, like it was the only forgotten house on the street. She gasped through her tears and wiped them away, angry that her random grappling had brought her here. Slowly descending out of the tree, she landed softly on the ground and walked toward the small home.

A cold winter fog rolled over the cul-de-sac as Elanor approached the front steps. She stopped and stared at the front door, wanting all of it to just go away. Casting a soft grappling spell around the porch beam, she pulled herself to a window and looked in.

Grayson was asleep on the couch. Elanor stared through the window and watched another loved one roll over in pain. The fog slowly leaked into an unnatural form and crept around Elanor. She caught her breath, knowing what was approaching.

"There was once a WishMaker who sent powerful wishes to the fairies of Paragonia. So powerful he was thought to be a candidate for WishingKing. But what did the two most talented Keepers do?" Erebus taunted as he swirled around her. His shadowy form grew into shape, towering over Elanor. She didn't bother to look at him, but kept staring at Grayson. "They destroyed him. Destroyed his love. And now look at him. Look at what you've done."

Elanor whirled around, drew her wand, stomped it hard at her feet, and filled the front porch with a blast of bright white light. Erebus shaded his eyes and shrunk in form. The light faded and Erebus regrouped, unfazed.

"It looks like I may need to up your dosage, my Elanor. Years ago, that might have ruined me, but thanks to you and your lost ones, now it's not so terrible." He flashed his evil smile as if to beg her to do it again.

"We did what we had to do!" Elanor yelled, trying to convince herself more than Erebus.

"But look at us now," Erebus said. "So many magical years of promise-keeping we've had. How fitting it comes full circle with the famous WishMaker. We made a deal, Ellie, my dear."

"This wasn't part of the deal."

"Oh, but it was. I allow a certain number of wishes to transcend and you bring me the rest. And out of the kindness of my heart, one in particular would allow you and your friends to go home."

Watching through the window, Elanor noticed Grayson wake, rub his sore, red eyes and walk to the window. Looking out, he didn't notice the drama unfolding mere feet in front from him.

"And you can return to your precious, handicapped daughter."

With a quick, enraged move, Elanor gripped her wand, but Erebus was ready this time. He whipped his darkness around her neck and raised her up, eye level with Grayson. "I win, Elanor! Accept it! Bring me the wish or our deal is off!"

He dropped her and she fell hard to the edge of the window, desperate for breath. Erebus morphed quickly into a thick black fog and revolved around Elanor. She suddenly stood upright, controlled by the curse. It whirled and whirled, waving Elanor's red hair across her pained face and, finally, her eyes swirled with blackness. Erebus and his fog retreated, leaving a stiff Elanor at the base of the window. She turned her head, looked up at Grayson and reached out her palm. It touched the cold, frosty glass as her eyes were swept up completely by the curse, overcoming her. The Captain had returned. She dashed off the front porch and left Grayson staring out the window.

About to walk away, Grayson looked down at the window's base. The warmth of a small handprint against the glass was slowly retreating and though he was sure he saw it, he rubbed his eyes and walked into the kitchen.

22
NO PIXIE

CLINK CLINK! Sweat dripped from Shea's brow as she opened her eyes, reacting to what sounded like coins falling on metal. She looked at her cell door and through its barred window. A guard rushed away toward the source of the sound as a skinny shaft of light beamed in through the opened door. *The opened door?* Searching the darkness, Shea didn't know where she was and the idea of an opened door wasn't making sense.

"Thane?" Shea whispered. "Hello?"

She stood up and a wave of vertigo swept over her. She sat back down and held her head. A headache pounded at her temples and, quickly, the memory of the night before rolled in. Unable to find her wand in the darkness, shuffling through the musty wet of the cold room, she hurried to the cell door. About to call out, she grabbed the handle and the door creaked open at the slightest tug. An open door. The guards were going to get an earful, or worse, for leaving it open, but Shea didn't have time or the care to worry about what might happen to her kidnappers. She crept out of her cell and into the open hall.

Four separate hallways broke off in opposing directions, torches lighting their way. The golden light of the torches cast thick ghostly images across cement walls, their flames flickering in a breeze. She looked to her right and saw a large, open, circular grey-stoned room. A mound of silver and copper coins covered every inch of the floor. Grey stone. Fallen coins. A constant drip from a vanishing point high above. It was slow to materialize, but Shea soon put it all together; she was at the bottom of the Lost Fairies' hideout. An ancient wishing well.

Two guards, wands ready, stood on top of the pile of coins, looking up, with their backs to Shea. A thin, piercing ray of sunlight beamed off of the mound of coins. Shea noticed a small wooden table a few steps away, just to the left of her and, next to it, a wrangled wish tied by a spell. The lasso spell was firmly wrapped around a metal hook that protruded like a lazy curled finger from the wall. The wish was huddling against the base of the wall, eyes closed and crying. On top of the nearby table was her wand and she knew that if she could just get her hands on it, she might be able to—CLINK CLINK!

A coin fell and crashed to the floor. Shea ripped her hand away from her wand, startled. She watched a sudden burst explode from the fallen coin—a bright blue Athletic Wish popped out of it and buzzed, bounced and zoomed around the bottom of the well. This gave Shea a chance to lunge for her wand, and as the Lost Fairies launched themselves up toward the retreating wish, Shea snatched it. Wand securely in hand and desperate to free the trapped wish, she started toward it, but quickly ducked behind the table as one of the Lost Fairies wrestled the new Athlete to the ground. Being far from gentle and borderline abusive, he had a wrangling spell squeezed tight around the little wish. It squeaked as the guard pulled it to the wall and tied the spell around a different hook.

Shea looked at the struggling wish, spying from under the table. She watched as the Lost Fairies had no regard for the amount of pain the little wishes were in. They simply stepped to the center of the well again, ready and waiting for more.

"Took you long enough," said one of the guards.

"Didn't know I was being timed," returned the other. "Ready yourself for the next."

Staring at the Athlete, Shea couldn't stand it. It was writhing in pain, trying to bounce out of the wrangling spell and escape. Finally, it gave up and closed its eyes. It was as sad as Shea had ever seen a wish, and anger flooded every inch of her. She wasn't worried about being seen anymore. No, she wanted a fight and was ready for it.

CLINK CLINK!

Another coin crashed to the pile, and just as a Money Wish exploded out of it, Shea yelled, "Hey!" The guards jumped at the scream, momentarily taking their eyes off the newly formed wish.

Shea exploded a wrangling spell around the wild, newly made Money Wish and attached to it. Using the momentum of the speedy wish, she swung herself up along the side of the well and ran sideways, dodging the incoming blasts from the suddenly surprised guards. They fired spell after spell, trying to knock Shea down, but she was too fast. Jumping out of the way of a close call, she tugged hard on the Money Wish, pulling it toward her. The guards continued blasting spells at her, missing by inches.

She released the wrangling spell and, in a free fall, dove to the wish and wrapped her arms around it. Freeing her wand hand, she pointed it up and cast a grappling spell at a flimsy wooden bucket dangling near the open mouth of the well. With a burst, and grunting with all her strength, Shea pulled herself up toward the exit.

The guards looked at each other in momentary awe, then launched themselves up. They gave chase, climbing the well walls with expertise, gaining on her. Lunging for her feet, one of the guards grabbed Shea by the ankle and pulled, refusing to let go in spite of Shea's flailing. She screamed as she and the wish started to fall, but with a final blast of energy, the Money Wish hurled them forward, pulling Shea and the Lost Fairy along for the ride.

Zipping up and out of the well, the wish carried Shea and her assailant into the cold winter sunlight. Running out of energy, the wish crashed to the snowy ground, causing Shea to lose her grip. The wish bounced away, exhausted, only to be caught once again in the Lost Fairy's wrangling spell. He yanked it hard and whipped the wish into his arms.

"Stop! You're hurting it!" Shea yelled as she quickly stood.

Treating her like just another rebellious wish, the other guard wrapped a wrangling spell around Shea, constraining her. "These wishes are for him, not your hopeless Keepers! Stop being a hero!"

"What do you mean, for him?" Shea said as she struggled to break free.

Barking through panting breath, the guard ordered his fellow soldier, "Get that wish underground. I'm right behind you."

"Him? You don't mean…"

"Captain ordered you to stay at base, so you're staying at base!"

He pulled her toward the well but though her arms were wrapped in the spell, her legs were free. She powered a kick right between the legs of the guard—he went down hard and fast. The wrangling spell disappeared and she pointed her wand at his face as he writhed in pain.

"Tell me what you're doing with those wishes."

"It's a fallow wish! A waste. And yes, him," he said, cringing.

"You're stealing them before they can cross over?"

"Welcome to the real world, pixie," the guard said through a clenched jaw.

This enraged Shea almost as much as did their theft and betrayal. She whipped another kick into the guard's stomach, knocking the breath out of him.

"I'm no pixie."

She hurried to the edge of the well, jumped onto the ledge and looked down. The other guard who was carrying the little Money Wish had vanished. She desperately wanted to help those little wishes, but she knew there wasn't time. She knew that, as important as they were, there was an even more important task at hand. She whispered in a rush, "I'm sorry," and dashed off toward the nearby park.

23
THE LOST FAIRY

As Shea ran through the pine needles, evergreens stretching over her, she tried to tie all of this together—all of what had happened over such a short period of time. She had known that there would be Lost Fairies and Erebus to deal with once she and Thane crossed over, but...

"Thane. If he's been turned into one of those things, I'll never forgive myself," she said to herself.

On top of that, did she really see her mom the night before? Was it just a figment of her imagination or an effect of the spell that knocked her out?

"Somebody took me to the Lost Fairy's hideout. It couldn't have been Mom. Stop it, Shea. Thane is in trouble and we have a wish to grant."

Her mind was made up about one thing. She was going to retrieve the True Love Wish, no matter what or who stood in her way.

She pulled herself up into an evergreen to get a better look around. The woods were thick and crowded with trees, and the snow that covered them made it seem like she was climbing through a sea of white. In the near distance, she noticed the trees had changed to oaks and maples, and just through them was what she assumed was a clearing of some kind. Her destination was at least confirmed: but then what? It was so quiet in the forest, the stillness made her uncomfortable. It was the kind of discomfort that was unique to a prolonged silence, as if a truth would be revealed that she didn't want to know. She continued on, climbing branch after branch and firing off grappling spells, making her way toward the clearing.

* * * *

At the edge of the forest was a large park. Swing sets, playgrounds, and teeter-totters were covered in snow, and not even a footstep had been made in weeks, leaving the snow untouched throughout. A circle of a couple dozen Lost Fairies surrounded Elanor in the middle of the park. She stood tall, lean and confident in the center as she calmly spouted orders. The Captain was dominating her again thanks to the recharged spell from Erebus.

"We split up into the three groups. Even though the wish abandoned its Makers, it will find its way back to one of them. Two groups will monitor each Maker, the other will…" She paused, halting her orders. The Lost Fairies looked up in the nearby trees as Elanor did the same. She sensed something—or someone—was watching and slowly reached for her wand. "Wands," she ordered, quietly.

WishKeepers dashed out of the trees and surrounded Elanor and her soldiers from above. Spells cascaded down upon them, but Elanor's defense was quick. Deflecting spell after spell, she and her troops dived, rolled, and grappled for cover.

Raising her wand straight up, Elanor sent a wide deflecting wall of energy over her troops. The WishKeepers' spells bounced off the wall, but bursting out of the chaos was Beren, wand outstretched. He blasted a counter spell at the wall, destroying it and knocking Elanor to the ground.

"Hold your fire!" yelled Beren.

Pulling herself onto a branch, Shea grunted and gained her footing. Just as she was about to send another grappling spell at a neighboring tree, a bright explosion shined just over the trees a couple hundred feet from where she was. She rushed to the source of the explosion.

Letting go of a grappling spell, Shea swung to the base of a scrawny, leafless bush and looked out into the park. Beren was walking, wand pointed, toward Elanor who was on her knees. Her hood was down and Shea got a complete look at what she had wondered was real or not. There she was—her mom, staring up into her dad's eyes. This couldn't be happening. This couldn't be real. A few feet away, the branches of the bush snapped. Thane was sneaking toward the scene. He didn't notice Shea, but she was too stunned to call for him. Then she heard her mom's voice.

"Lower your wands. Get in rank among your groups. This is a waste of time."

"Elanor!" Avery tried rushing to her, but Beren grabbed her. She was in near panic at the site of Elanor, on her knees, wearing all black. Those black eyes.

Shea watched, confused, as WishKeepers floated a few feet above Elanor and her troops. It was a standoff as Lost Fairies pointed their wands, ready for a fight. They finally lowered them at their Captain's order as Beren left Avery's side and walked to Elanor and stood over her.

He looked into his wife's eyes and knew that the explosion hadn't done the trick. Her eyes were swirling with the cursed fog, though a slight hope arose inside Beren when he looked closer. The whites of her eyes were noticeable and the blackness wasn't as thick as he remembered. He knew right away the curse was weakening, but he kept his mouth shut. She snarled at him when he reached out a hand to help her up. She stood on her own, grabbed her wand and walked away from Beren.

"Elanor. Please."

Quickly extending her wand, like a whip she cracked a powerful blast at Beren, knocking him back. The spell's light was so bright it melted the snow around them and the anger in Elanor's darkened eyes flashed with a ripple.

The Hope rushed Elanor, avenging the attack on their General, but she exploded a spell at her feet and launched straight into the air. Weightless and hovering, Elanor sent wrangling spells at each incoming Keeper. Her retaliation was so quick the Keepers didn't have time to react. One by one, they fell hard to the ground, struggling to free themselves.

Reversing her launching spell and pointing it at the ground, Elanor slowly hovered back down. Beren was the only Keeper not tangled in one of her spells. He stood through the pain and watched his wife raise Avery up into the air, a thick spell wrapped around Avery's neck.

"So foolish to leave your king behind," Elanor said, as she squeezed the spell tighter. It was crushing Avery. "He needed a new Regent, little Avery. Guess who he chose?" Elanor crashed Avery to the ground and released the spell. Avery cried out as a bone cracked in her left arm.

Elanor shook her head, fighting a sudden retreat of the curse as the fog swirled in her angry eyes. Elanor was in there somewhere, but The Captain wasn't letting her leave.

"Go home, Beren," she said, as she watched him rush to help Avery.

"Home? We won't have a home if—" Beren yelled.

"I don't care about the consequences!" she screamed, wildly.

"You know what has to be done and yet you listen to him," Beren continued.

"You're holding on to a hope that doesn't exist. I told you not to come back. That wish is his. We're done here." She turned away from Beren and Avery, snapped her fingers and ordered her troops to get in rank.

Shea watched, breathless, failing to take it all in. *Told you not to come back? The wish is his?* Suddenly a hand touched her shoulder and Shea flinched, falling back.

"Shea, thank goodness! You're alive! But, uh—" Thane said, excited but nervous all at once. He knew this had to have been a shock to her. Shea stood and backed away from Thane. She looked at him as if he was a stranger, suddenly unable to trust anyone, even him. Turning toward the park, she moved a branch out of her way, paused and stared at her mom and dad, then bolted into a sprint.

She had never felt more exposed as she stood in the middle of the park. It was like a nightmare. A bad dream where your parents are suddenly monsters, unrecognizable, foreign, and though they looked familiar they were nothing more than strangers. Even worse, the feeling of belonging and a sense of self that feels so natural when in your parents' company had vanished. It was one thing to feel alone, but to be alone with so many unanswered questions—questions these strangers wouldn't answer—fueled Shea's longing to just run away and forget it all.

"Mom?" Shea said with barely enough air in her lungs. She trembled as she stood. Her body wasn't ready for this.

"Shea!" Beren said as he took a few quick steps toward her.

"You've known all along. Haven't you?" Shea said quickly to her dad. This stopped Beren's approach. He was so relieved to see her that for a moment he had forgotten that this was all new to her. Unable to reply, he brushed his hands through his graying hair, muted.

Elanor turned to her daughter and looked at her with only a vague familiarity. The darkness in her eyes flickered, but she blinked through it. The curse still strong enough to keep her cold and distant and focused on the task at hand.

"You shouldn't be here." Something within Elanor forced her to approach her daughter. Shea was frozen to the ground. For so long she had wished for her mom to come home, to see her again, but who was walking toward her? Who was looking at her with dark, foggy eyes?

Shea tried to maintain her composure, but her chest heaved, searching for any amount of air it could find. She noticed her mother's eyes and the deep emptiness that consumed them. Reaching her hand out, Elanor ran her fingers through Shea's thick red hair, but when her eyes flickered and swirled with blackness, Shea flinched and pulled back, appalled and confused.

"We lost, Shea. He won. It's time to accept that."

Disgusted, Shea didn't understand. "What?"

"Don't listen to her, Shea! She's not herself," Avery called out.

Breaking her mother's stare, Shea looked at her dad. Though his eyes weren't black like Elanor's, Shea felt there wasn't much of a difference between them.

"Who should I listen to?" Anger and resentment overcame any feelings of confusion, and Shea backed away from her parents.

"It's time for you to go now, Shea," said Elanor, as dusty fog fell from her shoulders. Shea knew that her mom was right. She did need to go and she couldn't trust her parents. With one last look at Elanor and Beren, Shea turned and ran away into the thick brush of the woods.

Stone-faced and emotionless, Elanor watched her daughter run. Deep down there was a thought that she should be upset by what had just happened, but a numbness pulsed with every beat of her heart and she simply let Shea go.

"You're right about one thing, Elanor. We lost. You—" Beren said, fighting his own anger.

"I have a mission to complete. If you wish to try and stop me, by all means, try," Elanor said, without looking at her husband. "Form rank," she ordered her troops.

They followed orders and lined up behind their Captain. Beren could only watch as they launched themselves into the trees. The WishKeepers stared at one another, not knowing how to react or if they should go after them.

Beren simply stood still, staring at the ground. He had lost everything and he couldn't help but feel he deserved it.

*   *   *   *

Every muscle in Shea's body strained and cramped as she ran. She didn't care how her body felt, she just needed to run, to escape. It didn't matter where she ended up, as long as it was as far away from her parents as possible. She didn't want her family and she didn't care about her Makers. She just needed to go.

Finally breaking down but too exhausted to cry, she stopped near a small swing set and climbed up a snow-covered teeter-totter. Trudging through the smooth, icy snow, she reached the other end. It was raised a few feet off the ground and Shea looked down, catching her breath.

Thane caught up and spotted Shea. He didn't know what to say and wasn't sure if she noticed him. After a few moments, Shea wondered how long before he would say something stupid. She decided to speak first and save him the awkwardness.

"When I was little, the only thing I ever wanted was for my parents to be proud of me. 'Good job, Shea. You're the best Keeper Paragonia has ever seen, Shea.' What happens when *you* can't be proud of *them*?" she asked, knowing Thane was listening.

After a thoughtful moment, Thane replied, "My Gramms says that when you're lost in the woods, don't look to the stars for help. All they can do is wink at you, anyway." Though he was serious, the ridiculousness of the comment was obvious and Shea couldn't help but smile through her watery eyes. She shook her head as Thane floated to the ground beneath her. He looked up.

"I know. My Gramms is, well, Gramms, but it reminds me that I can rely on myself to get home."

With a deep breath, Shea sighed. She couldn't let go of what was happening and secretly vowed never to let it go, but the deep breath was one of resolve. What else is there?

"Can I do this, Thane?"

"I've seen you jump from higher places than this. Oh, you mean... oh, wait!" he said, excited. Reaching into his backpack, he pulled out Shea's aviator goggles and flew them up to her. They shared a smile as he wrapped them around her neck. "You dropped them when we crossed over. Come on. We'll do it together." He grabbed her arm and they jumped off the teeter-totter.

With a light grapple spell fired behind her, Shea grabbed the end of the teeter-totter, slowing her descent. With the help from Thane, they landed perfectly as a team.

"I was so happy when I saw her again, but then... her eyes. It was like she didn't know me."

"Then it's time she does," Thane said.

Shea smiled at how hopeful he was. Even though it was foolish, it was contagious.

"There's a wish to grant," Shea said.

"We didn't ask for their help when we started this, and we still don't need their help. And I have something else for you." Thane pulled a metal device from his bag. A WishRadar.

Surprised, Shea grabbed it from him. "Where did you get this?"

"Kinda stole it from your Dad."

"Kinda?"

Thane shrugged his shoulders. They smiled at each other and for the first time, neither of them looked away. There was something a little more to this smile and they knew it. Eventually, Thane coughed through the moment and took the WishRadar back. He pointed at the screen.

"So it doesn't say which dot is which WishMaker, but at least we can find one of them. This looks to be the closest."

Not listening, Shea quickly wrapped her arms around Thane. A hug that was unexpected but Thane happily welcomed. It was the only piece of familiarity Shea had left and it had never felt better. She held it for a few moments and finally released, placing the goggles over her eyes.

"We haven't lost yet, right?" she said, with a slight return of hope.

"Right," Thane said, triumphant.

24
TRUE LOVE'S HOME

A hazy sun set over a snow-covered backyard. A wooden play set, complete with a turret and a yellow slide, was doused with icy white snow behind a quaint ranch-style home. Two chain swings were motionless as the cold grey blue of another winter night settled in.

The True Love Wish floated to one of the swings, pausing to catch its strained breath. Shivering, it surveyed its surroundings, hopeful that this was its Makers' house and it had returned home. The True Love Wish huddled, freezing, along the swing's rusty chain. The swing acted as a reminder that this wasn't its Maker's home and it was still lost.

The wind turned dark, swirling around the True Love Wish with an unnatural fog. The panicked little wish hopped along the rubber edge of the swing's seat, attempting an escape, but the darkness circled, cutting it off.

"Well, well, well, it looks like I have to do everything around here." Erebus' deep voice laughed through the muffling snow and ice. "You're not far from home, little one. May I show you the way?"

The True Love Wish bounced away from the swing, and launched itself into the foggy wind. Pushing through and fighting the whirling, thick wall of Erebus' blackness, desperation cried from the wish's eyes. Although it pushed as hard as it could through the fog, it was no use as Erebus engulfed the retreating wish in complete shadow. For a moment, the True Love Wish vanished, overtaken by the malicious darkness, but just as quickly as it disappeared, a bright white light beamed from the center of the stillness.

A high-pitched squeal emanated from the fog and the light pushed back Erebus and his darkness. Squinting its eyes, pushing and pushing, the True Love Wish was reacting as though an automatic self-defense mechanism had been activated. Erebus was trying to wrangle the wish on his own terms, but as much as his black, foggy fingers swiped and tried to grab it, he knew he was unable to hold a wish prior to a Keeper's intervention. His frustration boiled.

"Don't waste your precious energy, little wish. If you're so desperate to find your loving Makers, then let me give you a little boost!"

Wind suddenly screamed through the neighborhood. A howling blast of cold whipped the True Love Wish up and into the sky like a lazy autumn leaf. Though Erebus couldn't physically capture the wish himself, he could still manipulate its flight pattern. His plan wasn't to keep it away from the Keepers, however. He had a better idea.

The wind swirled the somersaulting True Love Wish through the air, over frozen chimneys and icicle-ridden gutters until it finally nosedived into a snow bank along the edge of a quiet cul-de-sac. The True Love Wish popped its head out of the snow, shaking off the dizziness.

Taking shape from within the shadows of a large oak, Erebus and his darkness crawled across the yard. His black face appeared inches from the dimly lit True Love Wish.

"Welcome home. But don't get too comfortable."

At the sound of "home" the Wish looked up, past the staring red eyes of Erebus, and saw a quaint front porch with a snow-covered sidewalk. The steps to Grayson and Miranda's front door were a few feet away and through the window the True Love Wish spotted one of its WishMakers—Grayson—standing in his kitchen pouring some coffee. The red glow of the wish beamed a little brighter at the sight of him and it gasped with a happy smile.

The wish was smiling, and so was Erebus, but for a different reason. The shadow king swirled back into formless fog and, like billowing smoke, slowly surrounded the base of the house.

25
A WORLD IN NEED

In a scrawny elm tree, Shea and Thane ducked and crawled along a frozen branch. Thane hadn't moved his eyes away from the WishRadar since they left the park, following the movement of the closest red dot like a hawk. Shea's cheeks were wind-burned and matched the color of her wind-whirled hair, but her eyes were as alive and awake as ever. They were close and though they knew Shea's parents would be just behind them, excitement brewed as they spotted the rear entrance to Grayson and Miranda's house.

"This has to be the place. Here's us and here's the red dot. Now what?"

"What do you mean, now what? We go inside," said Shea.

"Inside? We're not supposed to enter a Wish-Maker's... "

"Has anything we've done lately been by the rules? Enough with the not-supposed-to. Come on."

Thane was fresh off his Keeper training and he was still hopeful that maybe if they followed the proper rules of WishKeeping he could at least cite that protocol was followed in the wish's wrangling. At least, this is what he told himself. In actuality, he was scared senseless.

Eager to get to the house, Shea readied herself for a grapple, but paused suddenly. From their vantage point within the tree, they could see all of the surrounding neighborhood and the winding street that lead to the small Abdera downtown.

It was their first clear view of The Other Side—something Shea had always wished to see. She stared out over the houses and through the peaceful haze of the winter evening. It was beautiful, she thought. It was a world she had only ever dreamed about and secretly caught glimpses of while spying on her dad at the F.I.A.: a world she always believed she would one day know by heart, where little pockets of it would be like a second home. As Shea stared into the distance, Thane looked up from the WishRadar and noticed her longing gaze. He joined her in the moment and waited for her to comment on what she was inevitably about to see next.

The sun wasn't completely set and its red-orange glow softly exploded along the horizon. A dizzying display of color. It was too early for the stars to come out, and it didn't quite register with Shea as to what she was seeing.

Small, twinkling lights hovered above all the homes—thousands of lights. The sky was filled, but it wasn't just the sky. The entire town was alight with bouncing, flashing wishes awaiting their WishKeepers: WishKeepers that weren't coming. This fact dawned on Shea, and a heaviness pressed against her chest. A rock-like lump formed in her throat as it settled in. A realization that all of these wishes were going to waste. Fallow, as she so painfully heard the Lost Fairy say earlier. WishMakers' hopefulness was alive, but there was nothing for it.

Thane stole a glance and though he knew what Shea was thinking—he'd had the same depressing reaction as well—he didn't expect to see how moved she was by it all.

Tears streamed down her cheeks as she stared at a world that needed help: a world that needed to be saved. A world that needed her.

A resolve within Shea that at one time had been just a fleeting thought grew into a determination of purpose. She blinked the tears away and once again focused intently on

Grayson's house. Without warning, Shea whipped a grappling spell to the back door. Swinging to a wrought iron railing, she pulled herself up. The door handle, and the next stage of her journey, was right in front of her.

Thane floated to the railing and joined her. He pushed his back against the plastic siding of the house, desperate to stay out of sight, while Shea studied the door. Though Thane understood where Shea's mindset currently was, he also understood where they were physically, and the reality of the situation quickly rushed in.

"Is it OK if I admit that I'm terrified?" Thane said, catching his breath and holding the WishRadar close to his chest.

"You don't have to admit it. I can tell. And you have more experience in wrangling Wishes than I do!"

"Lost Fairies are one thing, but WishMakers? Do we have a plan if we actually do get inside? Aren't we kind of going in blind? Maybe we should map it out. You take the left…"

CRASH! A spell smashed a hole in the door's window and glass splashed to the cement steps below. Shea's hand was outstretched and a wisp of smoke billowed from the end of her wand.

"Oops," she said.

"Oops? What did you think would happen if you fired a spell at glass?"

"I was aiming at the door handle. At least we can get in."

Footsteps suddenly bounded toward the back door from inside the house. As Grayson flung the door open, Thane tackled Shea off the railing, diving into the snow.

"Nice." Grayson spouted with frustration. He looked around his yard for any snowball-throwing kids, but of course didn't find anyone.

THE WISHKEEPER

Pulling herself out of the snow, Shea tugged on Thane's arm and rushed for the open door. She dragged her snow-covered friend inside. "Go! Go!"

Just as they snuck in around Grayson's feet, he slammed the door shut. Icicles fell from the gutters and smashed into pieces along the steps as a smoky fog billowed along the base of the back door.

*   *   *   *

Beren looked up at the sky. Darkness was slowly descending over the park and he knew it was more than just nature's way of ending a day. It wasn't natural. He barked orders at a handheld hologram rising up out of his WishRadar. His WishSentinel stared at him from the screen of the hologram, listening intently.

"The rest of the Keepers. Those who were so eager to volunteer. Call them all to The Other Side."

"Yes, sir. Right away, sir," the Sentinel replied.

Beren's Keeper troops were lined up behind him, listening. Avery was holding her broken arm, still in obvious pain.

"Avery, I think you should—"

"No," she quickly said. "I'm not going anywhere."

Beren nodded. He wasn't going to argue. He needed all the help he could get. "It will be dark soon. We need light, and lots of it." He looked at the Sentinel's hologram again. "Rendezvous at the cul-de-sac. I'll meet them there."

The Sentinel saluted and the hologram disappeared. Beren looked at his WishKeepers, knowing his plan would only buy them time—a mere step within a battle of an ongoing war. He nodded at them and at once they scattered into the night, following orders.

Avery stayed behind and stepped toward her General. "I'm coming with you. I left Elanor once, but there's no way I'm leaving Shea."

Standing at the base of the teeter-totter where Shea and Thane had recently been, he softly touched Avery's broken arm and smiled. He was happy to have her by his side. They looked down, followed Shea's tracks and flew off toward the cul-de-sac.

Deep within the forest, WishKeepers filed out of open Gates: hundreds poured into the thick wood and zoomed off in different directions. Flying through the small town and over the brick road main street, Keepers swept over holiday shoppers. As painful as it was to ignore the thousands of happy and excited wishes that bounced around the Makers' heads, they had their orders.

Sleepy chimneys billowed smoke from modest homes that rimmed the edges of a neighborhood. From house to house, Keepers flew in formation. A few Purity Wishes beamed and smiled brightly, following the Keepers. The soldiers looked at each other, cringing at their orders, but not a word was said and not one wish was wrangled. They sped off over the quiet town. Red and green Christmas lights twinkled within snow-covered bushes and the thousands of unclaimed wishes dimmed.

*   *   *   *

Sighing through his frustration, Grayson rummaged through a junk drawer in the small mudroom at the back of the house. Pulling out drawers and searching through cupboards above a washer and dryer, he hissed and snarled as he couldn't find what he was looking for.

Like dancing through an obstacle course and trying to stay out of Grayson's eyeline, Thane and Shea stepped around muddy boots, salty gloves and various winter shovels and attire.

"We made it. We're in!" Shea said, as she tripped through the bristles of a broom.

"Would you be quiet? If he notices us—"

"What does happen if he notices us?" Shea was curious, but more intent on meandering the maze of utility supplies.

"The connection of transport between The Other Side and fairydom will cease to exist!" Shea stopped and stared at him, not understanding, and her quizzical look begged for an explanation in plain English.

"The Gates will close. Forever," he said, flatly.

"Oh."

"Oh? And you want to be trapped here with Erebus for the rest of your life?"

Scooping a roll of black duct tape out of a drawer, finally finding what he was looking for, Grayson hurried to the back door. Stretching a few pieces from the roll, he taped over the hole in the broken glass.

Thane tugged Shea close, keeping her out of Grayson's sight. "Can we find the TLW and get out of here, please?"

"Well I don't see it anywhere, do you? He's leaving. Let's go."

Grayson shrugged off the tape job and made his way into the kitchen. Following as quietly as they could, Shea stopped at the base of the doorframe and pointed to a countertop above them. Thane nodded and floated up, landing safely behind a greasy microwave. Grayson rounded the corner of the small kitchen and was just out of sight as Thane waved Shea on.

Concentrating, Shea fired a grappling spell at a small cabinet knob above Thane and flung herself up, but as she swung, her toe kicked a sugar container. It wobbled and wobbled closer to the edge of the counter. Hanging on to her grapple spell, she dangled from the cabinet knob, holding her breath. If Grayson walked in, she'd be spotted for sure. She was frozen and powerless watching the container wobble closer to the edge until—CRASH!

Sugar and ceramic glass splashed along the kitchen floor and Grayson hurried back in. Noticing the broken container and spilled sugar, he threw his hands in the air and waved it off. Frustrated, he didn't even bother to clean it up, and left the room.

Dropping the grapple spell and landing on the counter, Shea wiped the sweat from her brow.

"Phew! That was close."

"He's just gonna leave the mess? It'll draw mice for sure," Thane said as he joined her, eyeing the broken sugar pot.

Ignoring Thane's distracted and obsessive-compulsive comment, Shea looked behind her and noticed a framed photograph. She turned and softly approached the photo of Grayson with his arms around a smiling Miranda. A major contrast from what Miranda and Grayson had recently been experiencing, though Shea was unaware. As she stared, soaking in how happy the Makers looked, her reflection in the glass of the frame slowly came into focus. Seeing herself, her smile faded, since all she could really see were her broken wings crossing the smiling faces of Grayson and Miranda. The future of all of the unclaimed wishes bouncing throughout The Other Side rested on her back: on her ugly, broken wings.

"Uh, Shea?" Thane broke the silence. "We might have a slight problem."

Turning to her friend, she noticed the worry in his eyes as they looked in the direction of the kitchen window. On the other side of the glass, Lost Fairies swung to the sill and surrounded the house. They hadn't yet noticed Shea and Thane, but it was only a matter of time.

Immediately, Shea whipped a grapple at the kitchen chandelier and swung herself into the dining room. One grapple after another, Shea was perfecting her skills as she flipped and flung across the house. Thane was simply trying to keep up.

"You're getting really good at that! Who needs to fly, when you can—"?

"Where did he go? We lost him."

They landed together on the top of a worn, flower-embroidered sofa. Behind them, more Lost Fairies grouped at the base of the kitchen window preparing to enter. Down the long hall ahead of them, a door clanked shut, slapping against its hinge.

"There!" Shea pointed.

The kitchen window slowly creaked open. Elanor was now standing on the windowsill while her troops pushed the window up and open. Shea's eyes met her mother's. Elanor stared, expressionless, and a shiver shot through Shea's system. It looked like her mom, but it sure didn't feel like her.

"That would have been easier than breaking in," Thane said, reacting to the slow opening of the kitchen window. Shea grabbed his arm, pulling him away from the sofa and grappled down the hall.

Two Lost Fairies had spells clasped to the base of the window, pushing it open as Elanor stood, patiently waiting. Out of the black, swirling fog that was now completely surrounding the house arose Erebus in full form. He hovered over the working Lost Fairies. Elanor's black eyes continued her hard stare through the window.

"It's time, Elanor. Bring it to me," he said as a sharp, dusty finger pointed through the window to the front door.

Just as his finger was fully extended, the True Love Wish rushed in through the closed front door. It zoomed in quick circles around the living room, happy to know his Maker was close. Thane and Shea had just missed it.

Elanor's eyes flashed at the sight of the Wish. "Beren and his Keepers. They'll be close behind."

"You have only one thing on which to focus. Your husband is not a concern," Erebus replied.

The wish stopped circling and caught sight of the Lost Fairies breaking in. It squeaked and flew off down the hall.

A nasty wind whipped around the house as Erebus expanded back into a massive black fog. Finally, Elanor's troops opened the window enough to duck in. One by one they entered, leaving Elanor the last to do so. She stared into the house. Her eyes flashed with darkness, and yet the swirling storm in her pupils seemed less intense than before. She blinked, rubbed her twitching eyes, and crept in.

Rumbling down the unplowed, icy street, a car slowly splashed its way toward the house. It stopped at the edge of the driveway, as if the driver were undecided whether to pull in or not.

Miranda looked out from the driver's seat, staring at the house. It wasn't just her house, but her home. She felt odd wondering if she should ring the doorbell, knock, or simply walk in. Turning the steering wheel, she aimed the car toward the driveway and parked. She took a deep breath, opened the door, and stepped onto the icy driveway.

Slowly forming along the edge of the house in complete darkness, Erebus stood watching Miranda approach the front porch. As dark as it was, a wicked smile could faintly be seen within the edges of shadow.

26
LIGHTNING IN WINTER

A WishMaker's home is not much different than that of a WishKeeper: everything is simply much larger. Sure, some of the materials are a bit foreign and, most Keepers would agree, wasteful. Shea, on the other hand, loved every bit of a Maker's extravagant living space, especially since everything was placed neatly on the ground. It didn't make her flight through Grayson's house any easier, however, since the size of the items forced her to grapple everywhere. As much as she wanted to stop and take in the sight of such a beautifully peculiar array of giant furniture, thick cloth curtains and tower-sized lanterns with strange, pear-shaped light sources, the door through which Grayson just entered was cracked open slightly, and she and Thane needed to follow him, and fast. Elanor and her troops wouldn't waste time sightseeing.

The door was much heavier than expected, but Thane managed to pull it open with a final grunt. Surveying the long hallway behind her, Shea didn't spot any intruding Lost Fairies or, thankfully, her mother just yet.

"What if the wish isn't down there? I mean, all of this could be a complete waste of time if it's with Miranda," Thane said, wiping sweat from his brow.

"It has to be. My mom wouldn't be here if it wasn't."

"TLW's aren't exactly easy to wrangle. You knock one more thing over, I'm killin' you."

"Thanks for the confidence boost. We'll have to be careful, that's all."

"Yeah, because we're really good at that." Thane kicked the door open a bit more. The hinges weren't quite perfectly level and had caused the door to slowly swing shut.

Shea smiled at Thane. He really was pretty funny when nervous, she thought, even though he constantly overreacted.

Without warning, a loud buzz and squeal echoed down the hall. The True Love Wish whizzed over their heads and shot down through the open doorway, lighting up the long dark basement staircase as it flew. Ten-year-old memories flooded back to Shea. The last time she saw a True Love Wish was when her mom destroyed Grayson and Miranda's first. She remembered the feel of its electrically charged, yet soft exterior, and the ecstatic smile and hopeful eyes. But as the memory continued, a recollection of the end result swiftly came into focus. Shea's mother was the last to touch a True Love Wish. She couldn't allow it to happen again. She wouldn't allow it.

Thane and Shea looked at each other. "At least we know it's down there," Thane said breaking the stare.

"Let's go!" Shea attached a grappling spell to a small bulb light in the middle of the arched ceiling of the staircase and flung herself down. Thane shot off like a bullet, tailing the wish.

Releasing the grapple spell and free-falling, Shea landed on and surfed down the railing, keeping pace with Thane. Lights were on in the basement studio where Grayson was hunched over a drafting table as Thane zipped past him.

The walls were lined with artwork: oil on canvas, pencil sketches, water colors, chalk etchings. Dozens of fresh pieces hung from a line that stretched across the long, narrow basement studio.

Just as Thane spotted the circling wish, he watched Shea slide down the railing, hurl herself up in a somersault and tumble directly onto Grayson's desk, crashing into an ink jar and spattering thick black liquid everywhere. Thane slapped his face with a frustrated hand and couldn't believe she did exactly what he just said not to.

With a quick grab and swipe, Grayson picked up his new painting and pulled it away from the mess before it could spoil it. He stood and looked at his ink-spilled desk. "What is going on?" Quickly but neatly setting his artwork down, he pulled a rag out of a utility sink and dabbed at the spill.

Even though Shea never thought of herself as a very lucky fairy, the stars must have been aligned for her since where she landed, dizzy and out of sorts, was perfectly behind a set of multi-colored paint jars and out of Grayson's view. Thane, however, was still near panic and waving at Shea, hoping she would wake up and hide, for crying out loud.

The wish lazily floated around the room, bouncing from pieces of art to Grayson's shoulder and back again, happy and content to be exactly where it was supposed to be.

Shea shook the dizziness out of her head and hid behind one of the jars, peeking out and searching for the wish. She spotted Thane instead, though it was impossible to miss his jumping jacks and arm waving. Next to Thane was a charcoal portrait of Miranda. Deep black hair fell over one side of her face as her other eye was closed amidst more deep gray and black shadow. Grayson had drawn such a beautifully heart-wrenching piece that it shocked Shea and stopped her for a moment. She was getting a glimpse of a sadness that hadn't yet been made clear to her, but when she looked at the other pieces hanging along the string, it was obvious—they were all of Miranda in dark tones and shadows. They didn't exude a sense of danger or threat, just a simple feeling of sadness. Though they were all obviously of Miranda, Shea saw herself in the paintings—sad, depressed, lonely. It was everywhere, the sadness. When the wish bounced within view, however, Shea snapped to and remembered why she was in the smelly basement in the first place.

The wish's huffing and puffing had settled. It was relaxing a bit and eventually settled near a small lamp to Grayson's left as he continued to blot and dab at the staining ink. The wish bounced and rested on the lip of the lamp, cozying up to the warmth of the bulb.

Waving to Shea, Thane pointed to the wish, signaling with his hands some form of a plan. Shea had no idea what he was saying, but she nodded anyway. What plan could there be? *Get the wish!* Pretty simple.

She crept from paint jar to paint jar, inching along the back of the desk as Grayson's rag suddenly pushed a small wave of the pooled ink. It splashed around her ankles and covered her boots. A new kind of pain rushed through her—she was not very happy to have her favorite boots so quickly ruined.

Thane was slowly floating behind paintings, staying out of the wish's purview. Inching closer and closer, he was now only a few feet away. Out from behind a small paint-spattered mug, Shea stuck her head and signaled Thane. They were both within wrangling distance. This was it.

They slowly and carefully removed their wands, raising them up and pointing the fizzing ends at the wish.

It fluttered for a moment, forcing its pursuers to catch their breath. It settled again and closed its eyes.

Sweat poured from Shea's forehead as she looked at Thane. His eyes were wide and shared her own combination of thrill and terror.

Ready... aim...

"Grayson? You down there?" Miranda yelled from the top of the stairs.

The wish sprang. Excited to hear its other Maker's voice, it didn't know how to control itself and zoomed in circles around the basement. When Miranda slowly climbed down the final step, it bolted to her and spun, dipped and rolled around her head and shoulders. It beamed as bright as they'd seen it—a sign that everything was right in the world. For the moment.

Shea slapped her knee in frustration and Thane dashed behind another painting. *Why did I hesitate? I had it right in front of me and had I just...*

"Hey. I didn't hear you come in," Grayson said with a look of surprise. He was still holding the drenched, black rag. It was dripping onto the cement floor as he stared at Miranda.

"You have a little mess there," she said.

"What? Oh, right. Yeah, a little clumsier than usual today, I guess."

It had been months since Miranda had been in Grayson's studio. When he had first cleaned it out and started using it as his art studio, she used to sit and read on the couch at the other end of the room. They simply liked being in each other's company, regardless of what it was they were doing. It just felt right, like a neatly organized counter where everything had a place and everything was in its place.

She was about to respond to Grayson, but after noticing the artwork hanging from the string, she paused. Each piece was of her, and while Grayson had painted her plenty of times in the past, it was a shock to see these. It was a shock because the darkness and bland undertones hit a nerve within her—a nerve that was a little too close to the truth as to how she was actually feeling.

"So, everything OK?" Grayson asked, even though he knew why she had paused.

"Yeah." She looked back at Grayson and forced a slight smile. "I mean, I don't know. Can we...? The fumes are pretty strong." Motioning to the stairs, she was afraid to have this conversation with Grayson. It was four years in the making and she still didn't know how to tell him.

Grayson tossed the rag back in the sink and wiped his hands on his apron. "Sure. Right." He knew what was coming, but something inside told him that this was a good thing. As difficult as it was, losing her, he knew he couldn't let her go so easily.

The wish zoomed up the stairs like an excited puppy, knowing its owners were headed in that direction. As Grayson pulled off his apron and placed it on his desk, he had to look twice at what he saw.

Tiny black footprints were tracked along the back of the desk. Had the upcoming conversation with Miranda not been in his near future, he wouldn't have shrugged it off so quickly. The handprint on the window and the sugar container breaking in the kitchen—peculiar, yes. But this? What was going on?

Moving in teams with military stealth, Elanor's crew of Lost Fairies made their way through the Maker's home. Only the light of the kitchen was on, leaving the living room hushed with shadows from the street lamp outside. Creeping along the edges of the wall, Elanor paused a few feet from the base of the sofa behind the long curtains that tickled the dark wood floors. Even before any danger or threat lurked within the darkness, it was a tricky assignment entering a Maker's living quarters. A WishMaker is much more in tune with and aware of its surroundings when at home. If something was out of place or a particular shadow didn't feel right, they knew it, and a WishKeeper, albeit naturally invisible to any Maker, needed to pay very close attention to its movements. One little mistake and it wasn't just the Keeper's life that would be threatened, but the existence and missions of all Keepers.

Hiding behind the sheer curtain, a floor vent was inches from her toes. She could hear Grayson's voice from below and held up a fist, ordering her troops to halt and find cover. She rubbed her eyes, trying to force the retreating curse to slow, but the headache was quickly settling in. The only positive effect of the curse was that it made the pain in her throbbing head go away. Her blurred vision refocused as footsteps pounded up the basement stairs. With her heart racing for what seemed like the first time in years, Elanor waited, knowing the True Love Wish would follow. Was she suddenly nervous? The curse was lifting, but did she want it to?

Miranda stepped out of the basement door first and then there it was. The Wish. Elanor's eyes flashed with a spinning cyclone of blackness again as she pinpointed it with sniper-like eyes. Concentrating on the Wish as it floated out of the basement, she slowly motioned for her troops to ready their wands. One by one, the Lost Fairies raised and pointed them directly at the excited wish. As Grayson emerged from the doorway, Elanor took her eyes off the wish and the cyclone of fog within them began to retreat once again. A different war was going on inside Elanor and at the sight of her WishMaker, the real Elanor seemed to be winning.

"You want something to drink? I can heat up some coffee. Made it this morning, but sure it's still good," Grayson said as he walked past Elanor.

"Let's just sit for a bit. OK?" Miranda sat on the couch, waiting for Grayson to join her. He was surprised to be so reluctant to do so and immediately felt unsure of how close he should sit next to her. Settling on the other end of the sofa, Grayson finally found some amount of comfort.

Climbing up and out of the stairwell, Shea and Thane regrouped at the base of the door, huddling near an unused electrical outlet. Elanor's gaze shifted to the little rebels and once again, her eyes flashed with darkness. A new mission was at hand for the moment, and she waved to her Lost Fairies.

"OK, well, they're settled at least. The wish shouldn't leave this room any time soon. Here's the plan," Shea whispered to Thane.

"Finally. A plan."

"It seems the wish wants to settle a bit closer to Grayson, but don't let that fool you. I have a feeling it will rest above both, possibly on that thing hanging from the ceiling."

"I think they call that a light," Thane said, sarcastically.

"Just, whatever. We wait for the wish to settle. You take to the air above Miranda and I'll—"

Wrangling spells crashed around Thane and Shea, trapping them on the spot. Two Lost Fairies stalked closer and closer with the spells connected to their wands as Elanor walked out of the shadow of the curtain and approached. She removed her black hood and leaned inches from her daughter's face. The curse was in full force, swirling in her deep black eyes.

"You never did listen. Always ignoring the wishes of your parents, but enough of this. You don't belong, Shea."

"Get away from her!" Thane winced as he tried to push back the strangling rope-like spell.

Shea stared at her mother, studying every inch of her face as if recalling a dream from her childhood. The vision she always held was of a youthful, strong and beautiful fairy. One that would toe the line between discipline and love and do it perfectly. She was always there, someone to run to and lean on and hug and be with in a state of wordless love, for there wasn't ever a need to define anything. It was simply in her eyes.

Her eyes. What happened? Wrinkles sagged under them, gray hairs curled over them, scarred skin stretched across her tired face.

"Mom. Where did you go? Please," Shea begged and suddenly felt like her adolescent self again. The bright, hopeful little fairy that for so many years she tried desperately to shed and be rid of.

Elanor pulled back at the sound of her daughter's desperate voice. Her eyes swirled once again—a storm retreating—but she quickly rubbed them, trying to shake it off. Her little daughter's voice rang between her ears and for a moment the shadow in her mind slipped away, but like a rush of a violent wave the darkness swept back in. She grabbed Shea by the arm, ready to pull her away.

"That wish needs to be granted, Mom! You know it!" Shea was desperate.

"How are you?" Miranda said from the couch. Elanor paused a moment, as did the rest of the fairies.

"How am I? My wife left me. Not so good. You?" Grayson returned. A pang of resentment was impossible to miss.

Miranda stood up from the couch and paced in front of Grayson as Elanor stopped tugging Shea and stared at nothing in particular, listening.

"We have problems, Gray. That's obvious. But don't you ever feel like there's just something missing?"

"I always feel that way."

"You do?"

"Of course. And when you left, it was obvious what it was," Grayson said, folding his arms.

"Don't put this on me. And I'm talking about something… else. I don't know, but it's weird. I know something is off, but I can't figure out what it is."

Tears were forming in Elanor's eyes as her grip on Shea's shoulder weakened. Leaning a bit closer, Shea noticed that the darkness in her mom's eyes was softening. Even though the confusion was still there, Shea could tell that whatever it was that was haunting her mom wasn't permanent. At least that's what she hoped.

"I thought they made a True Love Wish? It sounds like…" Thane said, but the Lost Fairy tightened his wrangling spell's grip.

Shea looked at her mother. "You still care. Don't you?"

A gliding tear was quickly wiped as Elanor's anger returned. She tightened her hold once again and pulled Shea along the base of the couch. Nearing the edge, a sudden violent winter wind rattled the house, flickering the lights. A winter storm was quickly brewing outside.

Getting up from the couch, Grayson headed to the kitchen. "Maybe we should stop trying to figure it out, Miranda. It's like all we do is try to figure things out. Do we have any candles?"

"In the pantry. I can't help it, Gray. There's something else. Something deeper is just wrong."

His voice trailed from around the corner as Grayson searched the pantry for a couple candles. "I know what's wrong, Miranda. My wife, the only person I've ever truly loved, isn't sure if she loves me anymore."

"Grayson, I…"

"Why is the window open?" he asked, as he set two candles on the kitchen table and pushed the window closed, cutting off a strong, cold breeze. Just before the window closed completely, he thought he noticed a flash of light fly in. Another blast of wind rattled the house, flickering the lights, and finally the window clasped shut.

Hiding behind a teapot, thoroughly out of breath, with rosy, wind-whipped cheeks, Beren and Avery landed and surveyed the small home. The wish was hovering near Miranda's shoulder. Jumping and crouching behind a salt shaker, they caught a glimpse of Elanor pulling Shea along the base of the couch.

Peeking around the corner of the sofa, Elanor spotted the floating wish. She pulled Shea in close. "This isn't a little fairy game. It ends now." She whipped her wand from her sheath. It immediately charged up, sparking light from its end.

Shea knew her mom was in there somewhere, but what could she do? She had come this far only to have the wish stolen out from under her.

A slow panic was building inside Thane as he watched the charging wand. He needed to do something, but what?

Shea closed her eyes, fighting the waterfall of tears, but suddenly felt a kick at the back of her leg. Thane was trying to tell her something, but if she tried to turn around— Dad!

Slowly landing on the windowsill behind Elanor, Beren crouched and nodded to her daughter. Thane's smile couldn't have been bigger as Avery joined him, but he quickly forced a frown as his captor gave him a strange look. He knew he had to keep the attention off of Beren.

"She does still care, Shea. I see it too," Thane said, attempting a distraction.

Shea didn't miss a beat. "The wish matters to you, Mom. It matters to you more than Erebus. Than Dad. Even me."

"You're catching on," Elanor said as she raised her wand to her daughter's throat.

"Dad!" Shea screamed, and blasts of spells fired from the ends of Beren's and Avery's wands, knocking Elanor and her Lost Fairies back. She dragged her daughter to the ground, but Shea wrestled to break free. Beren jumped, rolled across the floor and forced the Lost Fairies back with a defensive blast. Avery smashed The Lost Fairies against the wall and sprinted to Shea, helping her up.

"Thane! Behind me!" yelled Beren, and Thane quickly followed orders. He jumped behind Beren and the duo fired spells at the incoming blasts of the Lost Fairies. A firestorm of spells lit up the rear of the couch as Avery pulled Shea from Elanor.

"Go!" Avery yelled.

Shea fired a grappling spell at the light fixture in the center of the ceiling, swinging herself toward the Wish.

The Wish fluttered and buzzed as Shea chased it, firing wrangling spells at will. One spell crashed against a teapot, exploding it into pieces. Miranda screamed as the glass crashed against the walls.

Avery jumped on top of Elanor, trying to hold her down, but Elanor was stronger. She twisted Avery's broken arm, and popped her shoulder out of its socket. Avery cried out, and Elanor easily pushed her off, immediately firing a spell at Beren. He met it head on with an equal spell, but was thrown back by its force. Elanor watched her daughter gain on the retreating Wish, and panic over losing it set in. She shot off in the same direction with a grappling spell of her own and swooped through the house.

Beren and Thane flew after her, but the Lost Fairies' spells kept them from tailing too close and forced them to fire in defense. The cold, hard-hearted Avery suddenly returned. She popped her shoulder back into place with barely a cringe, and stood with a purpose watching Elanor flash spells at Shea. Avery could still fly, despite the pain. Floating slowly up into a ready position, she darted after Elanor.

The wish was masterful in eluding Shea as the little fairy swung from light fixtures, doorknobs and curtain hooks and left a path of mini-destruction in her wake. Her wild grappling, while perfect in the open air, wasn't suited for anything remotely domestic and Grayson's house was quickly turning into a war zone.

The Wish scurried out of the way of a powerful wrangling spell that exploded a small lamp. Elanor was gaining on it. Shea knew deep down that she was a better flyer than her mom, but this wasn't a contest. That wish needed to be wrangled by her and her alone.

The Wish landed on the fireplace mantel and a race was on as Shea rallied her strength and followed her mom's grappling pattern. A Lost Fairy lunged at Shea, but an explosion knocked him from the air. Shea landed on the mantel, looked back and saw Avery close behind with her deep, frustrated eyes peeking out from her dark cloak. If Shea hadn't noticed two healthy wings, she would have thought it was a Lost Fairy. Shea barely knew Avery, but she was happy for the help.

Thane suddenly grabbed her and woke her up. "Would you go, please?" He pushed her toward the Wish and Shea lunged. Another explosion just missed Shea and the wish, knocking Shea back. Reacting to the explosion, the Wish zoomed off the mantel just out of Elanor's reach as she tried diving for it. Shea knew this was her chance. She knew the wish would circle back to the center of the room and she needed momentum to cut off her mom's pursuit.

Hurling a grapple to the kitchen table, Shea flung herself and landed, getting a better angle on the fleeing Wish. Taking aim, she fired a spell at the chandelier and careened toward it. Reaching her arm out, ready to meet the Wish head on, Shea was knocked out of the air by a blast of light which flung her to the floor. Crashing hard, she rolled over her shredded wings and looked up through dizzy eyes, watching Elanor and Avery struggle for the Wish. They both had it in their arms and were falling fast.

When they hit the floor, the wish bounced out of their hands, dazed from the impact. It slid, momentarily slowed. Shea stood and ran for the Wish, but Elanor, again, was too fast. She shoved Avery off of her and flashed a perfect wrangling spell around the Wish, pulling it into her arms.

"No!" screamed Thane. He dived to Shea as he watched a Lost Fairy take aim and fire a spell square into Shea's chest. Shea fell back, immediately unconscious, and lay in the middle of the living room. Beren grabbed Thane, pulled him back, knowing what was to come next.

Elanor rushed behind a potted plant, holding the True Love Wish tight in her arms. Her Lost Fairies suddenly scattered and hid, and Avery rolled under the coffee table. The fairies were scattering, but what for? Elanor was about to escape as well, but quickly froze.

In the middle of the living room, Miranda and Grayson held each other, staring in fright. Their faces were pale white as they looked at something on the floor. Heaving breaths of confusion and panic, they didn't know what they were looking at, but Beren knew as he hid with Thane near the base of the living room window. He wanted to rush in and pull Shea out of there, but he was just as frozen as his wife. What now?

Shea groaned and pulled herself up from the floor, standing in pain and holding her chest. She looked at her fellow fairies. They were all staring at her, wide-eyed. Why were they staring at her? Turning her gaze upward, she quickly realized why: Miranda and Grayson were looking at a broken-winged fairy standing in the middle of their home.

27
RULES ARE MEANT TO BE BROKEN

The sky's dark clouds were swirling into a thick, black storm. Wind whipped through the frost-bitten trees of the cul-de-sac and hail bombarded the streets. WishKeepers pushed through the powerful storm as they approached the house. Their dark green cloaks waved wildly, but they stood their ground as they hovered, wands at their side. One by one, they formed a perfect circle around the small cottage— valiant soldiers at attention about to bring light to the threatening darkness.

Erebus and his thick black fog had all but covered the house, creating a wall of shadow. The shadow king swam back and forth within the thick of the blackness like a demented shark awaiting its prey. The WishKeepers eyed each other in disgust and fright as sharp black hands ripped out of the fog, swiping at them, taunting them to come closer. In unison, the Keepers raised their wands, two-handed, above their heads.

The house shook, and not just because of the powerful blasts of wind—the earth itself beneath Shea rattled as she looked up into the eyes of her Makers. Explosions echoed across the neighborhood as blasts of golden light shimmered through the windows. Gates were exploding shut, closing forever. The little fairy fell to the floor, unable to hold herself up as Miranda grabbed Grayson, trying to stay upright.

"Grayson!"

"I don't know! Just hold on!" Grayson yelled back.

"Shea, get out of there!" Thane yelled. Beren held him back from diving for his friend. The WishMakers had already seen Shea, but revealing a host of fairies to them would only make matters worse. As long as Shea doesn't—

"Miranda and Grayson! My name's Shea!" One rule had already been broken, and Shea was desperate. She looked at her mom. Elanor was huddled behind the potted plant, holding the True Love Wish tight in her arms with a look of utter terror in her black eyes. Even The Captain didn't expect this, and when Shea looked at Thane, worried, hurt and fraught with his own desperation, she knew there was no turning back.

Beren, wide-eyed and trying to force any kind of idea to surface, stared at his naive yet heroic daughter standing in front of two painfully confused WishMakers. He looked out through the windows and spotted his Keepers forming along the edge of the property. Another rush of wind crashed through the cul-de-sac and screamed between the cracks of the weathered storm windows. The lights flickered and buzzed, and with another golden explosion ricocheting in the distance, the lights went out completely.

Beren took the sudden darkness as a chance to make a move. He called for Avery with a loud whisper as she scrambled to her feet, cradling her shattered arm. Bolting out from under the coffee table, she flew to her General's side and looked out the window.

Goren and Foster were fighting the fierce storm, hovering with their wands held high. The one thing Avery had avoided with every bit of pained effort for the past ten years was the memory of Erebus and his torture, but there he was, in all his blackened glory. The demented WishingKing paced in front of the The Hope, daring them to try and enter: begging them for a fight. Avery stared, terror-stricken. Somehow knowing she was watching, Erebus stopped pacing and quickly turned toward the window. His dark red eyes pierced Avery's already fragile soul and a slow, black crease of a smile taunted her to join the fun. When she saw his face—that smile—every memory of her time with the traitor resurfaced as if caught in a blocked drain, bubbling up to the brink. But what she didn't expect to come up with the sludge was sympathy. A sudden rush of pity flooded her veins and very quickly she simply wasn't afraid anymore. She felt sorry for the old man who missed his wife. For the old man who dipped his hands too far into the jar of possibility and removed a black heart. Even Erebus could shatter his own heart if he let the pain consume him enough.

She looked at Beren, nodded and straightened her posture. After a salute above her brow—a salute that said 'goodbye'—she spun and whipped a spell at the window, breaking the glass. Without a second thought, she dove into the icy blackness and disappeared.

Miranda screamed again when the window broke. Wind blew in through the small hole as Grayson scrambled to light a candle, flicking a lighter, flashing shadows across the living room. The candle finally lit and he swung it to the floor in front of Shea.

Beren watched as his daughter, with her hands at her hips, looked directly up at the curious Makers. There was no plan for this. There was nothing to do, but to wait. He was just a spectator now. There was a long, anxious pause as Grayson stared at Shea, remembering all of the strange happenings from the past day. The coincidences were clicking in his frantic brain, but he just couldn't believe this.

"What... what is that?" Miranda asked with a quivering voice.

"Are you... alright?" he asked Shea. Seeing her broken wings, it was all he could come up with.

"Don't talk to it!" Miranda gasped.

There was one other rule Shea had yet to break. She had already been spotted by WishMakers and had addressed them directly, but responding to and conversing with a Maker—she didn't have a choice. Her mom, or whatever she had turned into, stood a few feet to her left, motionless, holding the most important wish that had ever been made. It was Shea's chance to define herself as the Keeper she had always wished to be: The Keeper no one believed she could be. Alter the flow of momentum: turn it back around. She needed to be in control, even if it meant destroying the Gates and never returning home. She had to break the final rule—interact with a WishMaker.

"I'm not alright, no," she said, looking up into the eyes of Grayson and Miranda. In the far-off distance, more Gates rattled the ground and exploded. Closer and closer the explosions came. Gates were closing at a rapid rate, like falling dominoes. "You made a wish, both of you, and it needs to be granted. There are powers, though, that want to destroy your wish and I..."

Before she could finish, the earth crashed with another quake and more explosions blew with even greater magnitude, seemingly right outside the window. Miranda held on to Grayson as the house was flushed with golden light, but the Makers couldn't stop staring at Shea. The trembling subsided and Shea remained determined, unfazed by the quaking ground beneath her.

"Fairies?" It was all Grayson could manage to say. Earthquakes, explosions, and a winter storm were one thing, but fairies?

"Please, listen to me," Shea tried to continue, but Grayson could barely make anything of his own thoughts, much less the words coming from the tiny, broken-winged creature standing in front of him.

"A wish?" he said.

"Yes, a wish. And I need to grant it."

"Shea, wait! Please," Beren called out from the windowsill. Miranda and Grayson whipped their heads in the direction of the small voice. They spotted Thane on his knees and Beren standing over him. Through the window, everything was revealed. A black, thick fog crept along the glass and other fairies were hovering in the wind, raising wands above their heads.

"What is going on?" Miranda slowly approached the window, unsure of what to examine first.

"No, Dad. I can't wait. I've waited all my life, but for what? To be told that I don't belong. That I'm not good enough. To be lied to." She looked again at Elanor, whose deep black eyes still swirled with the curse but were drenched in tears. "It's time to show you that I do. I do belong." Her knuckles drained to white as she gripped her wand.

28
AVERY'S RETURN

Avery rushed past the outstretched, black tendrils of Erebus and hurried toward Goren and Foster. As the Keepers raised their wands into the gale-force winds, Erebus arose out of the fog and towered over the circling soldiers. Like a black hooded dragon, he reared his head up and out of the darkness, high above the tops of the nearby homes, and stretched his tendril-like arms, preparing to collapse them down upon the Keepers. Rising out of the shadows of the cul-de-sac's every corner, Lost Fairies appeared, ready to assist their master.

"Keepers! Listen to me! Our king is nothing more than a man. A man who is just as lost as his thoughtless slaves," Avery yelled through the wind. "A light must be brought to his lonely darkness. To save him from his sadness."

Goren, with his wand raised high, felt that the speech sounded rehearsed. In all the time he'd known her, he had barely heard Avery speak a word. He looked at his friend and watched Avery Waterstone stare into the eyes of her one-time loving king.

The man with a pure, unbroken heart was gone, but she could still see the fear in his eyes: a fear that had turned to vengeance. Her empathy was no longer fueled by ignorance as it once had been, years ago. She knew, now, that the truest form of love came unconditionally and no matter how evil or angry her WishingKing was, she wasn't going to stop loving him.

For a moment, the wind stopped and the darkness rippled, and the Keepers saw their WishingKing standing tall but burdened amidst the retreating storm. Erebus looked into the eyes of his Regent. A long, hard look… and a smile, once again, creased the side of his shadowed face, and he leaned close to Avery. She didn't flinch or move as Erebus spoke, as if he were inside her head and reading her thoughts.

"The truest form of love, my Avery, is not unconditional, but relative to the one who has the power to control it. Only a fool relies on the blind faith of a wish. No more wishing, Avery Waterstone."

He pulled away and stood upright again, raising his long, black, outstretched arms left and right. He kept on smiling, with more confidence than the surrounding Keepers had expected.

"It's time to show you just how foolish you have been," Erebus said, and sent a wave of black fog whirling around the Keepers. The full brunt of it struck Avery and engulfed her.

The Hope closed their eyes, holding firm to their wands, but Avery kept her eyes open. There was a knowing deep inside her, a knowing similar to when she had first looked at Elanor. A knowing that was bittersweet. Erebus wasn't going to win this fight, but in the end, neither would she. Sparks of charged light cracked from the end of her wand she raised it above her head. Pure white light softly beamed, filling the area, joining the blinding light of her fellow Keepers' wands, but as the force of Erebus' darkness rushed her, only her wand's light was doused.

29
GOING ALONE

Shea stared daggers into Elanor's weeping eyes as she raised her wand. The Captain still had control over Elanor, but the pain in her heart was too strong for the evil to make a move. Keeping her pointed wand extended toward her mother, Shea slowly turned her head to her father. He needed to see this. He needed to see that his daughter wasn't going to stand idly by and watch her parents make the same mistake they had made years ago. Since her father would never allow her to prove herself willingly, she would simply have to do so with force.

Placing her goggles over her eyes, Shea sparked and charged her wand. "It's my wish to grant."

"Shea, no!" Beren yelled.

BLAST! Shea exploded a powerful spell at Elanor. It crashed into her chest, knocking her against the potted plant. Elanor's head smacked the ceramic surface and she slumped to the floor, unconscious. Just as the True Love Wish escaped from Elanor's limp arms, a white light exploded and blinded everyone inside the house, including Shea. The combined bright spells of The Hope filled the cul-de-sac with pure, radiant light. The Lost Fairies scattered and Erebus bellowed an ugly, painful growl. It echoed through the eardrums of every Keeper – a reminder of just how evil their WishingKing had become. His fog quickly retreated, scurrying away from the light, and rushed away from the brightly lit cul-de-sac.

Shea was so intent on recovering the wish and, with the help of her goggles, she was able, though barely, to keep the True Love Wish in her sights as the light shined through the windows. Miranda and Grayson cowered on the couch as Beren rushed to his wife's side, trying to shade his eyes from the blast. He ignored the True Love Wish floating away from Elanor. He ignored the WishMakers who were only a few feet away from him. All he could see was his slumped over, scar-faced Ellie, unconscious in front of him.

Watching the wish scurry overhead, Shea planted a perfect wrangling spell around it and grabbed hold. Using its momentum, she swung up to the wish, and wrapped an arm around it. She spotted Thane crouched along the base of the window, covering his eyes. She had to leave him. As much as she wanted Thane in her life, to keep her hand firmly placed in his, she needed to do this alone. With a final look, she quickly grappled toward the back door and flung herself, crashing through the duct-taped hole in the window, and was gone.

The light from the WishKeepers' wands quickly subsided and the house and cul-de-sac were quiet, save for the distant, echoing explosions miles away as more Gates continued to close. Beren quickly looked up, searching for Shea. Thane limped to his General. Elanor was unconscious and Shea was gone.

"There isn't much time. Thane—"

"Yes, sir. I'm right behind her." Thane started to leave, but Beren pulled him back.

"No. I need you to stay here."

"Sir, with all due respect, I was given an order to keep your daughter."

"My daughter is in trouble, private. Do as I say. Please." It was the first time since their journey began that Thane noticed a sense of true worry and anxiety in his

General. Though Beren was trying to stay calm, Thane could tell he was frightened.

"Yes, sir."

"I have to go. This is…" Miranda pulled away from Grayson and headed to the front door. The lights were still out and even though Erebus' fog had gone, the winter storm was continuing its assault.

"You're not going out in this. And I'm not sure if you've noticed, but there are fairies in our house!" Grayson rushed to the door and blocked her exit.

"This isn't real. It's a dream or nightmare or something! I have to go."

"Miranda, just wait!"

"Don't go out there. Please!" Thane yelled and flew into the faces of the WishMakers. "This is real. All of it. Believe me. I wish it wasn't."

"Just sit for a second. I'll get more candles," Grayson said as he walked a panicked Miranda to the couch.

Floating back down to Beren, Thane saw that Elanor was slowly and painfully waking up. "Is she OK?" he asked.

Carefully wrapping his arms around his wife, Beren helped Elanor sit up. He brushed the hair out of her face and wiped beads of sweat from her brow. Blinking awake and through the haze, Elanor's eyes were completely clear of the fog. While slightly bloodshot, they were mostly clear and white—a welcome reprieve from the recent madness. Shea's blast against her mother's chest, mixed with the pure white light from the Keepers outside, cured her mother of whatever curse had befallen her, at least for now. Beren had sworn to never come back for her, but when she looked him in the eyes, he knew that never returning had been the true mistake.

"Ellie. Ellie, we have to go," he whispered.

Elanor pulled her husband in close and wrapped a tight, desperate yet thankful hug around him. Deep down she always wished he would return and help her fight this curse, this disease. Quickly she remembered everything. "Shea. The Gates! Oh, Beren, she can't leave, and he knows!"

"Some of the Gates may still be open. Come on," Beren softly replied as he helped her up.

"What do you mean? Shea broke each rule. How are the Gates...?" Thane asked, confused.

"Stay with the Makers, Thane. Debrief them on everything. The Gates are closing, but there may be a few that haven't yet. We're beyond repairing what Shea has done. The Makers might as well know what's going on. We'll bring Shea back. I promise."

Thane watched his general help Elanor stand. Picking her up in his arms, Beren lifted off and flew out through the hole in the back door.

With a deep breath, Thane turned toward Grayson and Miranda. They stared back, confused, but waiting for a response.

"Oh, boy," Thane finally huffed.

30
SAFE AND SOUND

Beren helped Elanor to the top of a tall pine. They surveyed the forest in front of them, looking for any sign of their daughter. A soft red glow pulsed from within the woods a few hundred yards to the north. Shea was close.

"There. That wasn't a Gate," Elanor said, pointing.

"There are Gates all over this area," Beren said, studying the surrounding forest. "Right now, it's like a minefield. We don't know which ones will go off or when. We have to hurry. Can you make it that far without my help?"

"My daughter is out there. Of course I can."

Beren nodded and turned to go, but Elanor tugged on his arm. "How much time do I have?"

He looked in Elanor's eyes and while they were still clear, a faint hint of blackness swirled in the corners.

"It was barely a half-hour last time, but that blast was pretty strong," he said, trying to stay confident.

"I've been waking up at night. Not knowing where I am or how I got there. It lasts for longer and longer each time."

"It's lifting. We may have more time than I thought," Beren said with even more confidence.

"If I turn before we find her... "

"We're going to beat this, Ellie."

She pulled her husband's face in close. "Every day I lose my family, even when I'm alone. I can't go through it again."

"We'll find her."

Unable to hold back, Beren kissed Elanor. It was their first kiss in a decade and Elanor didn't want to let go. She had forgotten the flames of such a fire and how they burned so easily through any kind of fear or doubt. When he pulled away, she knew that this would be the last time she would ever allow the curse to affect her, even if it meant saying goodbye forever.

Elanor readied her wand and aimed it at a far-off tree, preparing to grapple. They nodded and Beren took off. She swung and propelled herself through the air, staying close to her husband. As she was about to swing and catch another branch, an explosion like a supernova went off a few feet to her right and her whole world was ablaze with a powerful golden light.

The light rippled through the forest and quickly vanished. The storm halted and for just a moment all was quiet and still, and then a brilliant white flash flooded Elanor's vision.

* * * *

Elanor knelt at Shea's bedside. Barely seven years of age, Shea dangled her little legs over the edge of the feather bed, and Elanor was removing soft white socks from her delicate feet.

"Shea, you really must get used to being barefoot. Fairies don't need to wear boots, honey."

She tugged and pulled a sock away from her dancing toes and playfully said, "Ahh," as if to show how nice it feels to let them breathe.

"See? Feels good to let your feet get some air, doesn't it?"

"Mom?"

Elanor did the same 'Ahh' with the second sock and smiled at Shea.

"Can I have a little brother? Please? Even a little sister would be OK."

"We've been over this, honey. It's not so easy," Elanor said as she tucked Shea's wings back and placed her head on the pillow.

"I just want someone to play with. That's all."

"I know, but listen." Elanor pulled the feathered blanket up to Shea's chin. "I don't ever want you to feel alone. Your Dad and I will always be here. I promise. OK?"

"Mom?"

Before blowing out the bedside candle, Elanor turned with one last smile. Beren's voice, filtered and frail, echoed through the room. She stared at Shea lying in bed, but her husband's voice kept calling.

"Elanor!"

*   *   *   *

His voice was weak and distant as he crawled through the snow. The storm rolled back through and Beren couldn't see Elanor, or much of anything else for that matter. Blood leaked from his forehead as he continued to search and call out his wife's name. The wind trapped and vanquished his yells. Gripping the bark of a tree for support, he leaned, out of breath and desperate, until finally he spotted her.

She was lying in the frozen snow, bleeding and having difficulty catching her breath. He fell to her, wrapping his arms around her.

"Hey. Hey! Stay with me."

"Shea… you have to… "

"Easy. Relax. Just relax. You're OK."

"Do you remember… the last time… you found me?" she asked through struggled breaths.

"I remember every time," he said.

"Don't stop looking. Please."

Her eyes swirled with a flicker of darkness. She could feel it and blinked, trying to ward off the impending curse.

"I'll always find you. You understand?"

"Thank you for keeping her safe," she said. Looking over his shoulder, she cracked a smile. "Looks like… you and Shea will have something… to talk about."

He looked and noticed his wing. It wasn't completely broken, though a noticeable, large chunk had been ripped out of it from the blast.

"Finally," he replied with a smile. "Come on. This isn't over yet."

He lifted her up through the pain. They stood holding on to each other as the wind and snow whirled through the dark forest.

31
SHEA'S CHOICE

The storm had grown into a whiteout blizzard. Shea could barely see through the thick, blowing flakes as she grappled from tree to tree. Stopping within an evergreen, she huddled against a thick branch with the True Love Wish secure in her arms—and cried. There had been plenty of tears through the years, mostly from frustration and anger, but these were different. There had been a deep, bottomless pit within which she had placed each thought of regret and sorrow she had ever had, and each revolved around the fear that somehow she was responsible for everything awful that had ever happened to her, to her father and to her lost mother. These tears were from that deepest part of her breaking heart, and she felt that they may never stop. She couldn't fight the feeling that maybe she shouldn't stop crying. That maybe she deserved these tears and that crying was a way to punish the broken-winged, handicapped fairy that would never become a Keeper.

The True Love Wish pushed itself against Shea and nestled its warmth firmly to her chest. Shea choked on her gasping tears and looked at the loving wish. Its big, round eyes looked up at her as if to say it was OK to cry, that it was OK to have regret and that it was OK to feel a sense of loss. A soft red glow surrounded them as they sat on the branch and the wind blew icy snow through the surrounding forest. While whatever was waiting for her on the other side of the evergreen's branches was danger personified, she felt a rising awareness of her mission: a mission that she needed to complete.

BOOM! An explosion rocked the forest and trees around her, sending ripples of golden light throughout. The Gates were exploding shut, one by one, and Shea quickly realized her time was running out.

"You're with me now. We're gonna be alright. Can you help me find a Gate?" Shea said to the wish as she wiped the tears away. It beamed a bit brighter, sensing Shea's growing confidence. "OK, little wish. It's time to go home."

Aiming her wand through the branches, she charged it up, ready to connect a grappling spell to a neighboring tree. As she was about to fire, a rush of black fog swept beneath her and swirled through the woods. The wish wiggled in panic and Shea knew she wasn't alone.

Trying to maintain her balance, Shea crept to the edge of the branch and aimed her wand. Blasting a grapple to a nearby tree, she latched on and swung herself over. Landing on another branch, she slipped on the icy bark. Trying to grab on to whatever she could as she slipped, she dropped her wand, and fell.

Crashing to the snow below, it being harder than it looked, she somehow kept the wish tight in her arms, but her pack and goggles were lost somewhere in the blowing snow. Her head was throbbing from the fall, but she didn't have time to feel any pain. She was out in the open and wandless. The True Love Wish beamed a soft glow to help navigate as she crawled.

A black wind rushed and circled around her, followed by a deep, foreboding laugh. Panic set in as she searched for her wand, clawing at the frozen snow. There! She lunged for it just as the fog thickened.

Behind Shea, Erebus slowly rose from the darkness and formed into a tall, black-hooded shadow. Shea spun on her knees and aimed her wand, but he only floated closer, daring her to fire.

KABOOM! Another Gate exploded a few hundred feet away, sending ripples of golden light through the forest once again. Erebus wasn't fazed and only smiled as he slightly bent over Shea. The True Love Wish wiggled and pushed itself as close to Shea as possible.

"Desperation. A hero's worst enemy. And it looks like we have a new hero," he said, taunting.

"Stay away!" Shea yelled, waving her little wand.

"But why would you want me to stay away? One who can give you all you've ever asked for. Grant all of your wishes."

"I don't want my wishes granted. I only want this wish..."

"Stop fooling yourself!" he yelled. "This isn't about that wish, Shea Evenstar."

Her red hair whipped in the wind as the wish cowered in her arms. She gripped it tighter.

"You're an outcast. No one has ever accepted you as you expect to be. Your own mother doesn't even believe in you."

"Stop it!"

"And what about dear old dad? Do you think he'll grant your wishes? He gave up on you years ago. You're what? Nothing more than a liability."

"Go away!" she gasped through gushing tears, and sprinted through the forest, pushing against the storm. It was useless, as Erebus swirled a tornado of snow and ice around her, knocking her to the ground. The wind howled and Shea gave up, falling, hugging the little Wish in her arms.

"How did you expect to escape? Through a Gate? Even if they weren't being blown apart by your foolishness, you're not a WishKeeper, Shea. And you never will be," he said as he leaned closer.

"I am a WishKeeper! I can grant this!" she screamed.

"Then let me help you prove them wrong, Shea. You can be the WishKeeper you've always wished to be."

Erebus pulled back and held out both of his hands, palms up. Images slowly materialized above them, flickering to life. Shea looked at the images, swiveling her head back and forth. What was this magic? What was he doing?

The visions formed and Shea suddenly knew what he was presenting to her. Two options. Above one palm was a ghostly image of Grayson and Miranda hugging, kissing, as happy as she had ever seen two WishMakers. Above his other palm was a bright blue and pink image of Shea—flying. Her wings were perfect, beautiful. Wind rushed against her ecstatic face. Two separate versions of happiness: Grayson and Miranda's on the left, and her own on the right.

"No," Shea choked. "It's not real and it's not…"

"Oh, it's possible," Erebus cut in. "But both are not. It's one or the other, my little Shea. Your mother made a choice once. And you remember how that turned out."

The image of Shea flying quickly changed to one of her as a little fairy crying in bed. She was lying on her stomach, both of her shredded wings protruding from her back. They were ugly, charred, skeletal. The little fairy girl crying uncontrollably in her bed, alone, hugging her pillow.

"Do you think everything will change, Shea? That suddenly you will be accepted by your worthless peers and allowed into the Keeper force? That Paragonia will be saved and all will be well again? Whose Paragonia are you saving? The world you live in will still be bereft of any hope that you may fly again. It won't be the Paragonia you loved to see from above. Your one and only wish to fly will still never be granted and you will forever be chained to the ground."

Shea tried to keep her eyes on the image of Grayson and Miranda. She tried to hold on to the image of her family's WishMakers living a life of love, happiness and fulfillment, but what about her own life? Every wish and every dream she had ever had in which she kept her perfect wings intact never came true. They were never going to come true… and it wasn't fair. It wasn't fair that she was the only fairy affected by that blast ten years ago, and it wasn't fair that she was the only one who had to carry the visible burden of weakness. The symbol of a dying Paragonia. Every time her fellow WishKeepers would look at her, they would see the hopelessness of their vanishing freedom. They saw their future and how dim it truly was.

A black hand reached out from Erebus' shadowed cloak and extended toward Shea. The images above his palms whisked away in the winter wind and she pulled the wish in close, not giving in. *He can't have it!* As horrible as it was that she represented such a dismal future, she had to hold onto hope. She had to hold on to the only possibility of ever living a life not in fear, but in love. Even if it meant she could never fly again.

Stretching closer and closer, Erebus' scrawny, skeletal, foggy hand caressed Shea's head, but didn't reach for the wish. For a moment she thought Erebus understood how difficult a choice this was for her. How impossible it was to exchange her world's last hope for her ability to fly. *Oh, to fly again.* To feel the freedom of weightlessness. To snag your breath upon the branches of your beautiful world that stretched out so openly beneath you, waiting for you to explore, to see, to love it as unconditionally as it loved you. *Oh, to fly again.*

Her thoughts rattled back and forth as she stared into the darkness of Erebus' eyes. Could he grant my wish? Could he really do such a thing? *I wish…*

As if he were listening and answering her question, Erebus slid his icy fingers along her broken wings and a slow, pulsating light emanated from them.

"A wish for a wish," Erebus whispered.

Shea could hear more than his whisper. She could hear the echoes of all of her unfulfilled wishes; every wish she had ever had rang in her ears as the shadow king caressed her ugly wings. My wings. The echoes stopped and only one wish flooded her mind. *My wings.*

Growing brighter and brighter, Erebus' spell lifted Shea off the ground and suspended her in air. Her arms were outstretched as her wings exploded with a fantastic purple light. She hung there, clasped in the fulfillment of a wish. Her thick, red-blonde hair danced in the freezing wind until an explosion almost as bright as the golden Gates poured through the forest. Breath left her lungs and she fell to the ground, gasping. On her knees, she slowly opened her eyes.

Reaching her hand behind her back, she felt something she hadn't felt since she was a child. It was something that was always there when she would dream at night, but which would quickly vanish when she woke, drenched in sweat.

Her wings were fixed. Both fluttered in perfect symmetry, like a butterfly.

The wind rushed back in and woke her from her dream-like state. She looked up at Erebus. He was smiling, standing over her, and the True Love Wish was in his arms.

"You're welcome," he said.

Shea gasped, realizing what she'd done. "No!"

With a rush of darkness, Erebus rocketed a wave of fog at Shea and sent her crashing into a tree. She fell, unconscious.

With a black flash, Erebus was gone.

32
INGREDIENTS

The windows of the little cottage rattled as the wind thrust its natural might against it with another blast. Half a dozen candles flickered throughout the drafty home as Grayson and Miranda sat in awkward silence, staring at a self-conscious and nervous Thane. He stood on the coffee table with his hands in his pockets while organizing a few magazines with his feet, lining them up in a neat and orderly pile. The wide-eyed stares from the Makers weren't making it any easier to begin the lecture he knew was necessary. Each time he looked up with a heave of a concentrated breath, ready to explain, all he could muster was an open-mouthed grunt.

Miranda and Grayson huddled close, staring at him. There was a tiny fairy standing on their coffee table. He was pacing. Sweating. Talking to himself. When he brushed his hand through his thick, wavy hair, a tiny battle of emotions stormed through their shivering bodies. They didn't know whether to laugh hysterically, or faint.

Nudging another magazine with his toe, he decided to start slow, though the beginning of such a conversation could have been better conveyed. "So. Made a wish, huh? Pretty cool."

Miranda immediately pushed the blanket off of her and stood. "OK, this is too much."

"What wish?" Grayson asked, studying the little fairy.

"There's a fairy talking to us and I just came over here to…" Miranda mumbled to herself as she paced to and from the kitchen.

"What happened to that other fairy and why were her wings broken?" The amount of questions that rattled Grayson's brain and begged for answers was almost too much for his mouth to handle.

At this point, Thane was reacting like he was watching a heated Ping-Pong match. Words were coming at him at such a rapid rate, for a moment he wished Lost Fairies were attacking so he didn't have to deal with this.

"Tea pots are exploding. Black fog is covering our house in the middle of winter. Little people with wings..." Miranda continued, barely able to breathe.

"They were fighting over something. One of them was holding some kind of light," Grayson said, leaning so close to Thane the little fairy backed away, thinking he might be blown over by his tackling words.

"I mean, I knew this was going to be a difficult conversation to have, but I just came over to..." Miranda continued.

Finally taking his glare away from Thane, Grayson's frustration with Miranda finally surfaced, "Why did you come over here?"

"I needed to talk to you, not a fairy!"

"I didn't think we'd have guests, ya know!"

"Guests? It's a fairy!"

"Well, let's talk then! Obviously we have a lot to talk about!" Grayson raised his voice for the first time.

"Hey! Hey! Please! I can explain if you two just shut up for a second!" Thane didn't like being called a fairy. He felt it was too feminine a description, but he also knew that if he didn't cut the two Makers off he might have to use his wand on them. Not a bad thought, really, but he quickly shook off the idea. "How did you two make a True Love Wish if you argue so much?"

"You keep talking about wishes. And true love?" Grayson calmed a bit as Miranda slowly walked over to the side of the couch, awaiting an explanation she knew she probably wouldn't be able to understand.

"I'll try to keep this short, but I really don't know where to begin," Thane said, as Miranda lowered herself to the couch cushions. She wiped her sweaty palms on her knees and listened.

"My name's Thane. I'm a WishKeeper. Well, not yet, but I will be. Maybe. We look after your wishes once you make them. Every wish is powerful, but a True Love Wish is, well, pretty important, as you can imagine. Or, maybe you can't imagine, but just go with me on this."

"And we each made one? A True Love Wish?" Grayson asked.

"Two, actually. Which is weird and has never happened before. Your first was made ten years ago."

The WishMakers looked at each other. To say they were confused would be an understatement, and even though it was difficult for Miranda to comprehend any of this, something dawned on her.

"What happened to the first one?" she asked.

Thane was apprehensive since his kind had never purposely killed a wish before. He wasn't sure how they would react. "Uh, well. It was destroyed."

Miranda leaned against the back of the sofa. Even though all of this was completely ridiculous, she knew that she wasn't hallucinating and that a fairy was standing directly in front of her. If all of what she was hearing and witnessing was actually true, the so-called missing link, the 'something' that was missing between her and Grayson suddenly made sense. It made sense, at least, on a completely and utterly outlandish level.

"You see, a TLW can't be made unless both Makers make the same loving wish for the other. Two unconditionally loving wishes combine to create one True Love Wish. It's very rare and, until now, Makers only ever make one in their entire lifetime," Thane continued. He felt that he was gaining momentum and his little lecture might be easier than expected. "The problem is, your wish is supposed to be granted, but there are others who…" he was cut off, much to his disappointment, since he was catching a groove. Grayson and Miranda were no longer looking at him, but instead tearfully looking at each other.

"I thought you didn't love me anymore?" Grayson asked his wife.

She looked back at Thane. "What happens if the wish is destroyed?" Her voice was quivering with equal amounts of excitement and sorrow.

"Our world grows weaker and… well, it's simple, really. The wish doesn't come true." Even though he personally thought it was simple, he quickly realized the Makers didn't.

"And our second wish: it hasn't been destroyed?" Miranda asked.

"Not yet," Thane didn't mean to be ominous, it was just the truth.

Grayson softly placed his hand in Miranda's. He wasn't listening to Thane anymore. His only concern was for his wife and marriage. Their eyes met and Miranda knew what he was asking.

"Of course I still love you, Gray. That's why I came over tonight."

Thane smiled while he watched the Makers hold hands. He felt most of his work was done here and it was rather successful.

"But that wasn't exactly what I wished for," Miranda continued.

Both Grayson and Thane looked at her with confused glares.

"Wait, what?" Thane chirped.

"What did you wish for?" Grayson asked, hesitant to hear the answer.

"Evidently we wished for the same thing, so you tell me."

Grayson looked at Thane for a little help, but the Keeper-in-training just shrugged his shoulders. This was beyond his realm of support.

"I just wish you were happy," Grayson whispered, heartfelt. He knew that his wish was one of selflessness: a wish for her happiness with or without him, and he understood that the real reason Miranda came over tonight was to discuss the latter.

Smiling through heavy tears, Miranda nodded. For so many years she knew something was off between them. There was something missing, and searching for it became as normal to her as breathing, but suddenly the possibility of discovering what that missing something might be was upon her. Even though she had planned to leave Grayson and wished he would find true happiness without her in his life, a weight was lifted. A weight so heavy the lightness of being was almost uncomfortable.

Although diffident about his approach to breaking the silence, Thane knew he needed to say something. This was all too depressing. "Look. Your wish is in trouble and even though I have no idea how, it needs to be granted and not just for you two, but for our kind as well. There is... well, it's a really long story, but someone wants it for himself and that really can't happen."

A burst of wind howled against the side of the house. The house shook as if a sudden earthquake had erupted and wouldn't stop. Miranda grabbed on to Grayson as the couch shifted and slid across the floor. Thane fell and braced himself along the edge of the coffee table.

The quaking finally slowed as a rush of bitter wind blew through the room, dousing the flickering candles. From pitch black, the room slowly brightened from a source of light emanating from the center of the room. Bigger and bigger it grew until, seeping in under the doors and through the windows, Erebus took shape. The light source was shining from his hands and cast an eerie, red glow, silhouetting his deep black cloak and pointed hood. Jumping to the couch and between the two Makers, Thane knew what this was and, though he drew his wand, fear clouded his eyes, awaiting the inevitable.

Grayson and Miranda watched in awe as Erebus formed in the middle of their home. Beyond disbelief, they simply watched, paralyzed with fear.

"WishMakers and a Keeper recruit. This won't help your ranking, Private Thane. Don't you know it's against the rules to fraternize with the help?" Erebus teased, as Thane eyed the True Love Wish in his hand. "Your dear friend, Shea, agreed to a trade. Very wise, that fairy."

"She would never do that. Where is she?" Thane yelled, pointing a shaking wand.

"Never, shouldn't, wouldn't, couldn't. It's all a waste of time. A WishingKing should never bring Makers to Paragonia, but it's exactly what I'm going to do anyway."

"Thane?" Miranda pleaded, begging for this to be fake or at least for an explanation.

"You're no king and you don't need them," Thane said as his wand sparked with a charge. Even though his initial assignment was to keep Shea, he had new orders and was ready to do what was necessary to keep the Makers safe, even if his efforts seemed futile.

Erebus simply smiled and leaned in close. "Oh, I admit. I do need them, master Thane." His shadowed fog crept around Thane and the Makers. "When you and your little flying friends brought me to your world, you gave me power. The power of a wizard, as some might say. Power that I intend to keep." There was a silent pause in the room as deafening as the storm outside. "I need them, Thane. I'm a wizard, and wizards need ingredients."

A wave of shadow blanketed them. It churned like a whirlpool in a giant cauldron and though Thane fired as many defensive spells as he could, it was overwhelming. The room filled with Erebus' fog. It spun and, quickly, they all vanished.

33
DRIFTED

Elanor's head pounded as Beren carried her through the forest, flying against a powerful headwind. Her body felt broken and useless in Beren's arms as he pushed through the storm. For Elanor, her inability to help was the most frustrating, and when a blast of wind pushed Beren to the ground, she knew he had to find Shea without her. She was only holding him back.

"We'll never find her like this. You have to let me go," she said.

"I'm not leaving you."

"I think I can grapple. I'm OK."

"You're not OK, Ellie," Beren said, watching her grip the bark of a tree. "The blizzard as bad as it is, we'll only get separated."

"It's not far from where that light blast came from. I'm fine, Beren. Shea is more important right now. Please."

He nodded, remembering how stubborn she was. "If it's too difficult…"

"Go. I'll be fine. I'll fire a flare to let you know where I am if you're not back soon." She waved him off, cutting through his hesitation. He kissed her on the cheek and jogged ahead through the driving snow.

Once he was out of sight, she leaned against the tree, gasping in pain. Every inch of her screamed in agony, but her determination to find her daughter was stronger; to explain everything to her, to apologize, to beg for forgiveness. For the past decade, each time the curse lifted, her first thought was of Shea. Waves of fear rushed through her alongside thoughts of how much Shea must hate her. Of how much she must despise everything she had done. Elanor couldn't help but be fearful that Shea was thankful her mother was gone. When Shea fired that spell at her moments ago, her nightmares were justified – such a look of hatred and resentment burned from her daughter's eyes as she pointed that wand. *Even if I do find Shea, then what? Would any kind of explanation suffice? Would any amount of an apology be good enough?* As Elanor pushed through the pain and searched through the snow-drenched forest around her, her soul begged that she would at least get a chance to see her daughter before the curse crept back in.

Limping over piles of drifted snow, her foot stepped on something solid, but it wasn't a branch. Kicking the object out from under its snowy grave, she took a moment to recognize what she was holding in her hands. Goggles.

She gasped, trying to catch her sudden bursts of breath, and a rush of tears overcame her. Her full-body pain vanished and adrenaline took over as she pushed further through the thick wind, rushing to find any other sign of her daughter. A brown leather sack was a few feet away. She fell to her knees to pick it up, terrified to imagine what separated her daughter from her pack.

The soft crunching of snow, footsteps that were barely audible, broke her from her search. Someone was approaching. Not now. Not when Shea is so close. She whipped out her wand and pointed it at the dark surrounding woods.

"Who's there?" she called out. "If you want a fight, it will be a short one, I can assure…"

Elanor didn't recognize Avery as she crept out from behind a mangled set of thorny bushes, with her dark cloak and black hair. She very easily could have been a Lost Fairy, but for her intact wings, and then Elanor remembered those eyes: eyes that stored a decade of pain.

At the sight of Elanor, Avery wanted to weep. A broken WishKeeper whose once-perfect face, always so alight with ambition and intent, was now scarred, tired and begging for help. Her Elanor was still there, though. No, not her Elanor. She wasn't foolish enough to believe Elanor could be hers like she had years ago, but the Elanor she fell secretly in love with was still there. Behind the blackened eyes was a mother, a wife, and a friend.

"Avery?" Elanor whispered, unsure.

Avery nodded quickly through tears, happy she even remembered, and ran to her. Elanor tried to stand, but Avery knelt next to her, lightly grabbing her shoulders. "Are you alright? Just sit. Sit," she said, and examined her like a doctor does a patient.

Elanor couldn't stop staring at her, not just because she was surprised to see her, but because the sight of her was slowly casting away the fog that covered up her memories. Seeing her was like drawing back a curtain and slowly revealing a forgotten past. She touched her cheek and they smiled, but the panic quickly returned. Elanor felt Shea's leather pack in her hands and remembered.

"Shea. Oh, Avery, she's here somewhere!" Desperation pulsed through her. "Please, help me find her. Please!"

It frightened Avery to see Elanor so panic-stricken, but what could she do other than help? They stood, Avery guiding the pained back of her friend, leaning her against the bark of a small birch.

Avery didn't want to tell Elanor that she had seen Erebus retreat from the woods, True Love Wish cupped in his palms. How, for years, she had been merely a coward and all she had ever wanted was for Elanor to be proud of her. It wasn't the time or place to explain anything. She only tried to help, as futile as that help may seem.

The wind had covered any remnants of tracks in the snow as Avery searched the ground for any sign of Shea. "She has to be close. Erebus wouldn't have let her get very..." she said, but was cut off by Elanor's scream.

"Shea!" Elanor yelled.

Clutching her wand and lying limp against the thick base of a maple, Elanor's daughter lay motionless, unconscious, across the floor of the woods a few yards behind them.

The pain didn't matter anymore as Elanor ran to her. Snow had drifted and almost completely covered Shea, and Elanor quickly wrapped her arms around her, pulling her out from under the icy blanket. "No, no, honey, please! Beren. Beren!" she yelled, and fired a red flare high above the forest ceiling.

Rocking her limp little fairy in her arms, Elanor mumbled pleas of hope. Though, thankfully, Shea still felt warm, she noticed her daughter's wings. They were perfect, beautiful, and this only made Elanor cry harder, knowing Erebus had tricked her. Avery stood over them, stoic, and too pained to cry.

Pulling her wand from its sheath, Elanor quickly arched a half-circle red dome over their heads. It glowed with warmth and melted the snow around them and all else Elanor could do was hug her daughter and beg her to wake up. Avery stood outside the warm dome, crossing her arms and taking a step back. She felt quick resentment that she wasn't included, but the look on Elanor's face—a look of complete and utter gratitude—was enough to erase the sudden selfishness, for now.

Elanor's shaking hands took the goggles and carefully placed them around Shea's forehead. She just wanted to see her baby again—the hopeful, energetic little fairy that was always so full of life.

"I'm sorry. I'm so sorry," Elanor gasped, choking through tears and rocking her close.

When Shea opened her eyes, a blurred image of the forest came into view and she could feel someone holding her. The warmth was strange as it contrasted with the frozen landscape that blinked in her eyes. It hurt to turn her head and look at whatever was wrapping itself around her, but when she noticed long, thick red hair, she panicked.

Elanor pulled her head back and looked at Shea. Her crying quickly halted.

Immediately, Shea pushed away from her mother's grip. Though the physical pain from Erebus' blast was still powerful, her fear of her cursed mother was even more so. Crawling away and trying to stay out of reach, Shea looked at Elanor. Her mother's eyes were clear and for the first time in years, Shea saw her mom. Flashes of memories poured through windows into a past that had all been closed. Her fear was still there, though, and forced her to doubt what she was seeing.

Elanor had imagined that reuniting with Shea wouldn't be easy, but she wasn't ready for fear to pour from her daughter's eyes. She was willing to accept resentment and anger, but there couldn't be a more hurtful cut than the one that dug into her—Shea's petrified gaze. Trembling, Elanor slowly reached out her hand, and though Shea flinched, Elanor took the goggles and pulled them over Shea's eyes.

"Goggles goggled?" Elanor asked with a quivering voice.

Shea was frozen, unsure of whether or not this was another trick, but she wanted to believe. She so badly wanted to believe this really was her mom kneeling in front of her.

"Check," she replied, hesitantly. "Wishes made?"

"Wishes granted," Elanor continued, trying desperately not to cry.

They rushed to each other and held on to one another as if at any moment the other could disappear. The red dome wasn't necessary anymore: the hug was more than enough. Avery gasped with a tearful laugh.

Pulling away, Elanor cupped her daughter's face in her hands and smiled. Yet, eyeing Shea's wings, a continued feeling of sorrow and regret pulsed through her.

Shea removed the goggles, noticing where her mother was looking, and remembered her fixed wings. "I'm sorry, Mom. I didn't..." but her mom stopped her.

"No. You're not the one who needs to apologize."

"Your eyes," Shea said, staring. A shadow of a shadow loomed within the corners of Elanor's eyes. Shea wanted to search. She wanted to look so deeply, to remember every moment she ever shared with her mother before she lost her, before her little world was flipped, before her wings were broken. Before...

Elanor looked away, self-conscious of what her daughter might see. "I am so sorry, Shea. There is so much to explain, but—I have missed you so much." She took her hand and though it wasn't enough to erase everything that had happened over the past ten years, it was enough for now.

Shea touched her mom's face and lightly turned it toward her. The corners of Elanor's eyes swirled with the smoky fog and though Shea's curiosity buzzed, the twinkle of familiarity was there.

"I don't have much time, honey," Elanor said, knowing that Shea must have so many questions.

"Erebus?" Shea asked.

Elanor nodded, wanting to say more.

"But the wish. It's over. He has it. I just—just gave it to him."

Avery cut in, wiping the tears from her cheek. "It's not over yet." Shea looked up, noticing another fairy was there.

"Avery?"

Avery nodded a pleasant but pained smile at the little fairy.

Taking her daughter's hand, Elanor agreed. "Avery's right. It's not over yet. Can you stand?" Elanor asked, as she helped Shea up. Shea's knees buckled, but she eventually stood.

"You OK?" Avery asked with a nod.

Shea nodded back, though not entirely sure if she was OK. "I did something awful, Mom," Shea said. "Erebus. He... I didn't know what..." Shea pushed her head against Elanor's chest, and hugged her, hoping it would make all of this go away. Hoping that the hug she had dreamed about for a decade would solve all of her problems as it once did.

Elanor held her daughter and shared a knowing glance with Avery. They knew that Shea was no different than they were now: another fairy that Erebus had tricked.

"We have more in common than you know, Shea. It's not your fault. None of this is," Avery said.

Pulling her face out of her mother's arms. "But what now? He has the wish."

"Even if the wish itself is gone, true love never goes away," Elanor said. She looked at Avery when she said this, and though Avery knew it wasn't a sudden admission from Elanor, she felt the burning again of the flame that was so strong years ago every time she had looked at Elanor.

"We may still have a chance," Avery said as they limped through the wind. "We have to find a Gate, and fast."

"We have to find Beren first," Elanor said.

"There isn't time, Ellie. We don't know how long he'll be and the Gates are closing faster than..."

Elanor quickly cut her off. She couldn't believe what Avery was saying. "We're not going anywhere without Beren. Nothing could make me leave him," she said, darting a frustrated glare at Avery.

Avery forced an understanding nod and held her tongue. In a way, Elanor knew that Avery was right. The Gates were closing and, by now, for all they knew, they could all be closed, but there was no way she would lose Beren all over again.

"It's time to show your father just how good of a flyer you are," Elanor smiled as she continued, reading Shea's thoughts. Shea felt a pain of regret. What would he say about her wings?

They smiled and Shea took her mother's hand. As they pushed through the wind, Elanor reached out and held Avery's hand too. Whether it was for simple support to help her walk, or not, the rush of adrenaline flooded Avery. Nothing was going to stop her from getting Elanor back safely.

It wasn't how Shea had always planned that such a reuniting would occur, but, then again, plans that fork off in new directions tend to be alight with better possibility. And now that she had her mom back, even just for a moment, the possibilities felt endless.

34
THE RETURN OF THE WISHINGKING

It wasn't long before Beren was lost. The blizzard made the world twist and turn and he was sure he had seen this particular oak tree not moments ago. He pushed off the ground and sped toward the top of the tree to get a better look at his surroundings. His slashed wing didn't make flying easy, to say the least, and, faster than expected, his understanding and acceptance of Shea's disability swept in. There was no sign of her, none whatsoever, and panic was starting to build. All of his life's training hadn't prepared him for such a rescue mission, but mustering the courage to remain composed and together was a necessity, not only in order to save his daughter from whatever evil had befallen her, but to simply stay sane.

So many thoughts ran through his dizzy mind as he gripped the icy branch and looked out over the park. He could see the water tower from where he was as well as the cul-de-sac barely a mile away. The fog had lifted and no evidence of a Lost Fairy onslaught was visible, but he also couldn't find his Keeper troops. Part of his hope of breaking off from Elanor was to find his team. Obviously, there was strength in numbers during a search and rescue attempt, and the lack of support, or much of any kind of hope, was weighing on his mind. The town was silent but for the creaking of the branches bending in the winter wind. Any time a thought surfaced of his daughter alone in this storm, lying unconscious, or worse, he pushed it away like a horrible memory.

He'd been away from Elanor for too long, he thought, but he needed to make one last attempt at finding Shea. Seeing the cottage sitting along the snow-covered cul-de-sac, his last-ditch effort was to check if, possibly, Shea had returned to the house. If nothing else, he would retrieve Thane and do the unthinkable: ask the Makers for help. He had begun this mission adamant about retrieving the dangerous wish and destroying it, but in a flash everything had changed. His daughter was all that mattered now.

Zooming through the wind, Beren sent red sparks into the sky hoping any remaining member of The Hope would notice. He was too far from Elanor for her to see the flare, but some of his team had to be close by. Landing along the sill of the kitchen window, he zapped a spell to lift it open with a grunt and hurried in.

The house was almost as dark as Erebus' fog and this immediately sent shivers of worry through him. The Makers wouldn't have blown out the candles: they needed some kind of light, and Thane, being Thane, would have begged for the same.

"Shea! Thane?" he called out, searching the living room. The house was empty, but how? It was barely an hour since he had left them. As he flew through the house, noticing the furniture pushed aside, toppled over and askew, as if a tornado had swept through, it quickly dawned on him—Erebus.

*　　*　　*　　*

Stars twinkled in a crystal clear night sky as the bright full moon lit up the Paragonian valley. A slight, warm breeze rustled the thick green grass as fireflies danced and blinked along the edges of the forest. Warm, golden lights from thousands of fairy homes rimmed the trees of the north end of the valley. Keepers throughout Paragonia were preparing for a restless sleep, knowing family and friends were on The Other Side fighting a war that could be their last, for better or worse.

A young mother was tucking her little fairy daughter into a plush, straw bed. She kissed her on the forehead and helped adjust her whisper-thin wings as she rolled on her side. They exchanged loving smiles and though the tiny fairy girl closed her eyes and gripped a small, round little doll resembling a wish, her mother didn't leave her side. A deep worried sigh left her lungs as she watched her daughter fall asleep.

Glistening in the moonlight, Castle Paragonia rested at the far end of the valley. It was unnaturally quiet as the old weathered castle sat amidst its weeds and overgrowth, haunted not by whispers of a troubled past, but by something more presently pressing. A light flickered from a large window in the middle of the castle, just above the closed gates. A large veranda stretched out with two double doors flung wide open. This was Erebus' potions room, and though the rest of the stone behemoth looked cold and dormant, a flutter of life glimmered from the center of it once again.

The room hadn't been touched in years. Dust and debris from years of neglect cluttered the corners and covered the wooden tables.

Inside a gyroscope, stuck in a spell, lay the True Love Wish. Its red glow was diminishing and its breathing was labored. There was no sign of Thane or the Makers as a breeze blew in through the opened veranda doors. It rustled the pages of an ancient book, browned and faded from years of use, as black fog curled away from it, sweeping toward the veranda.

Erebus stood along the aged stone railing, looking out over the starlit valley. The twinkling lights of the fairy homes were to his right, and though the Keepers were climbing into their beds with heavy thoughts of worry, little did they know the danger was at their doorstep. The wizard leaned against the railing and softly released a deep, low breath.

Fog crept out of him like a disease, seeping out over the valley in every direction. Spreading, it doused the bright stars and glow of the moon. It inched up and around the tree homes of every fairy, its fingers clawing at the doors and windows, bleeding in through thin cracks and down narrow chimneys.

Creeping over the still pond of The Nursery, the fog devoured the thatched roof barn, making its way along the base of the mountain. The few wishes that were in their pens cowered and huddled in the corners of the wooden fences. Some pushed away from the fog and tried escaping. One by one, the shadow devoured them, moving through the stables like a slow, demented tidal wave.

The light of the fulfillment pool at Exclamation Pointe was the only thing that repelled the fog. The darkness swirled around it like a whirlpool, spinning and spinning, lashing angry fingers at the stoic fairy statue. Erebus had covered the entire valley with his shadow and all that was left to control was Exclamation Pointe. In his mind it was only a matter of time, and he was going to enjoy every second of it.

The young fairy mother ran her fingers through her sleeping daughter's pink hair and gave her one last kiss goodnight. Just as she was about to stand and leave her little fairy to hopefully pleasant dreams, fingers of a black shadow hand gripped the wooden door and slowly pushed it open. The fog oozed into the small bedroom, clinging to the walls like thick black smoke. The young mother quickly covered her daughter as the fog collapsed over her.

Breathing in deeply, Erebus stood upright on the veranda, looking at his masterpiece. A black leathered smile stretched across his withered white face.

"It's good to be home."

35
LIKE FATHER, LIKE DAUGHTER

Shea's strength was slowly returning, but she knew Elanor's strenuous breathing wasn't a good sign. She didn't know just how much pain her mother was in, however, and Elanor intended to keep it that way. The blizzard wasn't helping matters either as Avery helped Elanor step by step, supporting her as she limped.

Shea risked running ahead in hopes of getting a clearer view, but there was no sign of the end of the forest or the cul-de-sac. They needed an aerial view, but the guilt that she felt over using her new wings kept her from mentioning it.

"Let's rest for a second," Avery said, as she stopped. "This damn blizzard just won't end."

"No, we need to keep going. Shea," Elanor said, calling her daughter back. Her headache was slowly retreating and that only meant the curse was returning. Something else she intended to hide from Shea. Avery looked at Elanor's eyes and noticed the black swirl was getting thicker. Catching Elanor's glare, Avery knew she didn't want her daughter to know.

"We need to find your father, get back to the house, and regroup. We can't stay out in this storm for much longer. You need to use those things," she said to Shea, referring to her wings.

Shea hesitated. Even though she so badly wanted to, she felt awful leaving her wingless mom behind. Avery nodded to Shea, giving her blessing.

"I'll be here. She'll be fine," Avery said.

Elanor took Shea's hand, knowing her daughter didn't want to leave. "Go. I'll be right here."

Fluttering her wings for the first time in over a decade, Shea stepped back and felt the forgotten, comfortable breeze her wings created when flapped. She looked at her mother and a slow, evolving smile rolled across her face. Elanor fought the urge to break down, and remained composed, if only to instill more confidence in her daughter.

"They're beautiful," Elanor said through a painful smile.

"I'll be right back. I promise," Shea said, and with a remembered joy, she buzzed her wings and lifted off the ground. For years, she thought that maybe she'd completely forgotten how to fly: that if by some miracle she could fly again, her wings wouldn't work, or she wouldn't be able to control them, or any number of other fearful reasons to keep her feet on the ground. When she looked at her feet, however, with her clunky boots dangling beneath her and the frozen ground retreating as quickly as her fears, it all came back to her. She was going to fly again. Oh, to fly again.

Floating in front of Avery and Elanor, Shea removed her wand, nodded her head and took off, like a bullet. She was a natural.

Once Shea was out of sight, Elanor collapsed. She fell to her knees and Avery cast the same domed warming spell as Elanor had before.

"Ellie?" Avery said, as she crouched next to her. "What can I do? Anything?"

Elanor turned her head. Her bare hands were buried in the melting snow, as she looked through darkening eyes at her friend. She cried out and arched her back. Thick, dusty fog poured off of her shoulders as she coughed and wretched. Avery barely flinched at the fog.

"You can't tell Shea. You understand?" she begged. Avery quickly nodded, tears forming in her deep eyes.

"It's almost calming, isn't it?" Avery asked. Her eyes were staring at the black dust that trickled off of Elanor's back. She knew all too well how Erebus' power could be so consuming. "When it returns, the fear grows so strong, so overwhelming, that shutting down is all you can do. After a while... it's all you know."

Elanor coughed again, though the release of the dusty fog was slightly less than the first. She looked through foggy eyes at her friend. She didn't want to admit it, but Avery was right.

Her friend slowly put her arms around her and hugged.

*   *   *   *

Shea's fingers grazed the tops of evergreens as the cold winter wind rushed through her lungs. She breathed in every bit of the weightlessness as she spun and twirled. The blizzard was just as treacherous and even more powerful above the trees, but Shea couldn't care less. Splitting the wind like a knife, her thick mane whipped across her face and she didn't fight the urge to laugh. It bellowed out of her uncontrollably and she realized quickly that the laughter felt even more foreign than flight. As she weaved through the trees, the laughter subsided and a sudden realization struck her like a brick wall. The years before her accident were spent completely unaware of how lucky she was. How thoroughly closed her eyes were to what she had, to what she was. Never again could she allow herself to take such a gift for granted. Her whole life had been a mistake: a mistake of self-pity, self-loathing and regret. The only mistake now was the one Erebus had made when granting her wish. As she blistered through the winter storm, barely affected by its might, it wasn't regret she felt, or fear or even guilt, but instead a driving need for revenge. The WishingKing was the fool now that Shea Evenstar could fly.

Red sparks in the near sky broke her from her thoughts. The flare showered over the tops of the trees a few hundred yards in front of her.

"Dad!" The wind muffled her call, but not the worry of what her father would say when he saw her wings. She was suddenly more afraid of her military father than she was of Erebus. Pushing harder and gaining speed, she found the tree from where the flare had come and dived into its branches.

Beren held tight to a small branch, bracing himself against the wind. His face was red with frostbite and stricken with worry and confusion. He was lost and he knew it. As he watched his flare blow away in the storm, his hopes for anyone seeing it did as well. He'd left his injured wife alone in this storm. Alone. He'd left her, something he said he would never do again, and he couldn't forgive himself. *None of this wishing business matters anymore*, he thought. His family. He'd taken for granted how lucky he was to have fairies in his life that cared about him. They loved him, and he loved them. Isn't that all that mattered, regardless of how difficult it was to keep them all together? To keep them safe?

A flash of light splashed behind the trunk of the tree behind him. Something had landed a few feet away and he realized how freezing cold he truly was—he could barely grip his wand as he pulled it from its sheath. His teeth chattered as he called out, "Show yourself!"

Shea leaned against the bark of the tree, nervous about stepping out. She glided her fingers along the edges of her perfect wings and took a deep breath. *He won't understand, but it's too late for that*, she thought. *If he never talks to me again, at least I brought him back to Mom. At least we're together again, even if he hates me for it.*

Stepping a cautious boot out in front of her, she revealed herself to her dad. Beren stood, shaking from the cold, pointing his wand and ready for a fight. His eyes popped open, unable to understand what he was seeing. It was his daughter... but, her wings. Shea. His daughter was standing in front of him, intact, in one piece. She was better than okay.

Her wings spread out wide behind her. Shea raised her worried eyes and looked at her dad and was surprised to see the worry reflected on her father's face. He unconsciously lowered his wand and stood in shock, taking it all in. Opening her mouth to release some kind of immediate apology, Shea only squeaked before Beren rushed and threw his arms around her.

He was no longer a general. No longer a leader, or coach, or disciplinarian. He was a scared father, relieved to hold his only daughter again. They held each other and Shea was thankful that he squeezed even harder than she did. At first, she didn't know how to hug her dad. They had never truly shown any amount of affection for each other. They were family and of course they loved each other, but it always felt more mandatory than automatic. Until now. As Beren pulled her in, she felt the love only a father could give: his strong arms cradling her, protecting her. She no longer worried about her wings, or the WishMakers, or even the stolen wish. For this moment, it was just her and her dad.

He finally pulled back to get a good look at her. It was difficult to look him in the eye as she noticed him surveying her wings. A deep, misty breath escaped his lungs and nothing needed to be said, much to Shea's relief.

He nodded, "You're safe."

"I'm..." Shea started, but Beren wouldn't let her.

"Don't. There is no time for apologies or regret. Your mother is injured," he said.

"I know. She was the one who found me," she replied.

At this, Beren hesitated. He was so happy to see Shea that he'd forgotten all of the secrets he'd held from her over the years. All of the lies he perpetuated in the name of keeping her safe. Safe from pain and sadness.

"I should have told you. Years ago. I just didn't know how," he said.

"Just keep moving forward. Right?" Shea returned. A smirk creased her lips and Beren nodded with his own.

"Know how to use those things?" he said, motioning to her wings.

"I've always known. Do you?" She eyed his chipped wing and flicked it with her finger. They both smiled and buzzed their wings.

"Let's go get your mom."

By the time they found their way back to Elanor and Avery, Elanor's bout with the curse had subsided. While far from perfectly healthy, she was at least able to stand on her own, despite the wicked wind of the blizzard. Avery still felt she needed to offer a helping hand, and Elanor didn't complain about having one.

Beren grabbed Elanor's hands upon landing and looked her in the eyes. They were much blacker than when he left her. Looking at Avery, he could tell they were hiding something and decided to keep it between them. Shea didn't need to know her mom could be leaving them shortly, and firing another explosion of light, even just at her feet, could break her—and not just of the curse. She was far too fragile to make such an attempt. Their only hope was to find a Gate, get back home, and stop Erebus from consuming the wish. Not exactly an easy task.

"I'm assuming the worst," Elanor said, not meaning to be so foreboding.

"You OK?" Beren asked.

"I'm fine," she lied.

"I went back to the house," Beren continued.

The others waited during Beren's long, drawn-out pause. Why was he pausing for so long?

"It was empty," he finally said, after a deep breath.

"But Thane. And the Makers?" Avery asked.

Beren shook his head. Shea didn't understand what that meant. Were they just missing? They left on purpose? Dead? After everything that had happened, she'd forgotten about her friend. How could she forget about Thane?

"We have to find a Gate and fast. Without a Wish-Radar, it won't be easy."

Quickly snatching her pack, Shea removed the WishRadar Thane had stolen and handed it to Beren. "What do you mean empty? What about Thane?"

"Your friend is in trouble, Shea, and I won't ask how you got this," he said as he flipped the radar device on. It buzzed and blinked. "Plans have changed."

"What do you mean trouble? You just left him at the house? With Grayson and Miranda?" Beren wasn't listening and Elanor and Avery weren't much help either. "Would you just tell me he's OK, please? What's going on?"

It was an unexpected kind of panic. The kind that was trying to cover up a mistake that she inevitably knew had everything to do with her.

Beren slapped the side of the radar as it continued to buzz and blink. The cold was keeping it from switching on, but finally the screen came to life. He wasn't listening to Shea, intent instead on finding any remaining Gate, hopefully one nearby.

The screen didn't show any red dots, much less any other color. It was a basic, grey map of the town with a small triangle indicating their position. Sweeping through the screen, searching, Beren finally found one little golden dot: a Gate a few hundred yards away on the other side of the woods.

"One Gate left," he said with a worried sigh. "Worse than I thought."

"Dad! Please!" Shea looked at Elanor and Avery for a little help. Weren't they just as worried as she was? "Is Thane OK?"

"No, Shea, he isn't! I'm sorry, but we won't be either if we don't find this Gate and find it fast."

"We can't cross over without him! We can't just leave him here," begged Shea.

"Thane isn't here. And neither are the Makers," Beren said, unable to hide the fear from his voice. He continued measuring the distance between them and the last Gate, studying the screen and then the forest around them. Elanor and Avery finally perked up. If they weren't here, then that meant they were in Paragonia. And that only meant Erebus took them.

"He took them. I can't believe he'd do that," Avery said, staring at nothing in particular.

"I can," Elanor said. "He's not going to destroy the wish. He's going to consume it, and he needs them in order to do so."

Shea waited for some kind of answer or solution, even a plan, but nothing came. Her dad just searched the woods and the radar.

"Well, we have to do something!" Shea finally cracked and broke the silence.

"We are, honey," Beren said. "We're finding the Gate and getting that wish. You'd better be ready to fly."

It was the first time her father had ever called her anything other than her name. It was odd to hear the term of endearment fall from his lips and, in a way, it frustrated her.

It made her feel like a little fairy again and she didn't want to feel that way anymore. She needed them to see her as an adult, as a force, not just some little fairy girl.

Avery could tell this angered Shea, and patted her on the back. She gave her a wink and smiled. It was so opposite to what the situation called for, but somehow it calmed her down a bit. "As frustrating as it seems, we have to do this one step at a time. Get ahead of yourself and you lose sight of your goal. We'll get Thane back. I promise," Avery said, calmly, and even if she was faking the confidence, it worked. Shea took a deep breath and followed her father.

"Ellie, we'll have to carry you," Beren said, as he tried to put his arms around his wife. She swatted them away.

"Carry me? I said I was fine, Beren," Elanor said.

He smiled at his stubborn wife, and nodded at a tree branch above them. "Let's go, then." Beren, Avery and Shea lifted off the ground and Elanor fired a grapple spell into the tree. They were off.

36
THE LAST GATE

"I have brought you all here today, to come clean. I must tell you something I am rather ashamed to admit," Erebus said, as he stood in the middle of his chambers.

Grayson and Miranda were tied to two chairs at the far end of the stone-walled room. Through the window, the WishingKing's fog lay thick across the valley and covered every inch of the landscape. Thane was tied up next to the True Love Wish, which was still stuck in the gyroscope with its light all but dimmed.

Erebus turned dramatically around, his black, dusty cloak swinging behind him like a snake, and calmly raised his right hand. His back was to his captors as he continued.

"I must admit that I cannot complete this mission of mine without your help. I know it is surprising, but it won't be that way for long." He smiled under his black hood and waved his hand to the right, motioning for something to open. Grayson and Miranda were beyond comprehending anything at this point and looked to Thane for answers. He was just as clueless.

As his hand finished its slow wave, the vast wall of books at the other end of the room vanished. A secret room was revealed behind the wall, but it wasn't only the crude magic trick that struck his captors.

A seemingly endless corridor appeared in front of him. It was lined with shelves upon shelves, hundreds of thousands that went beyond the eye's capability, and on each shelf, huddled closely together, were millions of glass jars. Each jar was filled with a wish.

Thane was awestruck. Outside of The Nursery, he'd never seen so many wishes all in one place. As he looked closer, he noticed that not all of the wishes were alive. Many were grey and lifeless, but nearly half were still buzzing bright with life.

Erebus turned back around and once again addressed them. "You see, I may consume all of the wishes to my heart's content. One by one, adding a little dash of power here and a little drop of strength there. In the end, however, it's futile."

"What's futile?" Grayson asked. He couldn't believe the words came out, but he also couldn't believe what he was seeing or experiencing. He was ready for some answers, even if they were asked of a crazy old man wearing fog as a cloak.

"Ah. The WishMaker speaks and not without a very good question," Erebus said. "I wished for true love once. I expect you didn't know that." Erebus looked at both Miranda and Grayson. All of this wishing business was still new to them, but they were surprised, nonetheless, to hear such a thing come from the monster in front of them. "For my wife. My Meredith. She asked me to never give up, to never let her go. As she lay there, coughing through the cancer that we couldn't cure, she made a wish for me. And I for her. It was the only True Love Wish I was able to make, and what happens? My wonderful Keepers deem it to be impossible. And what do they give me as a reward instead? The throne of a useless world. Destined to be nothing more than a manager, an organizer of other people's wishes. To sit back and watch as two Makers somehow get a second chance at true love. Their cruelty knows no bounds. And yet, they did give me some miniscule amount of power. But not enough."

He walked into the long, dark corridor, the light of the wishes being the only source of illumination, and fondled a few of the jars. "My True Love Wish will never be granted.

That much even I cannot change. But the Keepers of Paragonia owe me. They owe me something in return. The only thing that can match the granting of true love? The power that resides within it. You see, a wish is an interesting creature," he said, as he removed a jar from a shelf. He opened the lid. A bright purple Ladder Wish huddled in the corner, shaking, avoiding Erebus' reaching hand, but he easily snatched it up. Cupping it in his palm, he continued. "Pure intent, just waiting to be set free. It is my intent to do just that. To set such intent free. What happens, though, when intentions collide? The more powerful of the two consumes the other."

There was a crack as loud as thunder and Grayson and Miranda turned away. A flash of black fog stretched through the room, and then quickly reversed course. It flowed into Erebus as if he were a vacuum, pulsing through him as he consumed the wish's power. Breathing in, absorbing it like a drug, he sighed deeply and dropped the ashes of the dead wish from his palm. Wiping his hands together, he casually stepped back into his chambers.

"The reason I have brought you all here today is because a True Love Wish is a tricky wish to consume. I need the power of your intent as well. Inside of you resides the source of not one True Love Wish, but two. Now that is powerful. Don't you think?"

Miranda and Grayson looked at each other and though they couldn't shake the blur of everything that was happening to them, deep down they did know that they were special. But how had it come to this?

"The remaining question, however, is how powerful is true love, really?" he asked of no one in particular. "Tonight, I intend to show you that it is not as powerful as me."

Thane's eyes were wet with rage. *There has to be a way out of this. He can't win. He just can't.* "You're not stronger than true love, and you know it," he growled.

Swooping through the room, Erebus' black cloud swiftly revolved around Thane. Out of the darkness, Erebus stretched his evil face and smiled.

"Not yet."

*   *   *   *

Huddled in an evergreen, Shea, Avery and Elanor awaited Beren's next move as he stared at the radar. The screen was stuttering with static—the cold taking it over. Elanor's grappling was, admittedly, slowing them down and they needed to rest in every other tree just to regroup.

Beren slapped the radar again, hoping it would become unstuck, but the screen went dark. He placed it in his side pocket. "Damn. We're not far though. It's just through…"

KABOOM! A blast of golden light suddenly filled the forest, though much weaker than the other blasts. They ducked and managed to hold on. The force of the blast wasn't strong enough to blow them out of the tree, thankfully. A loud hum pulsed, emanating from the source of the explosion. HUMM… HUMM… HUMM.

"The Gate!" Avery said.

"I don't think it closed. That blast wasn't as strong as the others, and the humming… I think it's hanging on. We have to go. Now," Beren ordered.

They launched out of the tree and Elanor fought through every ounce of physical pain trying to keep up. Shea weaved through the branches and, for a moment, forgot her mother couldn't fly. She stopped and turned back.

"Shea!" yelled Avery.

"My Mom! Just go!" she yelled back, pushing into the wind.

Elanor's grapple wrapped around the branch of a leafless oak tree and in mid-flight she let go and whipped another, swinging her way to a neighboring tree. Landing hard on the slick branch, she cringed at the pain of her broken ribs. As Elanor knelt and tried to catch her breath, Shea jumped behind her and pulled her up.

"Come on, Mom. We can do this," she said, out of breath.

"Shea! You need to go. I'm fine."

"No, you're not fine and we don't have time. Please. We can do this together." Shea flashed a strong grapple around a tree and looked at Elanor. "Connect your grapple spell to mine and hold on to me!" she yelled through the wind. Hesitating out of pride for her heroic daughter, Elanor looked at her little redhead and nodded. Following her orders, their grapple spells wrapped around each other, and Elanor grabbed on to Shea. They jumped. Using Shea's wings and the pull of the grapple spell, they soared through the winter air faster than Avery and Beren could. The speed at which they flew sent a shiver through Elanor – they were out of control, at least she thought so. The vibrating hum of the Gate was getting louder, and they could feel the pulsing of its energy as they sped through the air. Firing a grapple behind them, Shea caught a branch and, like a parachute, slowed their flight and made a perfect landing at the base of a giant oak. High above them, the Gate pulsed with golden light, its hum almost deafening.

Beren and Avery caught up, landing next to Shea and Elanor. Beren pulled his wife in close and smiled at his daughter, thankful but surprised. He realized he hadn't seen his daughter fly since she was little, with or without wings. Avery, out of breath, smacked Shea on the shoulder and yelled through the din, "So much for needing those wings, huh?"

Shea smiled and blushed, or at least as much as the frigid winter air could allow.

Above them, the Gate was waiting along the edge of a thick icy branch. Still pulsing with golden light, the Gate fired out lashes of wild energy. Even if they got up there, it wouldn't be easy.

"We can't wait any longer. Ready?" Beren looked at his companions, each wind-battered, frostbitten and exhausted. This was it. Elanor raised her wand and fired a grappling spell high into the tree, launching herself up. Beren flew just beneath her as she swung her way up. Avery and Shea dashed off to either side of the tree and sped toward the Gate.

KABOOM! The Gate exploded with a powerful force, rattling the tree and shaking the earth. Elanor screamed as her grapple came loose. She fell and though Beren was right behind her, his frozen hands couldn't hold on. He tried catching her, but she slid out of his arms and fell toward the ground.

"Elanor!" Beren yelled.

Shea and Avery made it to the branch, hiding from the pulsating golden light of the Gate. They didn't hear Beren's scream, but when they looked down, two quick flashes of white light sped through the woods. Shea saw her mom falling, but she was helpless.

One of the flashes sped below Elanor and caught her just before she crashed to the ground. Goren grunted and pulled her up, zooming to the Gate above. Foster rushed to Beren and pulled his General back up into the tree.

They finally made it to the slippery bark of the branch, hiding from the pulsating light of the Gate. There wasn't time for thank-yous or health checks, and, anyway, since the hum was so loud, they could barely hear each other.

Elanor strained to get up, but looked at Shea right away. She pointed to the Gate, making sure Shea went through first, but Shea shook her head and yelled, "No! You first!"

"Injured first!" Beren screamed, and though it was barely audible, they didn't have time to argue. He grabbed his wife, looked at Goren and nodded. He saluted through gasping breath and Beren noticed his tunic was caked in blood. Quickly looking at Foster, he noticed the same. Foster was exhausted, kneeling and barely conscious, but still maintained a salute to his General.

Elanor saw the same thing Beren did and yelled, "Injured first!"

Avery suddenly grabbed her two friends and pulled them through the Gate. When they disappeared through the golden light, the Gate exploded again. Shea was just to the side of the Gate and dodged the force of the explosion, but it knocked Beren and Elanor off the branch, falling once again to the forest floor.

Shea didn't hesitate. She cracked a wrangling spell around her parents, catching them in mid-fall and though it tugged her out of the tree, she managed to stay afloat by buzzing her wings, pulling and pulling, tugging and tugging. The hum of the Gate cranked in volume, piercing the fairy's ears. It was closing.

With every ounce of strength Shea and her new wings had, she whipped the wrangling spell back up into the tree, throwing her parents through the Gate. With one hand, she grabbed hold of the branch and just before the Gate exploded for a final time, she jumped through.

37
WHEN AVERY DIED

Ten Years Ago

It was Wishing Eve, the night of the first True Love Wish's destruction, and the WishSentinel, Charlie, knocked on General Beren's door. He knew he needed to simply follow orders, but his curiosity couldn't help but buzz. *Why would the General, on Wishing Eve, assign me to guard his own house?* No one was home, and, frankly, very few Wish-Keepers were in Paragonia that night, anyway. He looked in through the windows and his assumption was confirmed—it was empty.

He stood upright, wand at the ready, and mocked a few high-stepped struts back and forth in front of the door. It was a cool evening with barely a breeze. Crickets scratched a tune in the thicket of the nearby woods. He admired his General's home. It was humble, yet strong. Fitting, he thought.

With a deep breath, he sat down on a knotted old tree stump just outside the front door and enjoyed the quiet of Wishing Eve.

Charlie was wrong, of course. Someone was home. He didn't see the frail body of Avery standing in the middle of the room. He didn't see that her hair had turned from a bright, hopeful pink to black – almost as black as her eyes. She stood motionless in the dark like a wraith caught between worlds, swaying in an invisible black breeze. Then the swaying stopped.

Her head and wings slowly lifted as if reacting to a silent call. Black dust trickled off her shoulders, and slowly her pale hand reached into a pocket and removed a long, crooked dagger. She walked in a trance to the front door, stopping to look through the tall, narrow window that rimmed the entrance. Charlie was sitting on the stump with his back to her, picking the petals off a dandelion.

As she quietly clicked the front door open, it creaked as she swung it toward her. Charlie jumped up, startled, and saw Avery silhouetted in the doorway.

"Oh, miss, you frightened me!" he reacted, pushing a giggle through the rush of adrenaline. "I didn't think anyone was home." He paused and took a slow step toward her, concerned at how frail, tired and sickly she looked. "Are you OK, miss?"

Avery smiled sad, weak and tearful, and stepped toward Charlie with open arms as if asking for a hug. The look on the poor girl's face was enough to make any fairy want to help, and while Charlie felt extremely awkward hugging the stranger, he obliged.

"Oh, come now," Charlie said, lovingly. "Everything will be alright. It's Wishing Eve…"

Her head was rested on his shoulder. Her arms were wrapped around him, and the dagger was slipped into the side of his neck. As she dug the dagger further in, her black eyes watered and filled up with silky tears that cascaded down her cheeks. No look of pain or sadness was on Avery's face, but deep down she knew. She knew it was the end of more than just one life that night. She knew that the old Avery was dead.

Charlie slumped to the ground, limp and lifeless. Stepping over him, uncaring and unfazed, Avery removed her wand, pointed it behind her back and cast a black spell around his body. He evaporated into thick black smoke, and she casually flew off across the valley, straight for Exclamation Pointe.

It was dark in the thick forest outside the Death Wish Cave, except for the light of two lanterns held up by the Sentinels standing guard. A crack of a stick. A rustle of leaves. The Sentinels looked at each other, worried for a moment. The quiet of the forest rushed back in and they smirked at each other for being so foolish. They were proud to serve their General and follow orders, but they both agreed there was truly no reason to stand guard at such a secret post.

Avery stepped out from the shadows of the wood and stood in front of the guards. Her black eyes set within her pale white face made it seem like they were floating in the darkness. The Sentinels raised their lanterns, barely able to make out what was glaring at them. Avery's cursed smile, and their WishingKing standing over her shoulder, was the last thing they ever saw.

38
WHEN THE WORLD ENDS

The explosion of the Gate tossed the escapees into the dark, foggy edges of the Paragonian valley. Though the blast's golden light was strong, it merely ricocheted, bounced and quickly dwindled against the powerful, thick darkness of Erebus' dense fog that had spread throughout the land. It took a few moments for Shea to gather herself. Not only was she exhausted, but the stark difference in temperature and climate was disorienting. She knew they had crossed over, but it was as if they'd slipped into a half-awake nightmare. Barely any of the Paragonian landscape could be seen through the fog and they knew it was midday only because the moon would not be able to cut through such a blanket of darkness. The sun itself was barely succeeding, though a slight silhouette was attempting to fight its way through the fog and into the afternoon. It did little to help them see much of anything—visibility was hardly ten feet and, for a moment, Shea felt a wave of panic slip over her when she couldn't find her parents.

"Mom! Dad?" she called out. The fog whittled away her words, muffling them as they escaped her lips. Could anyone hear her, much less see her? She called out again. Thankfully there was a response, though it sounded as if it came from another world, not from just a few feet away.

"Shea! We're right here. Where are you?" Beren returned. Elanor was on her knees, struggling to stand, the curse and her physical injuries having taken their toll.

THE WISHKEEPER

Goren tended to his friend. Foster was sitting, leaning back on his hands and grimacing through whatever wound he'd incurred after the WishKeepers had fought off Erebus in front of the house. Beren still didn't know what had happened and why only two of his Keepers had returned. He didn't know exactly how many faithful WishKeepers had come to help, but from the size of the light blast, he assumed at least a few dozen, not including the nine members of The Hope. He didn't have time to listen to a debriefing. His wife's health was quickly failing and, from the look of the surrounding fog, Erebus was moments away from consuming the True Love Wish.

Trying to brush the fog from her face, Shea crept toward the sound of her father's voice. Hazy images of her team finally came into focus; her mother on her knees, hunched over, and Foster cringing in the grass. Beren was kneeling next to Elanor with his hand on her back. The past few days had quickly shattered every preexisting belief she had about her parents. They were no longer the strong, unbreakable pillars she once thought them to be. For so long, and even after she lost her mother ten years prior, they were always two immovable forces, always right, always perfect, even if she disagreed at times. They knew what was right and could do no wrong, but suddenly, as the wafts of smoky fog briefly cleared around them, she understood that they were not any different than her. They were simply fairies struggling with their own inner fears, doubts and pain, and while some are lucky to experience a slow, evolving realization that parental figures are not as perfect as previously believed, Shea was forced to face up to it like a thrust of a hammer driving a nail. Nothing in her life for the past decade had been easy, but somehow, as she stood there looking at her equals who were supposed to be superior in every way, the heaviness of adolescence slipped from her shoulders and a new, even more distinct weight set in. Not only did her shoulders feel it, but so did her heart. The blind reliance that childhood so easily conjures was gone. They depended on her now and her life, like the onset of a sudden summer thunderstorm, shifted into adulthood.

As Shea came into the clearing, Beren looked up. She could tell his eyes were fighting back more than just tears. Shea noticed an odd, out of place look of pride in them. Goren stood, almost as if at attention, and Foster forced himself to do the same. Elanor raised her head and noticed them showing respect for her daughter. The swelling pride helped Elanor gather enough strength to stand, though she used Beren's hand for guidance. They all looked at Shea with reverence and, for a moment, she thought they were going to bow. *Please don't bow*, she thought. *Please stop looking at me like that.* It was unnerving to be shown respect, something for which she had wished for years, and now suddenly she couldn't help but feel it was undeserving. It didn't matter how she had found the strength to pull her parents up and toss them through the Gate. There was nothing special about her and, truly, it was her fault they were standing in the thick onslaught of their WishingKing's deceit. *Goren and Foster helped just as much as I did. Please stop looking at me.*

Finally, Beren broke the awkward silence and placed a hand on her shoulder. He could tell she felt suddenly exposed. Simply nodding in approval, he patted her once on the shoulder and, for the first time, Shea was thankful for her father's inability to express himself.

He purposely shifted the attention away from Shea and looked into the blackness of the nearby forest. The fog was so dense it blew in the breeze and wafted around the trees. The giant oak tree was a few feet in front of them, rising up out of the darkness and spreading its canopy of branches overhead. Right away, Shea knew this was Winston's Gate, and a rush of panic once again set in.

Peering into the tree, she noticed the small, ancient fairy standing guard, looking right at her. Winston tipped his hat to her and smiled just before he sat back down and rested his hands on his chest. Shea wondered if Winston knew what was going on. If he knew that his was the last Gate to close. She sent the old fairy a silent thank-you.

"The last one," Beren said, finally breaking the silence. The gravity of it all settled in as their little team stared at the oak. The last Gate. The last of a million gateways to The Other Side. For the first time, the WishKeepers were trapped. For the first time, all the wishes of the world were lost.

"Foster?" Beren said, as he looked at his wounded soldier. Foster knew it was a simple question of 'are you OK' and he nodded back to his General. "The blood?" Beren asked.

Foster glanced at his friend and Goren didn't have the heart to respond. "It's not mine, sir. After we cast the light spell around the house and Erebus retreated, we were ambushed by Lost Fairies. Somehow the light only made them fiercer. We were outnumbered, sir."

Beren nodded again, barely reacting to the news, even though deep down he was devastated. Something suddenly dawned on him as he looked at everyone. Foster and Goren were there, Elanor and Shea of course, but... Avery.

"Avery. She came through the Gate, didn't she?" he asked, swiveling his head from side to side, searching.

"Yes, sir," Goren said, suddenly confused. "She pulled me and Foster through."

They all limped uneasily through the darkness, eager to find their friend. She couldn't be far since the Gate had cast them all in the same area, unless she was unconscious, and with the blanket of fog being so crippling...

"Avery!" Beren called out. The rest of the team followed suit and joined in.

A faint voice woke Avery. She blinked her eyes open. She lay on her stomach: the left side of her face felt the cool moisture of the forest grass, tickling her cheek. Painfully, she pushed herself up, but she couldn't make it past a hunched position. She paused on her knees, caught in a rush of pain, and stared at the wet ground in front of her. There was an immeasurable amount of throbbing soreness that pulsed through her—something that was all too familiar. It had never really left, even after Erebus had been cast away ten years ago. At times, over the past decade, a fleeting wave of tenderness would catch her off guard, as if it was foreign to feel anything other than anger or resentment. There was another fairy somewhere deep inside her—the pink-haired, unconditionally loving creature that was blissful, joyful. The fairy that fell in love at first sight.

As she knelt, staring at the ground, the hairs on the back of her neck slowly stood on end. A quiver of goose bumps sped down her spine and she thought of Elanor. Elanor. A light that had been doused was suddenly lit again, but as the wave of emotion swept over her, so did the fog. Like water to a drain, it swirled as if it had been waiting for her, and swallowed any tender reminder of the pink-haired fairy that was trying to escape.

"No. Please," something, or someone, inside of Avery begged. It was a voice she hadn't heard for years, but something more resilient resisted it and forced it back down into its skinny, heart-encasing tomb. A rush of hatred bubbled inside of her, replacing the soft, desperate voice. Instead, flashes of Elanor crossed her memory and all she could see were images of her holding Beren's hand, kissing him, holding him, and looking him in the eyes with the love that was meant for her.

How dare Elanor cause her to feel such a thing? A thing that clashed hope against impossibility. Every ounce of Avery's heart was embarrassed, terrified and desperate to hide such forbidden feelings—such feelings that only felt true and right and inevitable. But, no: instead, she was doomed to long for the one thing she couldn't have. Nor could she tell anyone about it, nor share how sad and lonely she felt with each new discovery of love and longing.

The hatred boiled inside of her as the fog circled her little body. It wasn't fair. Her life wasn't fair. To witness the essence of love, but to be able only to watch it through cold, frosted glass, never to touch or feel or know what it's like to have it embrace you and comfort you with its warmth.

She tried getting to her feet, but the swirling fog kept her gripping the grass, head down. Grunting through the revolving re-emergence of the curse, she gave in and retched. Her back arched with every vomiting cough and with it spewed dusty remnants of the curse from her shoulders. Finally, the swirling fog calmed, and left Avery gasping. But like flicking on a light switch, she sat back on her ankles and slowly stood. Anger rushed through her like a relentless, cornered badger. She would die before she had to live another moment without the realization of her own personal wish. And so her secret intention was set.

"Avery!" Beren's voice called out through the fog. It was closer than before, but Avery didn't react. Pulling her black hood over her head, she stared into the denseness of the fog. Had the day been clear and sun-filled, one would have noticed her eyes filling up with a black, oil-like substance, but when Beren and the team finally found her, the combination of her heavy hood and the covering darkness hid her curse-filled eyes.

"Avery, there you are," Beren said, as she came into view. "I found her!" he called out. The rest of the team slowly made their way closer. Goren was the first to approach. With his hand outstretched, awaiting hers to meet his, he was thrilled to see his friend and teammate. It was also an attempt at a thank-you, but when Avery didn't return the handshake, he quickly remembered how quiet his friend had always been.

"Fine, then," Goren said, as he set his hands to his waist. "I'm still glad to see you, despite your inability to accept common courtesy. Or a thank-you, for that matter." A smile curled his lips and, like a mime, Avery did the same.

Her hand slowly took hold of Goren's forearm and for a moment, Goren felt an urge to pull back, but he fought the silly notion. He had never been afraid of her before and assumed it was simply the depressive nature of the situation that sent a shiver of sudden worry through him. She lightly squeezed his arm and Goren took it to be a sign of affection, or at least some form of 'you're welcome'. It was good enough for him.

"You OK?" asked Elanor. Avery cocked her head and looked at the limping, pained, broken-winged fairy, as if a sudden memory was trying to flirt with her mind. It quickly dissipated and she nodded.

Even though the fog was thick and her hood hung low over Avery's forehead, Elanor felt something was off. Avery had showed compassion, at least in some way, when she helped her find Shea, and though the darkness of the woods cast a natural gloom, Avery seemed different now. Like Goren, though, Elanor cast the thought aside and re-positioned herself, cringing at the pain in her side. Despite everything, her ribs were still broken and not much was going to help the pain.

"Dad, I need some answers," Shea broke in. It was quite a statement of demand and cut through the thickness of the air like a knife. It took Beren off guard, especially since Shea was suddenly ignoring the fact that they had finally found their lost teammate. He couldn't help but smile at his daughter's quick 'back to business' mentality.

"Oh? And what answers would you request, my dear?" He winked at Shea, which helped calm her a bit.

"I'm just... where is Thane? Grayson and Miranda? The fog? What do we do next? Everything!" she exclaimed. Her last word was a bit dramatic, though Goren and Foster nodded along. What was next? Now what?

"Avery, I'm glad you're OK, but we need to move. And fast," Shea said, looking at her father. Her dad nodded. There wasn't time for greetings or melancholy glances into the thick of the vanishing Paragonian woods. They needed to find Erebus and stop him. Simple enough plan, but the 'how' was a bit trickier.

"Like I said before. When I went back to the house, it looked like a tornado hit it. Grayson and Miranda were gone. So was Thane."

Elanor sighed. "It's not like the other wishes where he can just take them over. It's true love. A bit stronger than a simple wish for a new bike."

"But... Thane too?" Shea asked, not understanding. "Why would he need...?" Shea was suddenly cut off as Avery finally chimed in.

"He doesn't need Thane," she said, ominously. "Not for the wish, anyway." Her voice was deeper than before and as she spoke, she kept her eyes out of sight. "He needs the WishKeeper."

They all looked at each other, but only Elanor understood. Avery cocked her head up a bit, and Elanor looked at her, knowing she was right. Shea could see it in her mother's eyes that what Avery was saying made sense to her mom. She grabbed her arm and tugged.

"Mom? What is she saying?" she begged. No one said a word and Shea couldn't handle the silence. "Someone tell me what's going on!"

"In order for him to consume the wish, he needs the WishMakers and WishKeepers. The power within all four." Avery looked at Beren when she said this. "It will give him enough power to consume it and enough strength to harness it."

"Well, then we don't go! We leave him waiting there. If he needs us so badly, we—" Avery cut her off again.

"He will kill Thane. He won't hesitate. He will kill him, toss his lifeless body away like sewage, and move on. The forest is filled with plenty of victims. Thane is nothing more than bait," Avery said, and a hint of a smile creased her lips. The lights of the fairy homes in the forest across the valley were not visible through the fog, but the others knew what Avery was referencing. Erebus would run through the fairies one by one until they gave him what he needed. Avery was right. He wouldn't hesitate.

Elanor suddenly buckled over, crying out as if someone was torturing her. She fell to her knees, and, like Avery before, retched, coughing, sputtering desperate cries with each heave.

"Mom!" Shea tried reaching out, but Beren swiftly caught her, pulling her away. He fell to Elanor's side, but as he put his hand on her back, black dust fell from Elanor's shoulders. He recoiled.

"Beren," Elanor coughed. She looked up at him and he could see her eyes swirling with the cursed darkness.

"Dad? Mom, what is…?" Shea tried to push past her dad, but he wouldn't let her get near.

Elanor retched again in agony, and more of the curse fell from her shoulders. Beren slowly leaned and hunched over her, his face mere inches from Elanor's. Despite the oily blackness swirling in her eyes, he stared at her, begging her not to lose focus.

"Look at me," he said, but she couldn't fight the pain and looked away. "Look at me!" he yelled. His wife was leaving him and he couldn't let it happen again. "We're right here. You understand me? You and me," he said, pointing his fingers at his eyes. "And here. Always," he said softly as he put his hand to his heart.

Shea watched, staggering with confusion and fear. It was awful seeing her parents like this, and even worse that she was helpless. Her father was begging and her mother was dying. Nothing could match the fear of a helpless heart, but she wasn't about to just stand back and watch. Just as she was fighting the urge to pull her mother off the ground and yell at her for being like this—for being weak and, even worse, for scaring her so badly—Elanor stopped coughing.

Beren and Elanor stared at each other and even though it didn't lift the fog, or clear her eyes or erase any amount of pain in her body, it kept whatever dim flame was left in her still lit and faintly burning. Elanor leaned back and hiccupped through catching breaths. While her eyes weren't completely black, they were not the eyes Shea remembered seeing in the forest earlier. Her mother was holding on by a thin, black thread.

It started as a faint plea as it groped at her lungs, but Shea finally grabbed the scream and released it. She was past the point of desperation.

"Do something!" she screamed, angry, beaten and begging. It was a plea for everyone around her to keep her mom there. To keep her in front of her. To keep her from vanishing and leaving all over again. It broke the silence like the crack of a whip. Foster's shoulders jumped, reacting to the little fairy's scream. "Please," she said, as the tears flooded her eyes.

"We bring him what he wants," Avery said. There was no emotion inside her, or in the words she coolly presented to them. It was matter-of-fact and not necessarily in answer to Shea's plea. She was simply telling them exactly what they needed to do, unbiased, or so it seemed.

Shea was surprised to see her father turn and look at her instead of Avery. After all, it was Avery who just spoke and gave an answer. She knew her dad was thinking the same thing she was—do something, anything. He'd been trying to do something every day for the past ten years and there was yet to be any kind of true answer. Beren was looking at his daughter, not to comfort her, but to ask permission. He was asking her to be the decision-maker. To ask permission to die.

"No," was all Shea could mutter. It was a soft release of breath more than an actual word and more out of disbelief that such a thought could surface. Despite all that had happened and every mistake she had ever made, somehow her family was here, directly in front of her. Maybe it wasn't the kind of happiness of which she dreamed or the kind of togetherness her naïve little soul would conjure late at night, fighting sleep and the repeating nightmares, but by some impossibility her mom and dad were back together, and as her eyes danced back and forth between them, nothing, not even the end of the world, would tear them from her again. It was a vice-grip hold she had on such hope and even if there was a futility to it, her hope to keep it this way was all she had left.

Turning to Avery, whose dark cloak and hood virtually blended like camouflage in the fog, Shea, much to the shock of Goren and Foster, repeated what Avery said.

"We give Erebus what he wants."

A smile spread across Avery's lips as she watched the heroic little fairy agree with her. Goren and Foster shuffled their feet, wanting to disagree, but Shea wasn't done.

"We give him what he wants, but we take back what belongs to us. You don't have permission to die," she looked back at her dad. He had never seen such resolve, such intent, emanate from his daughter, and Shea's blind hope was uncontrollably contagious. He nodded and stared back, knowing that it was more than just a hopeful statement she was making. It was a plan.

"We'll give him his WishKeepers. Elanor," Beren said, turning to his exhausted wife, "He'll be glad to have his Captain back, but we need you to hold on a little bit longer. Let him think you've turned." He pointed his wand at his wrists and wrapped a thick, grey-streamed spell around them. Handcuffs. Elanor glared at her husband, took his wand and slowly nodded. "When the time is right, if you can hold the darkness at bay for a little while longer, we will take back what is ours."

Shea smiled and nodded her head quickly. While the plan meant putting her parents in the line of fire, she finally saw hope rise up and out of them again. It was a heavy hope. Not the resounding kind of hope that jarred loose flimsy fears, but hope, nonetheless. It was good enough.

"Goren and Foster. Avery," Shea said, addressing her teammates. "Go to The Nursery and find as many wishes as you can. The fog couldn't have consumed all of them. Those little buggers are pretty resilient. Bring them to Exclamation Pointe, just beneath the tip of the cliff. We need as much light as possible—it worked before. At least enough to give us time. I'll meet you there."

The salute Goren and Foster gave her didn't feel forced or fake. As she watched their hands fall back to their sides, an unfamiliar feeling of trust and strength burned in her stomach. They were listening to her. They agreed with her and, most of all, they accepted her as not only an equal, but someone worthy of giving orders. For a moment, Shea felt that a part of her life was suddenly complete, and as they darted off into the thick, black fog, she was surprised at her ability to suppress her rising ego. There was still work left to do.

Avery hadn't followed Goren and Foster into the darkness. She remained, statuesque in the fog, staring at

Shea. Her face was expressionless, thoughtless, and for a second Shea thought she was disobeying orders. A familiar sense of self-consciousness rushed through her. Maybe she wasn't so confident in her ability to give orders. Who was she to do so, anyway? Finally, Avery smiled again, but it wasn't one of comfort or acceptance, and as Avery floated into the fog, Shea fought the sudden strangeness. The smile was as if Avery knew something Shea didn't, but it was, nonetheless, the outset of a mission and she was thankful they were listening to her at all.

Shea approached her parents and released a deep breath. A long, quiet glance turned into proud smiles as Elanor and Beren nodded approvingly. There were so many years of brief conversations about their restless and rebellious daughter in between broken moments of Elanor's curse. Though they would discuss their sickening guilt over what happened and what they had kept secret from her for so long, they knew that even though those broken moments may soon be few and far between, their daughter just grew up right before their eyes. In a quick flash they both hoped and wished and dreamed they would someday be able to have a conversation again about their daughter, and instead discuss how extremely proud of her they were.

"It's time to go," Shea said, hoping to break the sudden possibility of a pep talk. With Beren's help, Elanor straightened up, despite the pain coursing through her body. She needed to act and look the part of the Captain even though the curse hadn't completely taken over. "We'll have to carry you, Mom. But once we get near The Pointe, you're going to have to grapple Dad up. Erebus can't see me."

"I'd prefer you stayed behind and didn't..." Elanor said. Shea knew what her mom was going to say.

"No more staying behind, Mom. We're granting a wish today. And I'm going to help." She reached for her mother's arm, attempting to wrap it over her shoulder and help her father carry her, but Elanor took her hand instead.

"Shea, I—" Elanor started.

"I know, Mom. I love you, too."

Elanor's arm softly cradled Shea's neck. Shea propped her mother up and nodded to Beren.

The world had ended for Elanor when she destroyed the first True Love Wish, and it continued to end, over and over again, every time she would wake from Erebus' curse and then fall back into it a few painful moments later. She didn't tell Beren and Shea that this time would be the last time her world would end, that she didn't have the strength to fight off the return of the curse, nor the resilience to wake from it again. But feeling her daughter's words resonate through her crippled body—the only words she ever longed to hear—stole away her fear and left it lifeless, never to return. If her world was to end again, she had the solace of knowing her only true wish had finally been granted.

39
EXCLAMATION POINTE

The wind whipped across the edge of The Pointe, pushing and pulling Grayson and Miranda as they stood, back to back, wrapped in smoky handcuffs. Completely surrounding the Wishing Pool, Erebus' fog circled the only source of light still left in the valley. Dim as it was, the Pool shined, forcing back the encroaching darkness and casting an eerie glow against the pained WishMakers' faces.

Grayson and Miranda were living, experiencing, and unable to shake off the oddity of such a moment. Fear, most often, comes from the well of the unknown: the unfamiliar happenings outside of one's own comfort zone. But even though Grayson and Miranda had been told what was happening and it was clear they were not dreaming, it was beyond their ability to control their fear. Barely a couple hours earlier, Grayson and Miranda had been discussing what was missing in their relationship—a seemingly difficult conversation at the time—but now, stuck on top of a mountain and handcuffed by fog, they were merely trying to hold on to any sense of sanity.

Grayson looked at Thane, who was to his left, at the other end of the Pool. The little fairy—so much smaller than the humans—was sitting along the stone edge, hunched over with his hands also tied behind his back. He was staring at the rippling water, and Grayson could see how defeated and hopeless his new little friend looked. Was there any hope left? Was the image of Thane mirroring the same feelings inside of him? As he felt Miranda release a deep breath, he could tell the same inner dialogue was inside of her, and the sudden inability to fight off a rush of determination burned inside of Grayson. He stood up straight and let the determination consume him. Despite all that had happened at home—his best friend walking out and his marriage in shambles—he couldn't let go of the rising belief that this wasn't over. He wasn't going to let it end like this. It needed to be on their own terms. If they were to end their marriage and go their separate ways, it wasn't going to be because of someone else's actions. Miranda was right behind him. She was still there and even though he hadn't the foggiest idea as to where exactly they were physically, he knew where his relationship was—balancing on the edge of a cliff.

"Grayson," Miranda said, breaking his mental pep talk. Grayson leaned toward her, letting her know he was still there. "We don't belong here," she said with a soft, sad voice.

He understood what she meant. She didn't mean this place, this cliff. He nodded, knowing and agreeing. "I know. Whatever this is, honey, we'll get out of it. We can fix it. I know we can."

There was a long pause after another deep breath from Miranda. She was looking out over the edge of The Pointe, and all she could see was the swirling dark fog lapping over the edge.

"How?" she finally asked. She could barely see five feet in front of her, but truly, it was the creeping fear clawing at her heart that she couldn't see through.

Grayson looked at Thane. The little fairy was still hunched over, his head hanging low. Thane finally met Grayson's glance. Grayson was hoping for some kind of reciprocal look of hope, but Thane just looked away, defeated. Miranda felt Grayson's lungs fill with air and then release. A deep, sad breath. An acceptance of the situation.

THE WISHKEEPER

Visions of their childhood fluttered through Miranda's mind. Ten-year-old Miranda pushing up Grayson's Coke-bottle glasses with a smile. The long, nervous stare they shared before their first kiss, and the electricity of pure emotion when he proposed. She held on to the memory of that feeling and closed her eyes. *Within Grayson's arms, their lips pressed against each other's for the first time and, recalling the vivid memory, she felt as if her feet were slowly lifted from the lightness of such a rush of love.*

Her heart fluttered for a beat, though fear of never feeling that love again crept back in. She didn't notice the light of the Wishing Pool brighten. She didn't see that it sparkled amidst the darkness of the fog.

But Grayson did. He didn't know why it suddenly glowed brighter, but he knew it was reflecting something and he knew he wasn't a fool for trusting his new sense of determination. He looked again at Thane, and saw that the little fairy was also watching The Pool. Quickly, their eyes met and for the first time in what felt like forever, Grayson watched a smile build across Thane's face.

The fog swept quickly over The Pointe and Erebus appeared, floating next to the WishKeeper statue. His gaze went from the pulsing glow of The Pool to The True Love Wish in his palm, dimly lit and shivering.

"So hopeful even in defeat. So much intent within the smallest of chances." Erebus crawled through the fog and stood, hovering over the brightness of The Pool. He lowered his hand and dipped it into the glistening water, then raised his dark, menacing face with a smile, looking directly at Grayson.

"Now you see why I want this wish."

Like a slow leak of oil, the bright blue water rippled with a black, oily ooze. It stemmed from his icy finger and spilled, dousing the glow.

"And why yours will never come true."

Miranda didn't bother turning her head. She could feel the brightness in her heart fading. She squeezed her eyes tightly closed, desperate to hold on to the memories, as a tear glided down her cheek and pooled at the corner of her lips.

40
AVERY'S WISH

Flying through the thick valley air, Goren and Foster rushed to The Nursery. Though there was no wind, not even a breeze, pushing through the fog was like running along a blustery beach. Their wings were heavy, and the moisture of the air gathered and dripped from their foreheads. Foster was having difficulty catching his breath, and Goren only agreed to stop since the Wishing Pond was a few hundred feet in front of them. They were close, and by some miracle of directional memory they had found the Wish Nursery despite the lack of visibility.

Cringing and holding his side, Foster bent over and dropped his wand, resting his hands on his knees. Goren surveyed the surroundings. The quiet was crippling and his eyes were tired from the constant need to refocus through the darkness. Goren peered through the fog, and saw the barely noticeable small dots of light within the main barn of The Nursery.

"There's some life left in 'em. I can see a few. They're not moving, but their light still shines," he said. He turned and looked at his tall, lanky friend, who was still hunched over. "There any life left in you? Or do I have to do all of this myself? Once again."

Foster turned his head and Goren's smirk was enough to give him a little energy, if nothing else but to return some of the slight trash-talking. He reached down, snatched up his wand and gathered himself with a wheezy deep breath.

"Even if my legs were lopped off at the knees, I'd have more life in me than you and that bulging belly of yours."

Goren patted his stomach. It wasn't Goren's fault that his stout frame came with an inability to keep off the weight, although this wasn't helped by his inability to stave off the constant hunger. He was known for snacking on Maker candies during WishGathering missions. Everyone needed a vice and Goren's was definitely that he had a sweet tooth.

"Let's get this over with so you can eat," Foster continued with a smile.

"Once again we've misplaced our third wheel. Where is that black-haired mystery fairy anyway?" Goren was of course referring to Avery, but they didn't have time to wait. As they walked along the edge of the pond, its water was still, and though usually it was lit by gliding Wishes, now it was black and motionless, like a muddy puddle.

The slow squeak of the front wooden gate of the stables resonated an eerie feeling through the two Keepers. Piles of silver dust lined each pen, and Goren and Foster refused to look at them directly. They knew what the dust was—dead wishes, reduced to nothing but weightless fibers of powder. Stepping through and along the path, they noticed a soft set of lights inside the main barn. Millions of wishes had at one time brightened this end of the valley, but now just a muted set of trickling light pushed its way through the cracks in the side of the barn.

As they hurried through the barn door, the low bass of its hinges echoed through the empty main hall. Massive in size and depth, The Nursery hall was lined with rows upon rows of shelves five stories tall. The circular space was massive, meaning the far side of the hall was almost un-noticeable, so far away was it from the front doors. Countless glass jars sat on the shelves, each with dusty fibers of consumed wishes at their bottoms. Empty, but for the remaining dust. Even though Foster and Goren were expecting to see some form of devastation, they were not expecting such desolation. Being the base of operations for all near-fulfilled wishes, never had the main hall of The Nursery been empty. Even if Paragonia had been slowly vanishing over the years and WishGathering had become more and more straining and difficult, the main hall had always been filled. There was never a need for any kind of artificial illumination, or even basic candles, since the wishes themselves would light up the hall just fine. Suddenly Foster and Goren were looking at a scene that was nothing short of a nightmare.

The jingling of glass bristled their ears. Quickly looking to their far right, they saw a small group of wishes bouncing in their jars, reacting to the Keepers entering the hall. They rushed over, sprinting along the ancient wood flooring of the barn, and counted the remaining wishes.

Nine. In the past it would have taken them weeks to count the number of glass jars within the main hall and now, shining as brightly as they could, all that was left were nine hopeful little wishes.

"All Purities," Foster said, holding back a rising panic. Indeed, all nine wishes were pink, though each was with its own discolored version of yellow. This was not surprising, as they had been sitting within the main hall for quite some time and were most likely going unfulfilled.

"Closest thing to true love, a Purity. Resilient, but..." Goren looked around him. Foster knew what his friend wanted to say. He, too, couldn't process the emptiness of the hall. It wasn't a hopeful "but:" it was one of confusion and disbelief. Only nine left.

The floorboards of the hall creaked behind them as the low creaking of the barn doors echoed shut. Goren and Foster turned, wands drawn, and quickly pointed at whatever had entered. They could barely see Avery in the looming darkness of the hall. As she stood, staring, in the middle of the massive room, the two Keepers lowered their wands, thankful it was just Avery and not something more menacing.

"Waterstone, you never cease to startle the living daylight out of me," Foster said, releasing a captured breath. "Care to join us, or are you just going to stand there? There's not much time." Goren said and looked at Foster. "Nor much hope."

As if pushed by a breeze, Avery glided slowly to them. Her wand hand was limp at her side, and her black hood covered a lifeless pair of eyes. Goren and Foster didn't share each other's thoughts, but both felt as if the fog itself was creeping toward them. Approaching with her head slightly tilted down and toes scraping the wooden floor, Avery finally paused in front of her friends. The balls of her feet gently landed on the floor and she stood, glaring at the nine remaining wishes.

"Shea's little plan isn't much of one," Goren said.

"She obviously didn't think there would be so few left. Cut her some slack," Foster returned.

"Well, there's nothing for it. If this is what's left, we do what we can with what we have," Goren said, aiming his wand at the glass jars.

Avery, suddenly and lightning quick, grabbed Goren's arm and stopped him. She was still looking at the wishes, but her grip tightened. Her hand shook as Goren grunted and tried pushing back. He was surprised she could grip his hand with such powerful force. He tried pulling back again, but she wouldn't let go. As strong as he was and usually able to overpower any Keeper, he couldn't undo the painful hold around his wrist.

"Avery. Stop, what—" he said, but when she finally turned her head and looked at him, he caught his breath.

Her eyes were black as a moonless midnight, bubbling with a swirling oil. Deeply set bags hung under her emotionless, and just as Foster tried to back away Avery smashed a hot black spell against the floor.

Thousands of glass jars tumbled and fell, breaking into pieces. The nine remaining Purities bounced out of their broken homes and Foster fell to his knees. Keeping her grip tight around Goren's arm, Avery aimed her wand straight above her head and looked at the fallen Foster. He finally saw the darkness in her eyes and all he could say was her name, astonished at how suddenly ruined their friend was, at how unrecognizable she'd become.

"These aren't the wishes he needs," she finally said, raspy and deep. An umbrella blast from the end of her wand cascaded over the top of them, devouring the nine floating wishes and obliterating them to dust. The powder slowly fell and dribbled over their shoulders as Avery released the spell. Quiet rushed back into the echoing hall, and Avery turned her thoughtless gaze back toward nothing at all. Lifting inches from the wooden floor, she floated once again and let go of Goren. All they could do was look, stunned and breathless. This wasn't the Avery they knew, and even though she'd always been distant, quiet and mysterious, she hadn't been evil. Not until now.

Foster's face burned red with building heat. His body flushed with anger and he pushed himself off the floor, forgetting about any pain still pulsing through his bones. He and Goren whipped and charged their wands, daring Avery to make a move.

She made a move.

Without hesitation, without even a steadied thought, Avery spun suddenly like a twister, rising up above them, trailing black dust behind her high among the shelves of the hall, and flashed a bolt of black energy from the end of her wand. In an instant, Goren and Foster were flung against the broken shelving, and fell face first into the shards of glass and spilled dust.

Quiet once again returned to the hall and Avery floated to the floor, arms limp at her side, toes scraping the floor boards, head tilted slightly down. She left her unconscious and bleeding friends and slowly floated out of the barn.

It was not the Purities she needed. It was a different type of wish Avery Waterstone needed, and they awaited her arrival within a dark, damp cave upon Exclamation Pointe. Though the pink-haired, blissful little fairy of her past was long forgotten, there remained a fleeting notion within her that this curse could be lifted. What could possibly lift such a thing: a curse she had battled for a decade?

Embracing it.

41
AT THE EDGE OF A MEMORY

Standing at the base of the mountain, Shea, Beren and a limping Elanor looked up. Towering overhead, Exclamation Pointe was barely visible. The light of the Wishing Pool was the only way they could spot The Pointe, but as they stared upward, the difficulty of their task was suddenly apparent. Rising up, the mountain was the tallest of any in the valley, and even though Exclamation Pointe wasn't at the very top of it, it still resided hundreds of stories above their heads. Getting a crippled Elanor up the side of the mountain would be daunting, but having her grapple on her own the final few feet before reaching The Pointe would be nothing short of a miracle.

They rested for a moment at the mountain's rocky base. Elanor leaned against a boulder. Her breathing was labored, and not only because of her cracked ribs. The black dust was visibly trailing from her shoulders now and Shea wondered at how painful it must be to ward off such a thing, even though she didn't understand it.

"I don't think I've ever been able to keep you in one place for so long, Beren," Elanor said, smiling through the pain and looking at the handcuff spell wrapped around his wrists.

He returned the smile and helped Elanor sit. "Shea, did I ever tell you about the first time I met your mother?"

"Do we have time for stories, Dad?" Shea said, even though she actually did want to hear this one.

"A moment for a breath. Plus, it's not much of a story." He winked at his daughter and Elanor gave a hearty laugh, knowing it was a bit of a joking insult.

"It was our first training session on The Other Side. It was known as a Live Performance Test at the time, but basically it was a Singulars mission—a Wish Wrangling Performance Trial as we call it today."

Shea nodded her head, knowing the term. She'd always wanted to try one. Very simply, it was an annual training session race between the top Keeper recruits to track and find one particular wish that was individually assigned to them and hidden somewhere on The Other Side. No one knew what region it was hidden in and the test famously lasted for weeks. The fastest to capture their Wish and return it to Paragonia automatically qualified for the Keeper force and this resulted in quite a bit of fame for the successful Keeper. The top five finishers were given a "legendary status" on their recruitment sheet. It was another little dream of Shea's: achieve legendary status among her peers.

"Where were we, Ellie? Prague? I think it was Prague," Beren asked Elanor.

"Hamburg. You always get the Maker cities screwed up. Your dad was never very good at Maker geography."

"It was Prague," Beren said, smirking at Shea. Elanor guffawed, fighting the urge to argue. "There is a giant timekeeping machine at the center of the city and I was certain the Wish was hidden there."

"They call them clocks, Beren. And, hmm, you might actually be right. There was a clock tower in the Prague city square."

"Prague," Beren said again. "As I floated to the top of the tower, there it was: The Wish. I looked around me in case any other Keepers were following, but I was alone."

"Or so he thought. I pushed him off the edge of the overhang," Elanor said, laughing. "That Wish flew away so fast at the sound of your dad's yelp, I'm surprised the Makers didn't hear him."

Shea laughed, but tried holding back when she met the annoyed eyes of her father.

"It wasn't a yelp. It was more of a cough. She hit me square in the wings. Very illegal move, and it forced the breath right out of me."

Shea watched her mom and dad stare at each other, as they silently recalled the moment with soft smiles.

"But, really, it was the sight of your mother's eyes that truly made me lose my breath," Beren continued. Elanor's eyes filled up with tears and, self-conscious from the building blackness currently swirling, she looked away.

She had never seen it before, but Shea noticed a slight brightness radiate from her parents' wings. Even though her mom's were broken and shredded, just a touch of light emanated from them, as from Beren's. Maybe this was what love looked like. Despite the gravity of their current situation, Shea thought it was beautiful.

As Shea was lost in her loving thoughts, Beren turned to her, reached out his handcuffed hands and took his daughter's.

"I want you to understand something," he said. "When two people love each other, time is the only thing that can change. The love always remains constant. No matter what happens tonight, we will always love each other."

"And we never stopped loving you, honey," Elanor said, looking up at her daughter. For the first time, Shea wasn't frightened when looking into her mother's eyes. She suddenly understood what her dad had said. Her mother's eyes were swirling with cursed darkness, but she was still her mother. Her mom was still there and she would always be there, even if the curse consumed her.

A long pause filled the quiet stillness of the air, and finally Beren sighed a deep breath. "I think that's enough reminiscing for now." He helped Elanor stand. "You say there is a small cliff below the edge of the point?"

"Yes, I used to hide there when you two would bring wishes to the statue," Shea returned.

"Ellie, we'll fly you to that edge, but you need to grapple us up from there. We cannot assist in any way after that point or he'll know."

She nodded and clutched at the rising trepidation inside her. She had no idea how she would do such a thing without at least grimacing, but the Captain didn't know pain. She was going to have to do the same.

"When you present me to him, during the exchange, you'll fire a wrangling spell at the wish. Shea, you'll need to free Thane and the Makers, but you have to wait until after your mom fires the shot. Like you said, Erebus can't see you. He needs to think we came alone."

Shea nodded and straightened her skirt. Just the sound of Thane's name made her heart beat a little faster. There were too many reasons why it fluttered, but she did her best to calm the incessant feeling that she missed him and was excited to see him again. She didn't understand the feeling as it pumped through her veins, but she thought it must have been some form of love. Trying to hide it from her parents, she looked over her shoulders, wondering if her wings were glowing as her parents' had before. They weren't shining and, surprised, Shea was a little disappointed.

They readied themselves for launch and put Elanor's arms over their shoulders. As they rose up along the side of the mountain, Elanor looked at her daughter.

"Thane, huh?" she smiled as only a knowing mother can. Shea couldn't help but blush. It was the only answer she could come up with.

42
THE DEATH WISH

A Death Wish is not always a wish for someone to die. That's far too shortsighted, and the Keepers learned early on that every Maker is capable of a negative wish. A wish of hatred, vindictiveness, jealousy or any type of unkind act toward or for another Maker is the basic construct of a Death Wish. There is an innate irony within any Death Wish, as it is technically a selfless wish, at least in that it is a wish for someone else to fail, or lose or, yes, even die. While it may, at the surface, be selfless, the major difference between a Death Wish and a True Love Wish is the unattached selflessness. When a Maker casts a Death Wish, it is inherent that they gain something from the negative wish even though it is made for someone else. A True Love Wish, therefore, carries the quality of detachment and in no way does the Maker intend to gain anything—even a returned measure of love—upon the wish's fulfillment.

As Avery approached the dark corner of the forgotten realm of Paragonia's woods, the light of the Wishing Pool cut weak streams of light through the scrawny trees. It was no accident that the Keepers hid the Death Wishes within a cave so close to Exclamation Pointe. Before Erebus' treachery, the light of The Pool and the power it held over the land helped keep the wishes calm and obedient. Like a tranquilizer, The Pool sedated the powerful wishes. Otherwise, the Keepers would not have been able to control them. Removing a Death Wish from the cave was always done in secret, never publicly reported, and done with a full force of armed Sentinels ready to support the WishKeeper's retrieval.

Standing in front of the hidden cave, Avery studied the jumbled mess of rocks, boulders and outcrop of vines and vegetation. The entrance to the cave was small enough that only for a fairy could enter and exit, and therefore very nearly impossible to see with the naked eye unless you knew where to look. It was nothing more than a rocky bulge at the top of the mountain, and very little upkeep had been done on the cave over the years, and yet Avery knew it all too well.

Since the destruction of the True Love Wish, Avery would wake in the middle of the night and unconsciously remove herself from her soft, feather bed and go to The Cave. The first time it happened, she woke from the dreaming flight and suddenly found herself standing in front of it, terrified and speechless. She could control it at first, but as the years progressed, a darkness clouded her mind more and more. By the time Grayson and Miranda had made their second True Love Wish and Shea was crossing over in an attempt to retrieve it, she had lost count of how many Death Wishes she'd retrieved for her WishingKing. A wave of panic would engulf her every time she thought of it while awake. To think her body was somewhere else at night without her knowing, taking the wish to The Other Side and blindly handing it over to Erebus. How many times had she done it? How much power had she unwittingly given her deceitful king over the years?

Staring at the small hole just beneath an overhang of moss, and above a sharp granite rock shaped like a pointed finger, Avery was aware of everything. Usually when she was here she was unconscious, sightless and thoughtless, but this time she was fully aware of everything she'd done and everything she was about to do. Somehow the curse had dug so deep within her little heart that the pure Avery she once knew wasn't just pushed away, but was instead converted, changed. No longer was she resisting the curse. The hatred curdled inside of her and she let it. She could taste the deep determination to have what she wanted: to no longer be a pawn in her WishingKing's game. It was time to end it. All of it. It was time to bring death into the light. Time to bring an end to her pain. Floating toward the small entrance, she ducked her head and entered.

Pitch black, not an inch of space in front of her could be seen. A constant, low buzzing echoed through the cave, as if she'd entered a sleeping hornets' nest. As she floated into the darkness and set her feet lightly upon the stone floor, the cave buzzed with a resonant wave. The wishes knew someone had entered and they expectantly awaited retrieval.

A snap from the end of her wand sizzled and Avery held it up, using the soft blue light to illuminate her surroundings. Every inch of the wet, shimmering cave walls was covered with Death Wishes. They weren't in any kind of casing or jar, but were clinging to the walls like bats, fluttering, and buzzing a natural hum. Their black light slowly trickled on as it reflected Avery's wand. Though Avery's wand cast its light around her, the cavern ran so deep within the mountain that the light of the wand was unable to span the full size of it. Even larger than The Nursery's main hall, the Death Wish Cave had an endlessness about it.

A Death Wish buzzed toward Avery and zipped past her ear, leaving a thin, red scratch across her cheek. Another wish spun around her head and scraped across her forehead. Blood lightly trickled over her brow, and yet Avery didn't move. One by one, the Death Wishes swooped and bombarded the little black-haired fairy and swarmed her. The humming buzz of the wishes was deafening as they swirled around her. Thousands swallowed up the light of her wand and consumed her.

BLAST! A force of purple fog protruded out from the center of the swarming wishes and pushed back the onslaught. Avery stood at the center of the force with her wand held high above her head, gripping it with both hands. The wishes slowed and moved into a synchronized swarm, zooming around her in a perfect circle. Thousands upon thousands of Death Wishes were suddenly controlled.

Gripping her wand tightly, with the purple spell still emanating from the end of it, she slowly lowered it and held it firm in both hands. Her face and arms were slashed with hundreds of scrapes and scratches. Red strips of falling blood painted her skin like a warrior, and yet a slow smile curled beneath her pitch black eyes. Her WishingKing was about to receive something quite unexpected. An equal.

43
THE PAIN OF A WISH

Cringing, Elanor was holding back with every ounce of remaining energy not to cry out as Beren and Shea set her on the ledge beneath The Pointe's cliff. Nauseated, Elanor knelt and leaned her palms on the cold wet rock. The black dust was now falling from her shoulders with every breath she took, and Shea was near panic.

"She can't even stand up, Dad. How is she going to grapple you up to The Pointe? And without your help?" she demanded. Beren was pacing, well aware of the situation. He stopped and knelt at his wife's side.

"Ellie? Do you have one more in you? I know it hurts..." he stopped as Elanor sat back and gripped Beren's shoulder. Pulling herself up off the ground, she held back the need to gasp through the pain and kept as straight a face as possible. Her eyes were drooped, bag-lined and creased. Her complexion was cold, nearly bloodless, but she stood and pulled the hood up and over her head.

"Just get over the edge of the cliff, Mom," Shea said. "Once you're in front of Erebus, all you have to do is wait for him to address you and make the exchange."

Elanor smiled at Shea from under the hood. Elanor knew it wouldn't be so easy, but she loved her daughter for trying to calm her. A strange turn of events, she thought. Her daughter was giving her advice and comforting her. Removing her wand from her sheath and holding Beren's in the other, she gripped the handcuffing spell, looked at her husband and nodded.

"Let's go then," Beren said. With that, Elanor took a deep breath and fired a grappling spell at the edge of the cliff above. It clung tight to the rock, and Elanor pulled.

It felt as if her body was ripping in two. The spell pulled her up to the cliff, but Beren's weight, dangling at her side, despite his slight support with an occasional flutter of his wings, hurt so badly her vision blurred. She was passing out from the instant pain, but the cliff's edge was drawing closer and closer. If she could just hold on. If she could just resist the pain for one moment longer.

Shea watched her crippled mom struggle with the grappling spell. Even though Elanor didn't think she was grunting or making a sound, Shea's eyes poured with tears as she listened to her mom crying through the pain. She didn't know what to do. Once again she felt helpless.

The fog suddenly swirled along the edge of the cliff, darker than it had been and swifter than if moved by a simple breeze.

"I was beginning to think you would never show, my Elanor," Erebus' voice rang out across The Pointe, and Shea ducked along the wall of her ledge, desperate not to be seen. Fear spiraled through her at the sound of the WishingKing's voice. "No," she thought. "He didn't see me. He couldn't have. He didn't see." She squinted her eyes tight, praying silent pleas that she hadn't been seen. She was their only hope to keep this mission alive.

The fog released from the edge of the cliff and swirled back up toward The Pool. Incredibly, Shea was thankful for Erebus, who guided his Captain to the edge, not questioning the situation and not peering over to see her hiding there. "We have a shot. Hold on, Mom. Just hold on. Goren and Foster, where are you?"

As Elanor was placed along the grass of The Pointe, Erebus moved back and stood at the center of The Pool. To her right, Elanor saw Miranda and Grayson standing, tied up, exhausted, and petrified. Her hood fell over her eyes enough so that Miranda couldn't make eye contact, but even if she had, the blackness in her eyes would be obvious enough to keep up the ruse they were attempting. Thane turned toward Beren and Elanor, his face scarred and hopeless, and it was all Elanor could do to hold back the hiccups of tears. Finally, Erebus motioned for his Captain to approach, and though Elanor was still conscious and not completely consumed, the curse that raged within her was still strong enough to make her obey. She felt her legs step toward The Pool, and her arm tug on Beren's handcuffs. She looked behind her and avoided her husband's eyes. She knew she wouldn't be able to withstand the emotion if they connected.

They walked to the base of the stone pool. Elanor looked up at her master and waited for her orders. In Erebus' palm was the motionless, tired little wish of true love and Elanor knew she had to focus on its retrieval and nothing else. She had to focus.

"Thank you, Ellie, for being here. I wouldn't want you to miss this. Then again, I suppose you can't miss this since you are such an integral part of my process." With a slight move of his foggy hand, Thane was forced back, thrown suddenly to the edge of the cliff. The explosion of Erebus' spell knocked Thane unconscious, and his head dangled over the edge. One more roll and he would have toppled over. If his eyes had been open, he would have seen Shea below him covering her mouth to avoid a high-pitched scream.

Shea sped up to him, holding his face, and staying out of sight. She clung to the edge of the cliff and carefully peered over, watching Erebus stand above The Pool.

Wrapping tendrils around Elanor and Beren, Erebus grabbed and threw them along the stone ridge, placing them in Thane's spot. Falling onto the hard stone, Elanor couldn't hold back the thrust of pain as it jabbed directly at her broken ribs. She cried out and let go of Beren's handcuffs.

Erebus didn't flinch. He watched his Captain writhing and listened to Elanor's cries. He watched without surprise as Beren huddled over her, whispering support in her ears.

"WishMakers, I would like you to see something. Please, feel free to look. Go ahead," Erebus said, asking Grayson and Miranda to watch.

They were, of course, already watching. Their faces grimaced in horror as Beren clutched his dying wife.

"Please! She's obviously in pain!" yelled Miranda. She couldn't help herself.

"Pain?" Erebus taunted. "Pain is exactly why I intend for you to watch this. To see just what pain really is."

The shadow king whirled around Grayson and Miranda, surrounding them with his thick black cloak. Bringing his face mere inches from Miranda, he placed his shadowy arm around her shoulders and motioned toward Beren and Elanor.

"WishMaker, Miranda Anderson. Pain, my dearest, is clinging to the notion that you may remember a forgotten thing. Pain is holding out for one impossibility among a million impossibilities. Believing that something lost will miraculously be found again simply by sitting idly by and waiting for it to return."

He glided over to Grayson and leaned in. Grayson recoiled, pulling his face away, attempting to stave off the shower of dusty fog cascading from Erebus as he stared, inches away.

"WishMaker Grayson Brady knows all about pain. Don't you, kind sir? The pain of wishing and wishing and never seeing such a thing come true. Casting your hopeful intentions across The Other Side only to be left waiting. Waiting for the familiar pain of failure to tingle up and down your helpless spine. The tingles of justification—proving correct your scared little belief that wishes don't actually come true."

Erebus pulled away from the WishMakers and floated, once again, above The Pool. Still cupping the True Love Wish in his palm, he continued. "You all know pain, because wishing is foolish. A wish is nothing more than the lazy attempt by the blindly faithful to acquire what it is that you want. It is foolish to believe in a wish, just as it is foolish to believe that I care whether or not Elanor Willowind is in pain." He darted a hateful look at Miranda and opened his palm. The True Love Wish was lying there. Its little chest was heaving its final breaths, and a furrowed bent of his brow made it obvious it had little time remaining.

Shea stared over the edge, wide-eyed and desperate. Erebus knew her mom wasn't The Captain and he knew they were only faking. Some kind of 'Plan B' was needed, but there was no sign of Goren and Foster, and she technically didn't have a Plan B. She grasped Thane's unconscious face and held it again, lightly slapping his cheeks. "Wake up, you idiot. Please wake up. Please," she begged as tears welled. Thane didn't move.

44
PIECES

Feeling something dripping on his nose, Goren opened his eyes. Blood was rhythmically falling from his ear, across his face and dropping into a puddle below the tip of his nose. Pulling his face off the glass-strewn floor of The Nursery's main hall, he painfully picked the shards out of his skin. To his right his friend Foster was lying, unconscious, but still breathing. He nudged him once, but nothing.

"Foster," he called out. "Foster, wake up." He nudged him again and an audible groan slipped through Foster's lips. Foster, too, was bleeding, but primarily from the pieces of glass stuck to his forehead.

Gathering himself, Goren stood and brushed the debris off. His back rippled in pain as he bent over and helped Foster stand.

"Avery. Why would she…" Foster said as he stood up straight. "It was her, wasn't it?"

"It was definitely her, but we don't have time to figure out why. What did she say again? About the wishes?"

Foster picked another shard of glass out of his forehead, grimacing. "Something about the wishes. She didn't need them. I can't remember. Damn!" he said, frustrated, as he pulled out another shard that had dug into his cheek.

"Right. She didn't need these wishes," Goren confirmed.

"*He* didn't need these wishes. That's what she said," Foster corrected him. At first it didn't hit them as to what it meant, but as the slow realization came to them, they quickly looked each other.

"He? These wishes?" Goren quickly breathed.

With a flash, they grabbed their wands and flew out of the barn, knowing just what their friend was retrieving for him.

45
THE POINTE OF A KISS

"But enough of my preaching," Erebus said, mocking. The wind picked up across Exclamation Pointe, and the fog billowed over the edge of the cliff like a black waterfall. It cleared the skies over The Pointe just enough to reveal dark storm clouds hanging low over the valley mountains. "We have only one final piece of this little WishPuzzle to complete, and she should be arriving shortly."

Shea listened as she gave up on trying to wake Thane. *She?* Shea didn't understand, but she also didn't understand why it was taking Goren, Foster and Avery so damn long. She needed to do something, but she couldn't just jump out and duel with Erebus. Suddenly a groan rattled out of Thane.

"Thane!" Shea whispered. She kept slapping him. "Thane, wake up. It's me, Shea! Wake up!"

He pulled his face away from her swatting palm and pushed her hand away. "Stop. Please stop hitting me."

"Don't move. Don't move!" Shea said, grabbing his face and squeezing his cheeks.

They looked at each other, faces inches apart. Thane was frozen simply because of Shea's sudden order, but when she lunged in and kissed him, his body relaxed.

His lips were dry, chapped, and his breath was awful, but Shea didn't care. Like a magnet, her lips simply needed to be pressed against his. She didn't know what it meant and she didn't know for how long she was supposed to keep them there, but she did know it felt right. Their wings didn't glow or brighten, but something deeper inside of her did.

He looked at her with wide, surprised eyes once she pulled away. Quickly he noticed her sprawling wings buzzing behind her, and how far of a drop it would be if they suddenly stopped working.

"What is… Shea? Shea, your wings are…" He tried pushing up off the ground, but Shea pulled his head back down.

"Don't ask," she said. "And you need to stay still! If he sees you moving or talking to me, we're done. You understand?"

"You kiss me and now I can't move? Torture."

"Might be the only way I could have gotten in there in the first place. Just don't move."

They smiled and he shook his head within her palms, obeying. That same rush of excitement bolted through her as he smiled again. The mixture of panic and happiness to see him was making her sick, so she had to pick one. Somehow 'panic' felt easier and more natural, and most likely why she needed to kiss him. It was the only thing she could think of, but it certainly felt good.

PULL! Shea quickly grabbed Thane's shoulders and pulled him down to the ledge, praying Erebus hadn't noticed.

"Ow!" He fell hard to the rocky base. Shea flung a finger over her lips, telling him to shut up, then slowly floated back up to the edge and looked over.

Erebus was tying up Beren and Elanor with his tendrils and tightening his grip around Grayson and Miranda. He hadn't noticed.

"We have to go around. He can't see us approaching from the front. Our only chance is to surprise him from behind," Shea said, dashing glances around either side of the ledge, trying to decide which way to go.

"Can you… Shea, can you fly?"

"I told you, don't ask. But… yes. You OK?"

"Fine. I think the ridge of the point curls around almost all the way behind Erebus. We'll need to find our way through the woods if we mean to come up from behind, though," Thane said.

"Alright," Shea said, but not with much confidence. She was looking out in the opposite direction, trying to peer through the thick fog.

"What?" Thane asked.

"Goren, Avery and Foster. I told them to retrieve as many wishes as possible from The Nursery, but I don't know what's taking them so long."

"There's something you should know about Avery," he said.

Shea looked at him, waiting for him to go on.

"She and your Mom have a little history."

"What does that mean?" Shea said.

"Well, no, not like a history, but…" he didn't know how to say it.

"Just, tell me on the way. We don't have time."

Thane was relieved he wouldn't have to look Shea square in the eyes when he told her about his experience after they got split up. How Avery admitted her love for Elanor and how Beren had known all this time. Maybe it wasn't important and maybe it was a bad idea to bring it up in the first place. He was just happy to see Shea again.

They darted off around the base of The Pointe, flying through the thick black fog. Wind raced through their ears and across their faces and Thane loved that he was able to fly right alongside her. She said not to ask about her wings, and he didn't, but he wasn't stupid. Shea had run off with the wish, and suddenly Erebus had it. It didn't take him long to put the pieces together as he watched Shea fly. Her wings were perfect and she was an even better flier than he expected. When he started to notice her hair whipping in the wind, her strong muscular legs dangling beneath her and her chest...

"So are you going to tell me about Avery or what?" Shea asked.

"Oh, well, yeah, I suppose." His thoughts were quickly forced to refocus. They flew around the final turn and came to where the edge of The Pointe met the rest of the mountain. A wall of rock was in front of them, and the thick evergreen forest was just above them at the final curve. Landing quietly, staying out of sight, they tiptoed into the trees.

"I guess I should just make it quick, but after you and I got split up, your dad and his members of The Hope found me. He wasn't real happy when I told him I lost you."

"Not surprised by that, but why in the world would you tell him?"

"It doesn't matter at this point, does it?"

Shea shrugged her shoulders and turned around the base of a baby evergreen.

"He explained everything to me, but in the middle of it all, Avery came storming in and almost killed him."

"What?" Shea stopped and listened.

"Well, I don't know about killing him, really, but she beat him up pretty good."

"Why?"

"I'm getting there," he said. They continued through the woods and spotted the Wishing Pool and Erebus through the trees. Thane lowered his voice. "After Goren broke up the fight, Avery said that she, well, she was in love with your mom."

A blank stare was all Shea could muster. She turned and looked at Thane, wondering if he was serious.

"Seriously," he said, knowing what she was going to ask. "To be honest, I don't trust her. There's something off with her. And it has nothing to do with how she feels about your mom."

"Like, love love?" Shea asked.

Thane nodded.

"Avery was Erebus' WishKeeper. Did you know that?" Shea continued. "I remember when I was little that my parents would bring her over for supper and tea. She always scared me a little. I didn't know why at the time, but something was wrong. My parents were always whispering about her. I guess now I know what about."

"She was Erebus' WishKeeper?" Thane asked, still thinking through it all. "She gave me the rules parchment. Before you and I crossed over. She was the one who told me to help you."

At this, Shea quickly turned her head. The wheels in her head were spinning at the sound of this. *"Why would Avery want Thane to help me? What could she gain by having me on The Other Side?"* she thought.

"At the time, I thought she was nuts, but she said that retrieving a wish goes beyond our rules of WishKeeping. Pretty devoted, I'd say. Couldn't help but agree, actually." He smiled at Shea, but the smile faded when he noticed Shea deep in thought. "Look, it happens. Love is love. It doesn't mean Avery and your mom—" Thane tried to continue.

"No, it isn't that. Thane, what if Erebus planned this? Avery was his WishKeeper. His Regent after that. If he could control my mom, it would only make sense if he controlled her too. She used to have pink hair."

Thane scowled at the last of Shea's thoughts. "What does pink hair have to do with it?"

"I'm just thinking out loud, I guess." A sudden chilled rush of wind blew through the forest, followed by a long, bass-filled hum. Unable to figure out what it was or where it was coming from, they searched through the dark woods for any sign. The hum turned into a deafening buzz that crashed against their eardrums. They covered them, ducking against the bark of the evergreen. Their eyes closed shut, hoping the buzz would subside, but suddenly two sets of hands grabbed them by the shoulders and pulled them into a thick brush of thorny bushes.

Goren and Foster pulled them in, their hands covering their own ears, and looked at Shea, nodding. Even if they tried to explain, they wouldn't have been able to hear anything. The buzz grew and grew until finally it was directly above them. They looked up out of the bushes and there she was. Avery floated slowly in front of hundreds of thousands of black Death Wishes. Like a general leading her army, she pushed through the fog toward Exclamation Pointe.

Still clasping their ears shut, Shea and Thane shared a wide-eyed glance. The buzz slightly dissipated and finally, Goren and Foster pulled them out of the brush.

"There's no time to explain!" Goren yelled over the buzz.

46
A LIGHT RETURNS

Grayson and Miranda heard it too. The buzz was deafening, and it vibrated in their chests as it drew nearer. They looked up at the darkened skies.

Erebus only smiled. Not even bothering to look, he hovered over The Pool with the wish in hand. The True Love Wish shuddered in fright, trying to push off of Erebus' palm. Its attempt at escape was futile as Erebus had it locked in an invisible hold. Though it tried to bounce away, his grip was too tight.

As the buzzing enveloped the entire Pointe, Erebus extended his hand out and moved the wish a few feet in front of him, paused in midair. Stuck like a suspended ornament for all to see.

Elanor watched as Avery—demented, wraith-like—floated to Erebus' right-hand side. The Death Wishes revolved in a slow-moving circle above her head like a flock of individual nightmares, but all Elanor could see was her cursed friend. The petite little fairy hidden behind a black cloak of forgetfulness, agony and sadness. Elanor fought through the pain that devoured her broken body, and stood. Avery looked out from under her heavy hood and her eyes met Elanor's. A sudden vibration ricocheted through the surrounding swarm of Death Wishes as Avery stared. She slowly raised her wand above her head and released a pulsing black spell. It slowed the Death Wishes' circling and quieted their hum. She was in complete control of them, despite the rush of heat generated by Elanor's eyes.

"Avery, my dear. Right on time," Erebus said. He looked up at the surrounding Death Wishes and smiled. "An even better crop than I expected. You always manage to exceed even my expectations. Bravo." He reached out his hand, waiting for Avery. "No time to waste, now that we're all here. Come, my dearest of dears. The final piece."

"Avery, please! Don't do this!" Elanor cried out.

She pulled her hood back from over her face, and Avery continued to stare at Elanor. Even in her sick and twisted heart, there was no other thing to look at now. While in past years a gaze between her and Elanor would soften the darkened corners of her cursed heart, somehow this look only strengthened her anger. It was an anger toward Elanor, but also toward everything. An anger toward anger.

From behind the Wishing Pool where the waterfall used to cascade from the Keeper statue, Shea, Thane, Goren and Foster watched as Avery calmly floated toward Elanor. They noticed that even Erebus was surprised at this – he dropped his waiting hand, impatient.

"We have to do something. If Erebus consumes all of those wishes on top of the True Love Wish..." Thane whispered.

"Look at the wish. It's just floating there. Now's our chance," Foster said. He fidgeted in place, eager to make a move, but Shea grabbed him.

"What is Avery doing? Erebus asked her to give him the wishes, but... she's not listening," Shea said.

"Well, we can't just sit here and watch!" Goren hissed. Shea gently placed a hand on his shoulder. She knew that this was something Erebus had not expected. Avery was disobeying orders and if she continued Erebus would lose even more focus on the wish. The wish was still mere feet from him and stuck in a spell. But they needed to wait just a moment longer.

"Foster and Goren, to the left. There is a nook just to the side of the Pool, near Grayson and Miranda, where you can set up a shot. Thane and I will go to the right. We need to release the Makers and my parents from Erebus' hold first. We'll need as much help as we can get when we go for the wish." They paused before obeying orders, thinking it through and surveying the area. "OK?" Shea said, impatient.

Nodding, Goren and Foster shot off through the thicket. Thane looked at Shea, worried.

"Shea, the only thing that's important right now is—"

"I'm not sacrificing everything just for the wish. There's more than a wish at stake here. Right?" she said, giving Thane a curled smile. "Move quick, but out of sight. I don't want those things spotting us." She was talking about the Death Wishes. Floating like sentinels, they showered an ominous tone over the area as if one quick move against their master would cause them to rain down their ugliness upon the attacker.

Stopping inches from Elanor's pained face, Avery's black eyes glared. Elanor fought the urge to recoil at the sight of her and instead reached out her hand, shaking. It slowly cupped Avery's cold, white cheek.

"This isn't you, Avery," Beren said softly. "This isn't the friend I made years ago. You don't have to listen to him." He flinched when Avery quickly turned her head.

"I'm not listening to him," she said through a crackled, raspy voice. "For once, I am listening to no one." Though pitch black, the corners of her eyes were a wispy grey. Beren and Elanor both noticed the retreating darkness in her eyes, but before they could say anything…

Elanor quickly pulled her hand back as a spark of black energy clasped suddenly at her fingers. The Death

Wishes, one by one, began their circling once again and small cracks of lightning bolted between them and Avery.

"Avery, if there is anyone who enjoys a little dramatics, it's me, but I ordered you to bring me the wishes and I expect you to obey," Erebus said. His black fog rolled off his shoulders and rushed to her. A Death Wish raced past Erebus, jolting a quick bolt of lightning around his head. His fog curled and stopped, but for only a moment. He scowled and pushed the fog harder, but Avery turned and looked at her master.

Crawling slowly to the edge of the stone ridge, Shea pulled Thane in with a gasp. The Death Wishes fired down from their circling swarm. They watched Avery spread her arms out to either side. Her wings grew larger and larger as each Death Wish exploded against her. Beren pulled Elanor away as they watched Avery consume each wish, one by one. Their black energy pulsed off her back, chest, legs—every inch of her body was sucking in each Death Wish. Her wings grew into black, sharp, dragon-like canopies stretching from her back, and she continued her hard stare at the watching Erebus.

Goren and Foster dived to the feet of Grayson and Miranda. The Makers had pulled their heads away, trying not to watch as lightning cracked and storm clouds raged over the top of them. Opening his eyes when he felt a sharp stab at his foot, Grayson looked down and saw Goren punching his shoe.

"Maker! I don't know you, and you don't know me, but it doesn't matter," Goren yelled up. "You and your girlfriend need to get the heck out of here. My friend, Foster here, is going to fly up to your cuffed hands and release that blasted spell, but you can't immediately react as if you're free. Maker girl! You hear me?"

Miranda quickly nodded.

"Miranda, you OK?" Grayson asked. "Hold my hands and don't let go."

The wind swirled through Miranda's hair as she squeezed her tearing eyes closed. Their hands clasped together as Foster pushed against the whipping wind and flew up to their foggy cuffs. Waiting for Goren's cue, Foster charged his wand and looked at his friend. Goren held up his palm, holding him in place.

Erebus rippled with anger. The fog rolled with a wave throughout The Pointe. The water of the Wishing Pool crashed waves over the side of the Pool's and poured over the top of Shea and Thane as they hurried toward Elanor and Beren.

"Mom!" Shea whispered. "Dad! Down here!" She motioned for Thane to run to their other side. He army-rolled to the base of the stone ridge, just beneath Shea's parents. He aimed his wand at their tied cuffs, but Elanor quickly shook her head No! Shea didn't understand, but as Avery spoke, it was clear why her mother wanted her to wait.

"To my WishingKing, whom I have followed into darkness," Avery shouted. Erebus stood up straight, watching the Death Wishes pummel her, one by one. "For all you have given me and taught me, I have learned only one thing." She raised her wand hand while looking at Elanor, and aimed it straight up. "If there is something you want, you must simply take it. And I choose freedom!"

"No!" Elanor screamed and dived to Avery. Avery's wand blasted with a charge and exploded a black spell into the swarm of Death Wishes. Beren and Elanor were flung from the edge of the ridge, crashing to the ground, unconscious.

More and more Death Wishes exploded into every inch of Avery. She grew in size, spreading her wings out across the Wishing Pool.

Shea and Thane ran to her parents, falling to their side. Beren groaned through an aching head and focused his dazed eyes. He was fine, but Elanor was waking up. All they could do was watch the quickening build-up of a battle between Avery and her WishingKing.

Foster held the charge aimed at the cuffs, but was so surprised by Avery's sudden shift, he didn't hear Goren yelling from below. Miranda kept her eyes closed, unable to watch, terrified. "Grayson! What's happening?" she yelled.

"Foster! Break it! Now!" Goren screamed.

Foster broke through his rising panic and released the spell against the fog-induced hold around the Makers' wrists. A bright white light flashed and broke the tie. Their hands were free and just as Goren had instructed them , they didn't run. They didn't move. Their hands desperately found each other's and they held on tight.

A slight, white glow rimmed the edges of the Wishing Pool, and the True Love Wish, suspended there amidst the chaos, quietly brightened with a soft red glimmer as Grayson and Miranda squeezed each other's hands tighter and tighter. No one noticed. No one except Shea.

47
A WISH DESTROYED

There were so many anxious thoughts pouring through her mind, but when Shea noticed the ridges of the water brighten, she quickly looked at Miranda and Grayson. She saw their hands clasped together and all other thoughts escaped her. Sprinting away from her parents and Thane, she ignored his cries to stop. All she could focus on was trying to figure out why the Pool suddenly shined and why the True Love Wish brightened, if only for a moment.

As she sprinted, she looked to her left and watched Erebus spread his arms out, releasing his fog and whipping it at Avery. She retaliated by sending hundreds of Death Wishes hurtling toward him. They cracked bolts of lightning around him, but he didn't flinch. His anger was too powerful to break.

Shea flew up to Grayson's shoulder and landed, catching her breath.

"Grayson! Miranda!" she yelled. They turned their heads at the sound of their name, and Shea flew back and forth between them as she yelled through the storm.

"Squeeze your hands a little tighter!" she continued. "Look at the Pool!"

Goren and Foster quickly watched the water of The Pool and as Grayson and Miranda listened, squeezing their hands together, they too noticed the water flutter with a white light.

"Shea, the wish!" Goren yelled. The wish brightened again, just as before, though it was still stuck in Erebus' spell. "Now!"

There wasn't time for second-guessing. It was Shea's chance to end this—to grasp the True Love Wish one last time and bring it to the Keeper statue. It had to be fulfilled. It was the only way to stop Erebus and keep Avery from sacrificing herself.

Shea's hair whirled around her head as she stared at the wish. Erebus was focused on Avery and not paying attention to the wish. It hung there, vibrating with a slight red glow, and when it looked at Shea, she remembered the last time the Makers' wish was destroyed. It had looked at her with such a sense of knowing, as if it knew that no matter if it was fulfilled or destroyed, everything was going to be okay. The weight on her chest from her panicked breaths subsided and she raised her wand.

BLAST! She put every last ounce of energy into her wrangling spell and as it exploded through Erebus' hold, it wrapped tightly around the wish.

Thane and Beren watched as The Pool glowed with a white light, but just as they were about to fly and help, Erebus roared. His bellowing scream raged across the valley, and he flung his darkness in every direction. With flashes of black shadow, he whipped tendrils around Avery's neck, and just as quickly wrapped another around Shea's waist. Pulling each of them in, despite the Death Wishes plowing lightning into him, Erebus wrapped his hands around the True Love Wish.

Foster and Goren fired spell after spell at the retaliating WishingKing. Their spells bounced off of him like annoying flies and Erebus laughed. "Enough of this! It is time to complete what I came here to do!" As he gripped Avery tighter and tighter, despite her growing size, her last available breaths were pushed from her lungs.

Tendrils gripped around Beren and Elanor once more, and Grayson and Miranda were raised up in the air by another. Elanor was still unconscious, limp. Cupping his hands around the True Love Wish, Erebus pushed his fog straight into the sky, enveloping the darting Death Wishes, consuming them all at once. A circle of fire burst up in a ring around The Pointe as Erebus pushed harder and harder on the Wish.

Its power flashed bright red energy through his shadowed body. His head reared back as he felt the rush of the power of true love pulse through him. His tendrils dropped the captors to the ground. Thane was thrown back and Shea was helpless as she watched his wings burn from the surrounding flames. He growled in pain and rolled, dousing them, but his wings were gone.

As he leaned on his hands, howling in pain, the wall of fire raged higher and higher and all Shea could do was stare in horror as Erebus sprung his arms out wide. His black, shadow cape spread across the cliff as he grew in height, towering over the mountain. The True Love Wish beamed a blinding red light at the center of The Pool, cracking and breaking, connecting itself to Erebus as he grew. Death Wishes careened down from the sky and exploded as they crashed into the True Love Wish.

A wave of energy rippled from Avery, and she was flung to the edge of fire. She wasn't moving. She was as limp and lifeless as Elanor.

Like the sound of a raging locomotive, Erebus roared with every sudden pulse of energy as the wish flashed and exploded, bit by bit. To her left, Grayson helped Miranda pull herself up from the ground and run for cover along the side of the mountain. Shea raced through the wind and floated in front of them.

"What did you wish for?" she screamed.

Miranda burrowed her head into Grayson's chest, holding him as if she might blow away.

"Shea, get out of here!" Goren tugged on Shea's arm as Foster flew to the other end of The Pointe, helping Thane and her parents take cover.

"No! Grayson! What did you wish for? Tell me!" she screamed again.

"I—I wished for her to be happy!" he yelled back.

"Wrong! You wished for true love. Not to have it or to keep it or to even give it away, but you wished for it to just simply be!" She flew to Miranda's hand and pulled it up to Grayson's.

"I saw it! Just before—" she braced herself as Erebus roared again. His dark black fog whirled over the point, completely taking over. The ring of fire burst higher—a wall of swarming heat. Beads of sweat trickled down Shea's forehead as she pulled harder on Miranda's hand. Their hands gripped tight, intertwining their fingers.

"This is what matters. Not the wish. Not anything else! Look at the water!"

The water beamed brighter than before, even as Erebus swooped out over the cliff and towered over everything. The wish was beaming brighter as well, but Erebus was so consumed with power he hadn't noticed the glowing white and red of the pool.

"Please! Come on!" she tugged on Grayson's arm and motioned for them to follow. They ran across The Pointe, dodging the sputtering flames of the ring and joined their friends. Beren was holding Elanor now—her body broken, falling in and out of consciousness. Shea rushed to Thane's side, holding him up. They had nowhere to go as the wall of fire surrounded and trapped them.

"Dad! What did you say earlier? About time and love. Do you remember?" she called out through the storm. He was about to answer, but Erebus roared above them and hovered above The Pool, wrapping his darkness around what remained of the wish.

"Keepers and Makers!" he bellowed with a deep, powerful voice. "I promised to show you that I could be as powerful as true love. You stripped me of my freedom when you placed me on that worthless throne. Imprisoned me in this secret realm and took from me what I cared for the most! It's time for retribution!"

Shea burned with anger as Erebus spoke. Without thinking, and only reacting to the flaming anger boiling inside of her, she flew up directly in front of Erebus.

"Shea!" Thane yelled, but Foster grabbed him.

"Stay here, you fool!" Foster yelled.

"We took nothing from you! But you've taken everything from us! From me!" Shea screamed. Her face burned hot and not because of the fire surrounding her. For so long she had blamed her parents for all that had happened to her. For her lonely, bullied life and her broken, pathetic wings. But Erebus was everything she'd grown to hate: a monger of power, control and the darkest nightmares. But Shea was done with it. She was done with it all. She couldn't watch her mom whittle away into agony any longer, nor catch constant glimpses of her once strong and capable father dwindling into nothing more than a fearful and hesitant fairy.

"Little Shea. So eager to make a name for herself. So willing to sacrifice everything not for one wish of true love, but..." He paused and swooped down directly in front of her face, his dark, shadowed face even larger and thrashing with flashes of red lightning. Shea didn't flinch like before. Fear was something she was not going to allow him. Erebus, though, was also unflinching. "Shea Evenstar was so willing to sacrifice the hopes and promises of a once again powerful Paragonia, just to fix her worthless, decrepit, broken wings.

You are to blame for all of this! You are the reason I am here before you. For that, I must thank you."

He rushed back high above them all and reached out his blanket of fog. Like a tidal wave, it rushed down the cliff of Exclamation Pointe and devoured all of the surrounding land. Everything disappeared behind a wretched covering of shadow and fog. All that was left was their spot high above the valley mountain, ringed with fire, and owned by evil.

Shea floated back, closer and closer to the wall of flames. Grayson and Miranda held each other tight. Thane looked up at her, proud yet terrified. Her mom was lying in her father's arms, incapable of moving and waiting to die. Below Erebus was the rippling water of the Wishing Pool, and along the edges of the small tips of its waves was a bright, white light, shimmering and dancing with each crest and fall. Shea stared at the water and called down to her father once again.

"Do you remember, Dad? What always remains constant?"

Beren followed Shea's eyes to the cresting waves of The Pool. Quickly, he realized what she was seeing and yelled up to his WishMaker.

"Miranda! Take Grayson's hand," he called up. She did what she was told as Erebus and his dark fog poured over the remaining edges of the world.

"Grayson, can you feel it?" Shea said. "Do you understand that what's important is not having or holding on to something, but letting something go," Shea cried. "Love is not what you can get or even give someone." Shea looked at Thane. "But what you can learn from them."

Shea floated down to Thane and looked at him. It had been barely a few days that they'd known each other, and they would probably both agree that in some ways they annoyed the other even more than they loved each other. They didn't know what love was, but as their eyes met a knowing was shared—they were willing to learn how, together. As he squeezed her hand, their wings—even Thane's blackened remains—glowed a bright, white light. He tugged, as if for her to rejoin their friends, their family, but she tugged back and shook her head.

"Time is the only thing that changes," she said with a purposeful voice. Beren hugged Elanor and looked up at Grayson and Miranda. The Makers watched as the fairies' wings also glowed white.

Exclamation Pointe was now floating along the edge of nothingness. The valley and land around them had vanished into darkness. The forest behind the Keeper statue was gone and Erebus was all that was left.

As the darkness covered The Pointe, Shea held on to Thane's hand and looked at his broken and burned wings. Thane noticed a kind of smile she had yet to share with him. She knew something he didn't. For the first time, true confidence gleamed from her radiant eyes. Shifting her gaze to the stone ridge, she watched Avery, small, delicate and freed from the darkness in her eyes, standing painfully along the edge of the fire. Her black hair was waving in the wind, and she was looking at her one-time king.

"Thane. Look around you. What do you see?" Shea asked quietly.

"Avery!" he shouted, but Shea held him back.

"Love. At least what I think is love. All kinds of love. I've missed out on this my whole life and there is no way that it could end now. Not with all of this around us." She smiled, squeezed his hand tight and looked at Grayson and Miranda.

"I don't know how to love you, Thane, and maybe I'm not supposed to, but I know it might be fun to try."

The white glow of the Wishing Pool suddenly brightened and beamed a soft beacon into the sky. It cut through Erebus' darkness and pushed him to the side. He watched as Avery looked at Elanor. Thane held Shea's hand.

The WishMakers held each other. Erebus' anger burst up from the deepest part of his blackened soul and he pushed his fog back over the shining pool. The darkness bounced off the light, breaking it like a knife. He pushed harder and harder, screaming with every thrust.

"Grayson. Miranda," Shea called out. "There are some things in life that you simply don't need. As much as you try to hold on to them, dreaming for them to come true, sometimes you just have to start over and let go of what isn't necessary."

Shea smiled at her mom, then up at Thane... and backed into the fire.

"Shea!" Thane yelled.

Her wings burst into flames. She fell to her knees, holding back the cries of pain. As she knelt there, wings lapping with fire, she looked up at Thane and fell into his arms. The beacon of light beamed even brighter and Erebus recoiled. His shadowed body rippled with energy. Cracks in his foggy chest broke open and shafts of light burst through. Pulses of energy exploded from him, ripping through the surrounding darkness. Patches of the world returned, one by one revealing the hidden land. Avery was forced to the ground, the fire lapping at her. Goren and Foster hurried to her side. Her body was frail and dangerously light. They easily picked her up and brought her to the group.

Elanor let go of Beren's hand and crawled to where they had placed Avery. Avery opened her eyes and saw her friend staring down at her. Nothing was said as they intertwined their hands. Elanor brushed the black hair out of her eyes.

"Thank you," Elanor said. Avery's chest heaved with sorrow as she couldn't hold back the tears.

Grayson pulled Miranda away, huddling behind a boulder. He held her with wrapping arms. "Maybe we don't know how to love each other either," he said through a laugh.

"I've always known how, Grayson. Maybe we just need more practice." Miranda smiled and pushed her head against his chest. He tucked his fingers under her chin and raised her mouth to his. It wasn't a kiss to end all kisses, but one that would be merely the seedling of a thousand more.

Erebus fought through his cracking darkness, but when Miranda and Grayson touched their lips together, there was an instant of sudden silence, followed by the brightest of light blasts.

Thane pulled Shea away from the fire and wrapped his trembling arms around her. The Pool exploded with radiance and a True Love Wish was granted.

48
PARAGONIA, PLEASE

"I think you should stick around. As a matter of fact, I think it's the best idea I've ever had," Shea said. She was sitting on a banister that rimmed the stone veranda of Castle Paragonia, dangling her legs over the edge. The valley stretched out in front of Miranda and Grayson as they giggled at Shea's little comment. The sun was a bright ball of warmth in the sky, and the fairy homes lining the branches of the Paragonian forest each had their windows open, allowing in the soft cool breeze of another perfect day.

Life returned to the valley when Erebus was destroyed. His darkness even left the most remote corners of their land, and reports from the Fairy Intelligence Agency brought news that WishingScouts had found forgotten regions—regions of Paragonia that had been lost long before even Erebus' rule. There was a rejuvenated sense of discovery in every little fairy and Keeper, and though not all of the Gates had reopened yet, WishGathering had returned at a very rapid rate. The Nursery was full again even though it had been barely three weeks since The Breaking. The fairies had a name for everything, of course, and when the fog was lifted and Erebus was sent away for good, there was a breaking of more than just the darkness. There was a freedom to be and do what the fairies of Paragonia were meant to do—grant wishes—and the crushing inability to do so was finally broken.

Shea knew Miranda and Grayson weren't going to stick around and, in a way, she was glad. Yes, of course, she wanted them to stay, but though she'd grown quite fond of the two Makers over the past three weeks, she understood that now that the Gates were reopened and safe enough for a Maker to pass through, Grayson and Miranda needed to get back to their life. A life that was waiting for a new beginning.

"We have some work to do at home," Miranda said, smiling at Grayson as he rocked back and forth in a wooden rocking chair. He had a pipe in his mouth and was poorly puffing smoke rings.

"I don't know. I kind of like it here," he said. A sudden spat of coughing came over him as he swallowed a bit of the pipe smoke.

"That was Erebus' pipe, ya know," Shea said, holding back a laugh.

Grayson curled his lips and lightly set the pipe down, wiping his hands on his pants. Miranda stood and took her husband's hand.

"Time to go home, Your Majesty."

Sprinting onto the veranda, Thane stopped and saluted. He was wearing a green tunic and, despite his burned wings, a look of wide-eyed excitement. Even though Thane hadn't yet been officially sworn in as a WishKeeper, he was on his way and loved every second of his military duties.

"Your Gate awaits, WishMakers." He lowered his hand and relaxed when Shea rolled her eyes. "What? Doing my job, here."

"Whatever," she sighed. She jumped off the banister, walked past Thane and smiled. When he smiled back, she stuck out her tongue and jumped away from Thane's playful swat. Leaving Miranda and Grayson alone on the veranda, they ran out of the castle chambers, laughing.

The Makers looked out over the sunny valley, deep in thought. What had just happened? What had they just experienced? Ridiculous, really, to consider everything they had been through over the past few weeks, but there was a slight tinge of a notion that somehow this place was not going to simply be left behind after they had gone. It was a fantasy of a thought that Shea had when she said that they should stay, but when Grayson and Miranda turned and looked at each other, the whole of fairydom beneath their feet, all they could do was laugh and shake their heads. They truly did have to get home. As much as they felt an innate connectedness to the land, they couldn't possibly belong there.

It was difficult for Elanor to feel at home in their little fairy cottage at the base of the tree. Most of her time after The Breaking was spent in bed, but she was feeling some of her strength return. Most of her strength came from her husband, however. The past weeks' nights had not been kind to Elanor—waking from nightmares, and vomiting from the sudden onset of crippling headaches. Beren was there for her without complaint, and she marveled at his ability to remain patient as she attempted to return to a normal life.

When she wasn't sick or fighting another headache, she would sit in Shea's room, looking out her bedroom window, wondering how many sleepless nights her daughter had had as well. How many hours were spent in anger and confusion as to what had happened ten years ago and why. Though Shea would repeatedly tell her mom that she understood and wasn't angry anymore, Elanor knew what it was like to be a teenager and couldn't help but worry Shea was harboring secret frustration.

Beren noticed his wife's depression right away. It was obvious, beyond the physical pain she was in, that she wasn't comfortable and it would take a very long time to pick up the pieces of her life. He once again found Elanor crouching along the edge of Shea's window seat, looking out over the green of the forest.

"The Makers left," he said, as he joined her at the window. He lightly rubbed her back as she continued to look out the window.

"We're still their WishKeepers. We'll see them again all too soon," he continued. She smiled without looking at him and placed her hand on his. "You look well today. Enough to go for a walk?" Beren asked.

"Did she ever talk to you about me?" Elanor asked. "I mean, really talk?"

His wife's eyes were glistening wet, and though they were sad, he would always be happy to never see the blackness return to them.

"We didn't have much of a relationship, you know. She kept to herself mostly. You know Shea. She—"

"No. I don't," Elanor quickly said. It was a sadness that propelled her to cut him off. She wasn't angry and when she squeezed Beren's hand a little tighter, he understood.

"Well, you have time do so. And she'll be happy to know you. Like I do."

"I think a walk sounds like a good idea," she said. "Was this Shea's escape route?" She tugged on the rope ladder that draped out the window and over the edge.

"Yes, but, honey, you really shouldn't..."

She just smiled at him and started to climb down. Beren followed with a slow float next to her, helping her grip and slide down. She landed, holding back the slight pain in her side. Her ribs were healing, but were not completely repaired.

"Where to?" she asked.

Beren and Elanor walked through the quiet trees and listened to the birds chirp and sing. Shafts of light of the afternoon sun cut through the branches, illuminating the forest floor with a golden hue as they approached a small cabin tucked away behind a tall, ancient maple. The cabin's chimney was lightly curling a bit of smoke into the air as Shea and Thane climbed out from behind a bush.

"Hi, Mom. You're out and about, finally," Shea said, excited. She took her mom's hand and helped her over a fallen branch. They couldn't fly and a forest floor was a bit tricky to maneuver, but Shea liked the idea of helping her mom. Whether she needed the help or not, helping her allowed them to reconnect, even if they weren't discussing anything of importance at the time.

Beren clapped Thane on the back and nodded at his WishKeeper uniform. "You still on duty?" he asked.

"No, sir."

"You'll eventually learn the delight of removing your uniform after a long day's work, Thane," he said.

"Is this a surprise walking party, or something?" Elanor asked.

They all looked at each other and smiled. Approaching the front door of the little cabin, Beren waited for Elanor to get closer.

"Sort of," Shea said. "For you, yeah, but more so for someone else."

As they entered the little brown cabin, Elanor saw in the far corner a comfortable bed with a white feather blanket covering Avery as she sat up and sipped tea. Her eyes beamed when she saw Elanor. Roots of pink hair were sprouting near her scalp, pushing away the black, and her hair was tied in a thick braid. Though she was thin and sickly looking, with inset cheeks and pale skin, the happiness that flowed through her was enough to erase any amount of remaining pain.

Avery had been bedridden since the night of The Breaking. The curse had affected her far greater than it had Elanor, and her nightmares had become so violent that they sadly had to keep her in a secluded cabin so as not to frighten her neighbors. Elanor was devastated that they needed to separate her friend from the fairies who loved her, but she agreed it was for the best, at least until she was well again. Beren, Thane and Shea would visit her every day and today was the first that Avery was able to sit up and consume any kind of liquid. Elanor had heard all about Avery's illness and to finally see her sitting up in bed and smiling was like feeling the sudden warmth of a fire on a cold winter's day.

Elanor hurried to Avery's side and took her hand, kneeling next to her. "Avery. Oh, Avery, look at you. You'll be up and retrieving wishes in no time. And your hair looks beautiful. Who did it?"

Avery blushed at this and giggled, looking at Thane. If Avery was blushing, Thane's face was on fire.

"Thane? Seriously?" Shea asked.

"I don't have much else to do, until I get my Keeper wings and all," he shuffled his feet. The group snickered and Elanor turned back to her friend.

"I never got the chance to apologize, you know," Elanor said.

"Apologize? Why would you apologize? Ellie, I was horrible." Avery was legitimately confused.

"I've had a lot of time alone the past few days. With my thoughts, anyway," she said, looking at Beren. He joined her and knelt next to Avery.

"I always knew what you were battling with, Avery. Before everything happened, I could tell how you felt and, to be honest, I was frightened."

Avery's eyes glistened and she couldn't keep eye contact with Elanor as she spoke. She'd always been ashamed of the feelings she'd had and wasn't ever able to truly vocalize them.

"But after everything that's happened, I want you to know that you will always be a welcome addition to our family." She choked through the last part. "You will always mean so much to us. To me."

Shea took hold of Thane's hand and pulled him over to Avery's bedside as Elanor and Avery hugged. As Shea stood there, watching her mom hug Avery, her father with a supportive hand on her mother's back and Thane next to her, for the first time in her life she didn't have anything to wish for. She had a family now, and whatever adventure might follow, she would welcome it with confidence.

EPILOGUE

An afternoon sun splashed through the young, skinny trees of a crowded city neighborhood, illuminating the smooth, brown facades of brick apartment buildings. Grayson paused in front of the stone steps of a five-story, dusty complex that was pushed tightly between two identical buildings. With an audible sigh, he wondered what kind of new beginnings he might have here.

The passenger door of a moving van creaked open and Miranda reached out her hand. "Uh, a little help, Mr. Brady?"

"Oh, God, sorry. Here, wait a minute." He hurried over and grabbed her hand, wrapped his other under her arm and helped her down.

Miranda's belly was bulging just enough to show the developing new member of their family, but Grayson was acting like she was ready to pop any day. She kissed him lightly on the cheek as she plopped down on the hard cement. They arched their necks and looked up at their new home.

"Can't see much of the sun. Stars probably won't be shining much · either. All these lights," he said. Slowly turning his head to see her reaction, he knew a pair of rolling eyes would be waiting for him. They laughed and took a shared step up the cobbled stairs. As Grayson opened the door for Miranda, he took one last glimpse at his neighborhood, smiled and followed, but not before a bright pink Purity Wish popped to life above his head and followed them inside.

THE WISHKEEPER

Within the narrow alley alongside their complex, a white-bearded homeless man sat among greasy trash bags. A young woman pushing a stroller walked by, ignoring him. A purple Ladder Wish circled her head and for a moment swirled down toward the old man.

He opened his eyes, dark and ageless, and reached a hand slowly out of the blanket of newspapers. A wisp of grey fog danced along the edges of his fingertips and the Ladder rushed back to its Maker. A smile slowly crept across Erebus' pale white face.

Here ends Book One of The Paragonia Chronicles.

THE WISHMAKER

Read on for bonus content, the intriguing first chapter from
the forthcoming
Book Two of the Paragonia Chronicles,
The WishMaker

Chapter 1
Family Secrets

To my Little M --

There are things in this world that are difficult to explain. Things that can be seen and things that cannot. I have seen plenty that I wish I hadn't, but I have seen even more that I will always cherish. Your blossoming family is one thing I wish I could see more of, but not all wishes can come true.

Creating a will can be such a depressing process—to whom do I leave my most prized possessions? Do I even have possessions worthy of such a loving family as my own? Your grandmother always wished for you to be a mother. She and I knew that you would one day be a lovely one. Since that wish has already come true, I wonder what greater gift I can leave for you when I pass. There is one thing, and though it does not carry the worth of our little Ada, your young family will, I'm sure, find a good use for it.

Our family has held a one-acre plot of land in the city for three generations. It is needless to say that we have been offered sizable sums for the land, and yet I have not been able to part with it.

M, there is something special about the acre that I cannot share with you here. But since it now belongs to you, I am confident you will realize its importance soon enough.

I will see you on the other side.

With the truest of love,
Grandpa George

P.S. Ada will know

*   *   *

Miranda set the letter on the end table and sat back on the couch. She sighed, hiccupping through the aftermath of a good cry. Her grandfather George was 93 years old. A World War II veteran, he had stormed the beaches at Normandy, survived the Battle of the Bulge, and fallen in love with his high school sweetheart. Grayson had called her earlier in the week to give her the news that Grandpa George had passed away and even though her grandpa's health had been slowly failing, it was, nevertheless, a shock.

"Oh, God, I'll miss him," she sighed, as Grayson joined her on the couch.

He placed his hand on her knee and joined her in a heavy breath. "I didn't know your family owned an acre of land. In the city? I can't believe they held on to it for so long," he said. "And 'Ada will know'? What's that mean?"

"Grandpa George loved riddles, even though he was terrible at telling them," she giggled. "He left an address. It's actually not that far from our apartment. I can't believe my mom never told me about it."

"We'll take a look over the weekend," Grayson replied.

Miranda leaned her head on Grayson's shoulder. They stared at George's letter and Miranda's portion of the will. It was strange that a man who had lived so fully was now just the simple contents of an envelope.

THE WISHMAKER

*   *   *

When George Anderson returned home from the war to his young wife and a changed world, he never told a soul what he experienced while on the battlefield. It wasn't just the carnage, death and violence that he intended to keep to himself, but something more peculiar, something more mysterious. He made a wish while at war. In the middle of a French forest, evergreens toppling and exploding from shrapnel, one of the bloodiest battles of the war was in full tilt. His friends and fellow heroes beside him were shivering in the frigid cold, and he just wanted it all to end.

When the final syllable of his wish danced from his lips, he saw something—something that even until the final days of his life he wasn't fully able to believe. A small, winged man held a ball of red, flashing light. The ball of red light smiled at him, and the mysterious little man softly saluted.

George Anderson saw his WishKeeper that day, and yet he refused to tell a soul. But a month before his death at 93 years of age, George's great granddaughter gave him a gift. The gift shined in the little girl's palms. It gleamed a bright blue light and an unmistakable smile radiated from the little ball of blue energy.

He watched in awe as his great granddaughter handed him a wish.

Maximilian Timm is an author, screenwriter, consultant and instructor who shepherds the careers of screenwriters through his work as the Director of Community Outreach with the International Screenwriters' Association (ISA). With over a decade of teaching experience, Timm has supported thousands of writers in the film, television and entertainment industry.

He attended Holy Cross College at the University of Notre Dame before moving to Columbia College Chicago to study screenwriting and entertainment producing. Through his work with the ISA, he hosts events and multiple podcasts through its Curious About Screenwriting Network, and runs a screenwriting class, the ISA's Master Class, in Los Angeles and online.

Timm has devoted his life to the craft of writing, and with his debut novel, The WishKeeper, he intends to inspire the young adult audience to embrace their imperfections and pursue their dreams. He specifically wants to send a message to teenagers that not only do they matter, but so does every wish they make.

You can follow him and The WishKeeper on Facebook, Twitter and Instagram in order to stay tuned and updated regarding details of Book Two of The Paragonia Chronicles, *The WishMaker*, set to release in early 2017.